Questred's Question

"Will you tell me that you love Tom?" Sidney Questred demanded.

"I . . . we . . ." Pamela faltered.

He cut off her protest. "You may tell me that you love him, but I'll not believe you. You have not remained a stone statue beneath my kisses, do not tell me differently. If you loved him, would you have responded? Would you have come here in the first place? Would you?"

He was standing so close to her. His hands were hard on her arms. His fingers were biting into the flesh, but she did not mind the hurt. She wanted him to be closer yet. And all she could say to try to stop his mouth from coming down on her lips again was, "I do not . . . know."

(For a list of other Signet Regency Romances by Ellen Fitzgerald, please turn page. . . .)

AMOROUS ESCAPADES

Ellen Fitzgerald
The Heirs of Bellair

A SIGNET BOOK

NEW AMERICAN LIBRARY

SIGNET TRADEMARK REG.U.S.PAT.OFF. AND FOREIGN COUNTRIES
REGISTERED TRADEMARK—MARCA REGISTRADA
HECHO EN CHICAGO, U.S.A.

SIGNET, SIGNET CLASSIC, MENTOR, ONYX, PLUME, MERIDIAN and
NAL BOOKS are published by New American Library
1633 Broadway, New York, New York 10019

First Printing, January, 1987

1 2 3 4 5 6 7 8 9

PRINTED IN THE UNITED STATES OF AMERICA

1

Miss Pamela Cardwell sat on the first landing of the stairs leading up to her father's observatory, a large name for the small room housing his star maps, a few astronomical treatises, and an elderly telescope. Indignation warred with impatience, and intermingled with these two emotions was pity for Arthur Bellairs, who was being forced to listen to one of Sir Robert's lengthy discourses on planetary movement.

She exhaled a short impatient breath. Sir Robert had appropriated Arthur the minute he set foot in the front hall. He had not even given his little daughter the chance to exchange a greeting with the boy she considered her good friend despite the ten years that stretched between them. In the month Arthur had been home she had not spoken to him at all and she had seen him only once—at his mother's funeral.

As she remembered the sad occasion, Pamela's eyes filled with tears. Arthur's mother was also Tom's mother and he was her very special playmate, although her governess, Miss Pringle, regarded him with a rather dubious eye, saying that Tom invariably led her into mischief. Miss Pringle had threatened to speak to Sir Robert about it but had yielded to argument as she usually did. However, it would not have mattered much if she had spoken to him. As long as Pamela did not invade the sacred precincts at the top of the stairs, he little cared what she did. As she had gleefully explained to her governess, the less Sir Robert saw of her, the better, her arrival in this world having coincided with her mother's departure.

"I shall never have a child," Pamela whispered to herself. Mrs. Bellairs had been ill ever since Tom's birth, which had taken place just six months before Pamela had made her appearance in what Miss Pringle lugubriously termed "this vale of tears." Of course, Jocelyn Bellairs had been old when Tom was born—thirty one. When Arthur was born she had been twenty-one and in good health. It was her husband who had died. He had been delicate, and Arthur too. Arthur was still delicate—or that is what his mother had believed. According to Tom, his father, who was Arthur's step-father, had very little patience with what he termed Jocelyn's *cosseting* of the lad.

On the occasion when Arthur was home from Oxford, he ate too well and slept too much. That was what Edmund said, not to her, of course, but to Tom. It was true that Arthur was lethargic in his movements and also far too heavy, but he had such a sweet disposition and he was so kind. Pamela cast a long-suffering glance at the head of the stairs. Undoubtedly he would be listening patiently as Sir Robert droned on, and it was getting late, cold too, very cold for spring. Arthur would be walking back to Bellair soon, for he believed the night air unhealthy, which meant that she would not have a chance to say more than a word or two to him! And despite his stepfather's arguments, he would be re-turning to Oxford at the end of the week!

Arthur was very good-natured but he was also stub-born. Despite Edmund Bellairs' insistence that he remain here and learn to manage the estate he would eventually inherit, Arthur was determined to finish his studies. Tom had told her that, and added in an imita-tion of his father's disgruntled tones, "Though what he will do with philosophy, Latin, and Greek, I cannot imagine!"

Yet, if Tom parroted Edmund Bellairs, he loved Arthur—one could not help but love him. As Miss Pringle had said, "He is a truly good person. I do not believe he is capable of an unkind act." She had added distressfully, "It is a pity that people twit him about his girth—though perhaps he ought to exercise more. I expect his mother would not allow it. Poor lad, he will miss her." Pamela sighed. He had looked so sad at his mother's funeral. She had longed to throw her arms around him—though such a gesture would hardly have sufficed, given a figure that was almost as broad as it was tall.

Voices overhead aroused Pamela from her thoughts. She glanced up the stairwell. Sir Robert was finally bidding his guest good afternoon. She held her breath—would her father accompany him down to the hall? No, the descending footsteps were those of Arthur, she was sure. In another few minutes, she sped down to the ground floor as a tall, heavyset young man came down stairs which shook with each ponderous footfall. He was, she noted, holding tightly to the balustrade, a habit with him, for he was not surefooted. As his young brother unkindly said, it was doubtful that the bulge of his stomach allowed him to see his feet. Indeed, for a youth of twenty, he was surprisingly weighty, and it seemed to Pamela that he had acquired another chin!

"Arthur!" she called.

"My dearest Pamela." Arthur Bellairs' gaze had been grave but it brightened at the sight of the child. "I had been hoping I should see you."

"And I thought Papa would never cease to talk to you about those horrid stars," Pamela exclaimed. "I think he must know each of them by name."

"And I think that highly unlikely even for so wise a man as Sir Robert," he said with one of his warm smiles.

"Oh," Pamela giggled. "You know what I mean." She sobered instantly. "I am so sorry about Aunt Jocelyn." Though she was no relative to Mrs. Bellairs, Pamela had always addressed her as "aunt" by reason of the close friendship Mrs. Bellairs had had with her mother.

"I thank you, my dear," Arthur said. "It was a sad

loss for us all. I did not think her quite so ill." His eyes, a deep brown, almost black, and quite his most attractive feature, being thickly lashed if small in his plump face, were suddenly wet. "I would have come home sooner, if I'd known."

"I do not believe anyone knew. She never said anything about feeling poorly. That is what Tom said," Pamela assured him.

"I am sure she did not," Arthur sighed. "Her thoughts were all for others." He glanced toward the window and added regretfully. "The sun is descending. I expect I should go home."

Pamela was equally regretful, but since she had anticipated such an announcement, she nodded. "I expect you must." Then she continued, "Tom says that there have been smugglers hiding in the woods, that stretch between here and Bellair."

"Smugglers—in our woods!" Arthur frowned. "In from Romney Marsh, no doubt. A dastardly set of rascals. Too many people hereabouts shelter them and provide other means of protection."

"Oh, yes, I know," Pamela said wisely. "I expect it's because of the brandy and the perfume. Tom says that the duty on it is very dear."

"And so they'll harbor those miscreants who think nothing of murder if it suits them." Arthur's gentle voice was unusually harsh. "Those who furnish such protection are no better than common criminals."

"That is what Papa thinks," Pamela said. "Oh, Arthur, I do hope you will be able to come and see us again before you leave. Tom says you are going back to Oxford."

"Yes, I have that intention," Arthur said firmly.

"Tom was sure of it." Pamela nodded and looked down quickly. She was a sensitive child and she did not want Arthur to know that they had discussed his plans because probably he would guess that those plans had been greeted with disapproval.

"Papa," Tom had told her, "does not think Arthur appreciates Bellair as much as he does. And it does not seem fair that he is our grandfather's heir, especially since Papa has been managing it all these years."

"Pamela," Arthur broke into her thoughts, "will you walk with me a short ways?"

"Oh!" she said delightedly. "I would like that above all things."

Arthur's gaze, which had been somber, was lighted by his smile. "Come, then . . ." He opened the door and they came outside. As they walked slowly across the broad lawn toward the trees, Arthur said, "What have you been doing these past months, my dear?"

"Lessons." She rolled large greenish hazel eyes.

"And going riding with little Tom?"

"Oh, yes, but I have been reading too."

"What have you been reading, my dear?"

He acted as if he were really interested in the answer she would give him. That was what Pamela particularly liked about Arthur. He was kind and he listened when one spoke to him. He did not grow impatient, as Papa was inclined to do, or quiz her about her pronunciation, as Miss Pringle did. He was truly interested, as Aunt Joceyln had been before her last and final illness. Poor Arthur must miss her sorely—but he had asked her a question. She said importantly, "I have been reading *Le Morte d'Arthur*."

"Knights and beautiful ladies?" He smiled at her.

She grimaced. "I do not care so much about beautiful ladies, but I do like Launcelot, Gareth, and Gawain."

"And do you imagine yourself a captive maiden in a tower window with a dragon snarling and spitting flames below—as you wait for the right knight?"

"Captive maidens are all silly," Pamela announced. "They have long blond hair. Mine is red."

He laughed. "That would not prevent a dragon from capturing you or a knight from rescuing you. Your hair is very pretty, little Pamela. And it does not owe its curl to rags, I am sure."

"It does not," Pamela agreed. "But I would rather be in armor and slay the dragon myself."

His dark eyes gleamed with laughter. "You will change your mind when you are older, my lady fair."

"No, I will not," Pamela said positively.

"Tell me that in ten years . . ."

"In ten years . . . why, then I will be all grown up," she marveled.

"That is very true," he said solemnly.

Pamela came to a stop. "I wonder . . . what is it like, being grown up, Arthur?"

He, too, stopped. "It depends on how you grow."

She glanced at him. He was frowning, or did he merely look unhappy? "You are all grown up, are you not, Arthur?"

"I am."

"I do wish you might have waited for me."

His frown vanished. "Do you know, my dear, I wish I might have too. And if there were a good fairy about, I think I might ask her to wave her wand, but as there are none present, we will both need to be content with our lots. And now, my dear, I think you have come far enough."

Pamela looked around her and saw they had reached the trees that bordered the property. "Oh, dear, so I have," she said disappointedly. She added, "You will come again before you return to Oxford, will you not?"

"Of course I will, child." He kissed her on the cheek and then went down a slope toward the trees.

Pamela waved until he was out of sight. She was disappointed that he did not turn to wave back. Generally he did. However, she reasoned, he must be eager to get home. It was getting darker.

Arthur was not, however, eager to get home. In spite of the gathering twilight, he did not direct his steps toward Bellair. Reaching the boundaries of the property, he went deeper into the woods in the direction of the little stone house he called his "sanctuary." He had discovered or, rather, rediscovered it many years before, having come across a mention of it in a volume that contained a description of the property as it had been circa 1660. The Sir William Bellairs of that era had used the cottage as a refuge from the marauding Puritans. He had spoken of two rooms and a cellar, adding that the house had been built at the command of one Sir Anthony Bellairs, a Catholic turned Protestant at the time of the Dissolution. It was thought that Sir Anthony's loyalties had been divided. He had paid lip service to the Anglican church but aided fleeing priests by hiding them in the cellar of the stone house. Later, he had ridden with them to Dover.

Though Arthur had not been an adventurous child, he had thrilled to the tale of brave Sir Anthony and he had been intrigued at the idea of the cottage and had forthwith set off to find it. He could still remember his excitement when after many false turns and not a few scratches from forcing his way through thick foliage and close-growing trees, he had sighted walls barely visible behind another grove of trees. His excitement had increased to mamoth proportions when he had found it still largely intact, and from the condition of the rooms and cellar, possibly unvisited since Sir William had been allowed to return to Bellair from exile in France. He had never told anyone about the cottage, not even his mother, and in those unhappy years after she wed Edmund Bellairs, it had served as his refuge too.

He was thinking about his stepfather as he made his way through the thin-trunked ash trees, dense in that part of the woods. Walking wearied him and his heart seemed to be pounding in various parts of his body. Such symptoms appeared whenever he tried to hurry. They had always worried his mother, but his stepfather persisted in saying that he did not get enough exercise.

"He's a lazy lout," he had overheard Edmund tell his mother. "You've given in to him far too much."

"Dr. Lacy says he has a delicate constitution."

"Which would be strengthened if you were to cease from pampering him."

"But he must be careful . . . his father also had a tendency to quinsy, and later, as you know . . ."

"Will never let his various illnesses stand in his way. He rode and swam, too. We were boys together, Jocelyn. And I can tell you, he never would have wanted his son to be kept in cotton wool!"

Remembering that inadvertently overhead conversation, Arthur shuddered. He had an inexplicable fear of water, which his stepfather had tried to cure by tossing him into a lake and inviting him to swim to shore. He had been going down for the third time when Edmund had rescued him. The latter had not scrupled to show his contempt at what he had dubbed Arthur's cowardice. He had been equally contemptuous of his stepson's fear of horses. Still, if Arthur had never been able to conquer a terror of water extending even to the crossing of bridges, causing him to hold his breath and shut his eyes until he was safely on the other side, he had learned to ride. Indeed, it had been one of his few accomplishments until a recent increase in his girth precluded his finding a horse strong enough to bear his weight. That had been Edmund's expressed reason for denying him a mount, but of course it was not true. Heavier men than he rode, but Arthur was glad of any excuse that kept him from joining Edmund Bellairs in long rides around the estate he would inherit when his frail grandfather died. He knew, had always known, that his stepfather burned with rage because his own parent had been a younger son. He loved Bellair and had been managing it for most of his adult life. He administered it very well, as if, in fact, it were his own.

Arthur had moments of wishing he might break the

entail and give it to his stepfather and his little half-brother. He was fond of Tom, and despite Edmund's barely concealed dislike for him, he thought the boy was fond of him. Only this morning he had said wistfully, "I do wish you would stay, Arthur."

There had been tears in Tom's eyes. He had taken his mother's death much to heart. Possibly Tom's sense of loss was as great as his own—no, not quite. Tom had a father he adored. The misery Arthur had been hard put to keep at bay during Sir Robert Cardwell's endless droning about his heavenly observations swept over him once more.

"What shall I do without you, Mama?" he whispered, staring up at the dimming sky. Once more he wished that he might rid himself of the burden that was Bellairs. If it were up to him, he would have preferred to remain at Oxford among his books or, barring that, to purchase a cozy residence in London, where he might join some literary and scientific societies and also obtain subscriptions to operas, concerts, and the theater. His inheritance was a sore burden, but in the name of his father and his grandfather, he must needs return to Bellairs at the conclusion of his last term and learn to administer the property.

He shuddered at the thought of that instruction. Edmund would be his tutor, and Edmund who, without the alleviating presence of his wife, would give full rein to the contempt with which he had always regarded his stepson. All that remained between him and that misery was a year, and despite the pressure from his stepfather, he would not relinquish that. He knew that his stubbornness had surprised Edmund. That pleased him, yet despite this small victory, he was thinking of endings rather than beginnings. The time would pass swifty—far too swiftly. He paused in his unhappy ruminations. At last he had reached the stone house.

As always, the sight of it warmed his heart. It was with a feeling of having really come home that he approached its vine-shrouded door. Though a decade had passed since he had discovered it, a vestige of his original excitement upon viewing it remained. Mixed with that, however, were those feelings of trepidation that seized him at each visit. What if someone else had found his sanctuary? Hard upon that fear, he heard a cracking sound . . . a footstep behind him?

He turned and stared into the dimness but could discern nothing. There were always sounds out here, he recalled. However, he had yet to encounter anyone in this part of the woods. At the same time, he wished that he might have been better able to secure his discovery. Unfortunately, he was not good with his hands and the bolt he had pounded into the door had come off within a week. A second try had proved equally futile. There were, however, those vines growing over the house, and these he had always pulled in front of the door prior to leaving it. They had not been touched, he was sure of that. Pushing them carefully aside so as not to tear their tendrils, he thrust back the door. It moved with a rusty squeal of hinges, and at last he was in his sanctuary. It was with a wonderful sense of homecoming that he looked about his two rooms, seeing no changes in them other than the dust, and the leaves and twigs blown through the windows by the autumn, winter, and spring winds.

As usual, it smelled faintly of mildew. He moved to a small cabinet he had dragged in years before. In it would be candles and a tinderbox. Finding them, he lighted a candle and thrust it into an old brass holder. There was his chair and the cot he had also managed to bring there long ago—and there was the small stack of books he had appropriated from the library, bringing them here one or two at a time, his favorites, not excluding *Le Morte d'Arthur*. Remembering that it was among his collection, he smiled, thinking of little Pamela, lonely little Pamela, who had found the same joy in the reading of knightly adventures that he had himself, all those years ago. He, too, had envisioned himself as an armor-clad knight riding forth to rescue his fair lady, not realizing in those days that he would have more in common with one Shakespearean knight, the fat Falstaff, dunked in the river by a host of merry wives. He had garnered his share of laughter in his time. He could think of a moment at an inn near Oxford when a pretty barmaid had aroused feelings he had not known he possessed.

He also remembered her derisive smile at his faltering attempt to make conversation. Her wide eyes had traveled to his bulging belly and she had subsequently exchanged a laughing glance with mine host. That abortive effort had been his first and only attempt at a possible flirtation. Inadvertently he thought of little Pamela again. She was a lovely child and she had always adored him. She had said, "In ten year's time, I will be all grown up." She would not only be grown up, she would be beautiful with her wide hazel eyes—green in some lights, gold in others. Her hair was not "red," as she had phrased it. It was a dark auburn and very thick. Would a grown-up Pamela find him a figure of fun too? Undoubtedly she would. He could not imagine that his girth would decrease with the passing years, and why was he thinking along such odd lines? He seemed to be seeing in the child the woman she would eventually become. He had an answer for that. Her uncomplicated adoration of him was as foreign to him as it was sweet. She seemed to know him as none save his mother ever had. At this idea, a bitter laugh escaped him. He was being ridiculous. Pamela was only a child and had no more conception of the sensitive man he really was than his stepfather! With the death of his mother, he had lost the one person who really knew him, and he would not find her like again, not in this world! He tensed.

Hard upon his laughter he had heard something—what? He was not sure. An unexpected rustling in the trees outside—not a wind, because at this moment no breeze was stirring. Candle in hand, he rose and moved to the window, and lifting the light up and down, he peered out. He saw nothing. Yet he still felt tense, as if, indeed, he were not alone in the cottage. He had often been prone to such sensations and had been proved wrong. Still . . . He looked toward the stairs leading down to the cellar. These were stone, and many of the treads were badly cracked. They were also narrow. The idea of going down them did not appeal to him. Undoubtedly he was giving far too much rein to a well-developed imagination. He went back to his cot, and taking the blanket to the door, shook out the dust. Spreading it over the cot again, he settled down and picked up one of his books. It proved to be an old favorite. Kant's *Kritik der Reinen Vernunft*. Kant, he remembered, had died the preceding year, full of honors and at a ripe old age—eighty. He had been born in 1724!

Arthur marveled at all that had happened within Kant's lifetime. George I had been on the throne when Kant was born, his reign having thirty-six more months to go. Louis XV was on the throne of France and lived his whole life without ever dreaming of the fate awaiting his hapless grandson Louis XVI. And . . . Arthur stiffened. He was hearing sounds outside and he was reminded suddenly of little Pamela's mention of smugglers—was it possible that some of that dangerous fraternity could have discovered the stone house and stored some of their goods here? He rose and started to the door, but in that same moment it was thrust open and he found himself looking into the cold eyes of a militiaman. Before he had a chance to question him, he was pushed roughly back against the wall, while other members of the militia rushed into the cottage.

Finding his voice, Arthur gasped, "What is the meaning of this, please?"

"It means, young sir, that I arrest you in the king's name!" came the stultifying and astounding answer.

* * *

The ship, an ancient square-rigger, was anchored, he did not know where. He knew nothing save that he was chained to a hook in the noisome hold of the vessel, where he lay on the reeking floor. Others around him had hammocks. He had not been able to secure one for himself, but had been pushed away because he had yet to learn how to fend for himself. Furthermore, he had other matters on his mind, fractured memories of events that had taken place since that moment six months earlier when he had been arrested for consorting with smugglers and storing their contraband goods in the cellar of his sequestered cottage.

In vain he had protested his innocence. No one had believed him. They had believed a man he had never seen before. This man, Jonas Culpepper, swore that he, Arthur Bellairs, was hand-in-glove with the smugglers, that he had "offered" his cottage as a haven in return for money and brandy. In the melee that had followed the invasion of the militia, someone (he did not know who) had splashed brandy on him, and someone else (two other men, in fact) had pinioned his arms behind his back and forced his mouth open while they poured brandy down his throat, poured it even though he choked and gagged upon it, but he had swallowed a quantity of the fluid and had been dizzy and reeking of it when dragged before a justice of the peace who claimed to know his grandfather and who had read him a homily regarding his fine background and his betrayal of it. He had not heeded Arthur's dazed response that he had been wrongly accused. He had ordered him thrown in the first of the many cells he had occupied until they had brought him on this ship.

His stepfather had visited him in jail and had appeared to believe his protests of innocence. He had promised to help him but he had never returned. A month later, he had been brought up at the assizes and heard another young man, a prisoner like himself, swear that Arthur's cottage was known as a "safe house." He had spoken of payments given to Arthur in goods and gold. In return for giving this evidence, he had had a prior sentence commuted from hanging to transportation. Arthur, hoarse from protesting his innocence, faced that judge and heard himself condemned to ten years at hard labor in Botany Bay. He had been told that he had been given a lenient sentence because this was his first offense. He had also been told that his fate would serve as a warning to the other wild young sprigs of the gentry who betrayed their families and backgrounds.

Images of all he had endured in the past six months swam in and out of Arthur's mind as he lay there clad in the garments he had worn on the day of his visit to Sir Robert Cardwell. These were filthy and he was filthy. He was hot and cold by turns. His teeth chattered, and his body, no longer as ponderous as it had been, quivered. Dreams invaded his mind, and dominating them were three faces. The most prominent of these was that of his stepfather, who, he was positive, was responsible for his plight. The face of one of the men who had given evidence at his trial was familiar to him —he had seen him in the company of his stepfather. The second face he would remember was that of Sir Harry Bowers, who had presided over the assizes, Sir Harry, who had sat in court with a scented handkerchief to his long, thin nose. He, too, was a friend of Edmund Bellairs', a very good friend, a most obliging and accommodating friend. He had ordered Arthur taken from the court when he had screamed out his innocence. The third face belonged, of course, to Jonas Culpepper. But there were other faces, including that of the prisoner who had lied and was somewhere on this prison hulk and was, like himself, awaiting transportation to New South Wales. Arthur was feverish now—but he would not die of it. He was quite sure that Edmund Bellairs and his cohorts, knowing his terror of water, were sure he would die, but Edmund had underestimated his stepson and second cousin.

"I will live," Arthur muttered. "I will live, I will live, I will live. And then, Edmund Bellairs . . ." His voice rose to a scream.

"Stow yer gab," someone yelled, accompanying his command with a string of oaths.

Arthur lapsed into silence, but in his hate-filled mind, the litany continued. "I will live, Edmund Bellairs. I will live, my dearest Cousin Edmund, and I will return to claim the inheritance you've wrested from me." For that, of course, was the reason for his plight. His stepfather had coveted the property over which he now presided and would doubtless continue to preside for the next decade. But after that . . .

Arthur's chains rattled as he raised his fettered fists.

2

Pamela Cardwell sat at her mirror as Lucy, her abigail, combed her auburn locks, exclaiming as usual at the tangles. She also had some sharp words for the book which lay open on her mistress's lap and was glanced at from time to time.

" 'Ow am I to comb yer 'air wi' yer 'ead down like that?" she complained.

Meeting Lucy's reproachful glance in the mirror, Pamela said contritely, "I am sorry, but it is so interesting. Indeed, I prefer this to anything Mrs. Radcliffe has written."

"Ummm, it'll be all full o' spooks 'n the like, I expect," Lucy commented dryly.

"And dark passages and mysterious monks too," Pamela giggled.

"I wouldn't be able to sleep if I was to read that nonsense," Lucy said with the license allotted one who was but six months older than the mistress she had served since both were fourteen.

"It is not nonsense, Lucy," Pamela said defensively. "In fact—" She broke off as the door was flung open and a tall, fair girl with wind-tangled blond hair which would have been the better for Lucy's tending rushed into the room, startling the abigail into dropping her comb.

"Pamela!" the visitor shrieked. "You will never, never believe it!"

"Oh, law, Miss Edith," Lucy said, retrieving her comb.

"I am sorry, Lucy, did I startle you?" Edith

20

Courtney, who was Pamela's best friend, had a concili-
ating look for the abigail but a tragic one for Pamela as
she continued, "Hadley Hall has been purchased. It is
too dreadful! Now we'll not be able to ride in the park
anymore." Her glance fell on the book in Pamela's lap.
Scooping it up, she turned it over and read the title on
the spine. *Cavernor or: The Wild Hunter.* "Oh, I am
next to read that. Are you nearly finished?"

"I have another volume to go, but you may have the
first two," Pamela said magnanimously. "Who has
purchased the Hall, and why, I wonder? There are other
properties about in much better repair. Oh, dear, I
agree, it was a lovely place to ride. The carriageway was
wonderful for racing."

"You wouldn't catch me there. It's 'aunted," Lucy
commented with a shiver.

"Yes." Edith nodded. "I wonder if the new owner
knows that the last of the Hadleys was done to death
thirty years ago—in the front hall?"

"I do not imagine that anyone told him," Pamela
mused. Her eyes gleamed with sudden laughter. "I
wonder if he'll be found white and gibbering madly in
the vestibule—the way the purchaser of Twelve Trees
was discovered in *The White Abbey*?"

"Oooooh, Miss Pamela." Lucy produced an
elaborate shudder.

"The White Abbey?" Edith questioned. "Did I read
that?"

"You gave it to me!" Pamela reminded her.

"Oh, yes . . . and he never recovered his senses, the
poor man, did he?"

"He wasn't a poor man." Pamela giggled. "He had
done the heir of Twelve Trees out of great sums of
money and at length he won the estate in a card game."

"I remember now!" Edith exclaimed. "He cheated!
And that is why Sir Ulric D'Arcy, the family ghost,
persecuted him."

"Precisely. And who is the new owner of Hadley
Hall?" Pamela demanded.

"A mysterious stranger, of course." Edith winked. "He really *is* mysterious, too. No one I was able to quiz knows anything about him, save that he is a lone gentleman from foreign parts."

"How foreign?" Pamela asked.

"Foreign." Edith shrugged. "That is all Sukey knows."

"Sukey?" Lucy looked annoyed. " 'Ow'd she 'ear about it an' not me?"

"You must ask her, and if you learn more, tell me," Pamela advised.

"I will that, Miss Pamela." Lucy moved toward the door and stopped, reddening. "I 'aven't finished wi' yer 'air, Miss Pamela." She took up the comb again.

"Ouchhh, Lucy, do not pull!" Pamela protested. "And you may go now, if you want to visit Sukey. You have my permission." She glanced at Edith. "I hope you do not mind."

"Not in the least," Edith said quickly. "I do hope you can learn more than I, Lucy."

"I 'ope so." Lucy bobbed a curtsy and hurried out.

"It was bound to be sold one day." Pamela shrugged.

"I expect so." Edith also sighed. "I wonder if he will have the graveyard removed?"

"He'd not dare!" Pamela exclaimed. "That would be desecration."

"Still . . ." Edith murmured. "I should not like to have anyone else's ancestors on my property, particularly if they proved restless at night . . . like Lady Hermione, who drifts through the ruined chapel, supposedly."

Pamela giggled. "In spite of all her evil deeds, I'll warrant she and the husband she is supposed to have poisoned sleep peacefully enough. And it is a lovely chapel, especially when the sun shines through those stained-glass windows. How fortunate they were that the Roundheads did not smash them. Oh, dear, I will miss it. I had always intended to make a drawing of it. When is this stranger coming to take possession?"

"Sukey did not know. However, he's not here yet, which is why I should like to ride over there today. I know we'd planned to go toward the sea, but . . ."

"I am all in favor of a final visit. Do let's go!" Pamela exclaimed.

"I was hoping you'd agree." Edith smiled. She added diffidently, "Shall we ask Tom if he would care to accompany us?"

"Tom has gone to Bath . . . Oh, Edith, I quite forgot to tell you. Our wedding might be postponed again—because Mr. Bellairs wishes to remain at Bath. He is still feeling poorly and needs to take more of the waters." Pamela's tone was more relieved than sympathetic. "Consequently, I might have several weeks more of freedom."

"One would almost imagine that you did not want to be married," Edith observed. "And it's not as if you aren't fond of Tom." She could not quite restrain a sigh, which she hoped her friend had not noticed.

"I *am* fond of Tom," Pamela stressed. "But to be promised in marriage without so much as consulting me. It is not fair."

Edith had turned away. She stared down at the riding crop she still grasped. "Have you ever preferred anyone to Tom?"

Pamela rose and took a turn around the room. "I have not been given an opportunity to prefer anyone else," she complained. "In the seven months we have been home from Miss Minton's, I have been to only three assemblies, and each time, Tom has accompanied me. You know that. And even before we were officially affianced, it was agreed we would be. I could not persuade Papa to give me a London Season even though I told him that nearly everyone at school expected to have one."

"I have not had one," Edith pointed out.

Pamela stamped her foot. "You know very well that we are not talking about the same thing," she said bitterly. "Your mother's too ill to chaperon you, but your aunt will do so when she returns from Scotland.''

"Next year," Edith reminded her. "And then I shall be close on twenty."

"That is not ancient and you are very beautiful. You might even be declared an Incomparable. You have a sizable dowry and probably you will be wed within three months."

Edith moved to the window and stared out. "You are kind to say so, but I do not anticipate so early a wedding. All the girls at Miss Minton's fell in love with Tom when he and his father came to visit you that day last year. Thalia Penderbury said he looked every inch the Byronic hero."

"Ha!" Pamela retorted bitterly. "It's a pity they did not have more of an opportunity to converse with him. He does not have a scrap of poetry in his soul. He thinks Byron's a 'dashed loose screw' and said I was a ninny for sympathizing with him, and he also said that England is the better now that he has gone abroad."

"He never said such a thing!" Edith protested.

"Oh yes he did. You do not know Tom the way I do." She sighed. "I know him through and through." Pamela ran a hand through her hair, completely undermining Lucy's work.

Edith still continued to stare out of the window, and thus Pamela was unaware of the envy in her friend's limpid blue gaze as she said, "But you do love him."

"I am very *fond* of him," Pamela stressed.

"I certainly do not understand you." Edith turned to face her. "Tom is so handsome, and wealthy besides. Consequently you can be assured he is not marrying you for your dowry."

"He is marrying me because our fathers have long favored the match," Pamela stated. "He did not even question their decision. Practically his every waking thought is centered on Bellair. I am quite sure that he loves the estate even more than his father does. It is in his blood, and now that the official confirmation of

Arthur Bellairs' death is on its way from New South Wales, he is finally assured of the inheritance. Consequently he is anxious to settle down and put some of his agricultural theories into practice and, incidentally, marry me.''

"That is a dreadful way to describe it and I do not believe it is true. It is obvious to me, if not to you, that Tom is extremely fond of you. I do not believe he has ever looked at another female.''

"Very well," Pamela sighed. "I will allow that he is fond of me. But I want . . . oh, dear, I do not know what I want.'' Meeting Edith's uncomprehending stare, she said defiantly, "No, I do not know what I want. I want someone to love me passionately, and that Tom will never do. He does not have an ounce of passion in his whole body!''

Edith laughed. "You have been reading too many novels. I think it would be intensely uncomfortable to be loved 'passionately,' to be cast into the depths of despair and then lifted to the heights of rapture. I am positive that in real life we would both find that a dead bore.''

"I would not!" Pamela cried. "I think it would be wonderfully exciting, but could you ever envision Tom arranging a secret rendezvous or bearing me off to Gretna Green?''

"He does not need to do either," Edith pointed out. "And as for Gretna Green, I would not care for that at all, being married 'over the anvil' by some horrid drunken blacksmith!''

"In *A Midsummer Marriage,* Elsie Debray, the heroine, was—''

"I beg you will not keep referring to those silly romances," Edith interrupted. "They have nothing in common with real life.''

"You read as many as I do," Pamela accused.

"I might read them, but I do not expect to live them," Edith said coolly. "And you might be surprised,

Pamela, once you are married to Tom, to find him a great deal different from what you had expected.''

"I do not see how. As I told you, I know him—''

"Through and through, yes,'' Edith retorted. "However, I do not believe that anyone ever knows anyone else that well. We are close friends, but you cannot see into my head any more than I can see into yours. But no matter, if we are to ride to Hadley Hall, we had best start as soon as possible. It is easily a league from here.''

"I have only to put on my boots,'' Pamela said as she went to her armoire.

As they came outside and headed for the stables, Edith said curiously, "When did you learn of Arthur Bellairs' death?''

Pamela said in some distress, "Two months since. Mr. Bellairs had heard nothing of him in the last five years. Consequently, when he learned that an old friend of his was going to be an administrator in one of the townships, he asked him to find out what he might about Arthur.'' She shuddered. "Oh, Edith, he wrote that Arthur had been in some sort of trouble for which he had been *flogged*!''

"Flogged!'' Edith's eyes mirrored Pamela's distress. "From what you have told me about him, that was enough to kill him.''

"Yes . . . it seems to have so done. He is known to have been very ill afterward, and greatly weakened, and in spite of that, they sent him back to the roads, and a man who labored with him said he died. It is too horrible. Mr. Bellairs was shocked. He told Tom that he had written to the man who was governor when Arthur was sent to New South Wales—Bligh his name was. He had requested that Arthur be given some clerical position. He had cited his fine education and he was positive that the governor would make use of it. It is highly unusual that men with university educations are forced to do manual labor—particularly since it was a first offense. Mr. Bellairs said he never dreamed that Bligh would be so cruel!''

"It was cruel," Edith agreed. "But Papa insists that he betrayed his class by consorting with common criminals and deserved all he got."

"I do find that hard to believe." Pamela sighed. "I have never forgotten what he told me on the very afternoon of the day he was arrested. He said he did not approve of smuggling."

"Naturally he was trying to throw dust in your eyes."

"The eyes of a child?" Pamela frowned.

"Undoubtedly he said the same thing to everyone."

"That is what my father contends. It is a good thing he cannot hear us talking. He has forbidden me to mention Arthur's name. Yet, no matter what he did, it is hard to think of . . . of him being flogged and dying of it—far from everything he loved, and in that inhospitable land."

"I beg you'll not dwell on it," Edith said. "Do let us go."

Hadley Hall, finished in the middle years of Elizabeth's reign, stood three stories high and was built around a small courtyard. It was fashioned from time-mellowed red brick, and through the small-paned mullioned windows it was possible to see rooms with paneled walls, one leading into the next, and not entirely bare of furniture—an odd chair here, a table there. An old banner descended from a balcony in the main hall and an angular staircase led to the upper floors. The chapel, also on the ground floor, stood open, allowing a glimpse of a shattered altar; and on the floor, a slab with dates which had been obliterated was purported to be the final resting place of one Robert Hadley, whose head had been struck off and placed on a pole over Traitors' Gate in the Tower of London. He had met his end by engaging in an abortive plot to save Mary of Scotland. It seemed odd to Pamela that it was not his ghost that was supposed to roam the forsaken corridors

of the Hall rather than that of Lady Hermione, the wife
of the seventeenth-century Hadley. Evidently the
powers-that-be had deemed treason preferable to the
murder of an aged husband.

Pamela had brought her drawing pad, and while
Edith, who preferred to be outside, wandered through
the garden, Pamela sat down in one of the remaining
pews of the chapel, took out her charcoal, and began to
sketch. As she worked, she was still feeling regretful
about the Hall. Though she had not visited it overmuch
of late, she had always loved a house which typified the
sort of haunted mansion to be found in the books she
borrowed from a circulating library in Hythe. As she
sketched in a window, she sighed, thinking of Lady
Hermione, who, wicked though she must have been,
was also beautiful and unhappy.

She had been, Pamela knew, married at sixteen to a
widower of fifty-six who had a son over four years her
senior. It would be very difficult not to be "wicked"
under such circumstances, particularly since Lady
Hermione had been wed for her dowry, as Pamela
herself was going to be.

"No," Pamela whispered, her charcoal coming to a
stop. "That is not true." Tom, she reflected, was
affectionate and he had often said he loved her, but he
was so offhand about it! No one could ever call *him*
romantic. She was positive that he had her dowry ear-
marked for buying a farm adjoining Bellair. He could
not touch the inheritance until they were positive that
Arthur was dead. And, as she had told Edith, it did take
such a long time to receive messages from New South
Wales. Furthermore, one of the ships had gone down
and Tom was gloomily positive that it must have carried
the confirmation of Arthur's death.

Pamela shuddered. As always when she thought of
the man who had been so kind to her all those years ago,
her eyes grew wet. Fortunately, he did not come to mind
very often, but she could still remember him on that last

afternoon, for she had stood and watched him while he went down the hill, his huge bulk casting a long, wide shadow on the grass. He had told her he was going home, but he had lied. He had gone to the stone house in the forest, where he had helped the smugglers hide their goods. Why? He had not needed the money! However, it was his stepfather's theory that Arthur was a secret drinker. He had been three-parts drunk when they had found him in the cottage, and there was no brandy finer than the French—or more costly.

Footsteps interrupted her thoughts, and without turning, she called, "I'm not quite through, Edith." She picked up her charcoal again.

"Edith?" questioned a voice behind her.

Pamela rose swiftly and turned to see a tall dark man standing at the back of the chapel. Her drawing pad and charcoal dropped from suddenly nerveless fingers. "Oh!" she cried. "I did not know anyone was here."

"I fear I have startled you," he said.

She was more than startled. She was frightened. He was so very tall, and though he had spoken politely enough, he had a bold black stare which, for reasons she was not quite sure, caused her to feel most uncomfortable. However, it would never do to let him know that. She said, "You did startle me, a bit." She caught a breath as he suddenly moved forward, and bending down, retrieved her pad and charcoal. "You are an artist, I see," he said as he proffered them to her.

"Thank you, sir." She took them and continued, "I come here to sketch sometimes, but I am not really an artist."

"I beg to differ." His smile exposed very white teeth —or possibly they seemed so white because his skin was so deeply bronzed. "I would say that you are extremely talented, Miss . . ."

"Pamela!" Edith called from the door to the chapel.

Pamela's tension increased. She had had no notion of divulging her name to this stranger. He was far too bold. Indeed, there had been something perilously close to the familiar in his address, which, she reasoned regretfully, was not surprising, considering the manner in which they had met.

"Pamela?" he questioned, his dark eyes roving over her face.

"Miss Cardwell," she corrected coldly. She glanced at Edith, who had come to stand beside her. "And this is Miss Courtney, sir. I do not have your name."

"It is Questred—" he began.

"Questred!" Edith exclaimed. "But I have heard that name before. You . . . you are the gentleman who has bought this property! Oh, dear!"

"*You* are the new owner of the Hall?" Pamela felt her cheeks burning.

"I am," he acknowledged, with another flash of white teeth.

"Oh, dear, and we are trespassing," Pamela said apologetically and, at the same time, with relief. She had feared . . . But she could not quite trace the source of those fears. She knew only that he had made her feel very uncomfortable.

"We must go." Edith was also blushing. "We . . . we have been wont to come here to ride and to sketch," she explained. "We had no idea that you would be in residence so soon. This was to be our last visit to the Hall."

"I hope that you will see fit to remand that decision," he said with a slight blow. "I am delighted to have made the acquaintance of two such charming young ladies."

Pamela stiffened. The way he looked at her bordered on effrontery, she decided indignantly. Clearly he was not quite a gentleman. Yet his speech was certainly cultivated. He bore himself well, too. Her flush deepened as she realized she was staring at him, something she feared he may have noticed. "You are very kind, sir," she said coolly. "But we must go, and I pray you will excuse us for trespassing upon your property."

His dark eyes were bright with amusement. "I do forgive your trespasses," he murmured.

"Oh!" Edith choked back a giggle. She, too, blushed. "We will leave you, sir. Come, Pamela."

"Good afternoon, sir," Pamela said with an exaggerated politeness.

"Good afternoon, Miss Cardwell. Dare I hope that I will see you soon again?"

His attitude absolutely demanded a set-down, and Pamela was not in the least reluctant to provide it. She met his bold glance with an equanimity she had not known she possessed. She said, "I think that rather unlikely, Mr. Questred." Taking Edith's arm, she hurried her across the courtyard and out to the tree where they had tethered their horses. They made haste to mount, and it was not until they were some distance away that Pamela dared to look back. She did not see him, but she had an uneasy feeling that he was watching them. She urged her horse ahead, outdistancing Edith.

"Gracious," the latter said as she caught up with her. "That man . . . ."

Pamela, feeling safer now, reined in her horse. "A rogue!" she exclaimed.

"Yes, indeed," Edith agreed. "But extremely handsome, did you not think?"

"I did not notice his appearance," Pamela said coldly. "His manners, however, left much to be desired."

"Indeed, they did. He was far too familiar, I thought. And yet . . ."

"And yet what?" Pamela snapped.

"We were rather at a disadvantage, you know, having come there."

"A *gentleman* would not have taken advantage of that disadvantage," Pamela returned loftily. "I cannot think that *he* is a welcome addition to our community."

Edith fixed surprised blue eyes on her face. "Good gracious, Pamela, I have never known you to take so pronounced a dislike to anyone so quickly."

"Did you not find his manner obnoxious?" Pamela demanded.

"Not . . . entirely obnoxious," Edith said thoughtfully. "He was bold, true enough, but I had the oddest feeling that he was laughing at us."

"He was deliberately provoking us!" Pamela exclaimed. "And what gentleman is so familiar upon such short acquaintance? But enough, do let us be on our way, please!" With the determination of putting as much distance between herself and the man who had made her feel . . . She really had no name for the disquieting sensations he had aroused. All she knew was that she had no desire ever to see his bold gaze and his amused smile again! Once more, she urged her horse forward.

"Pamela," Edith called. "Not so fast through here, please. You know . . ." Whatever else she might have said went unheard as Pamela cantered down a path that wound through high bushes and close-growing trees.

"Pamela!" Edith shrilled. "That branch . . ."

Her warning coincided with the slap of a low-hanging branch and a neigh from her horse that bordered on a shriek. Pamela felt something rough and hurtful slap her chest, and in that same moment the reins slipped from her hands. She made a desperate grab at them, and then, falling, she knew no more.

"Please, you must not be alarmed, Miss Courtney. She is only unconscious. I doubt that she has sustained much hurt."

Pamela, aware of an aching head and various other aches, wished to disagree, but even as she opened her mouth to do so, confusion descended. What had happened and where was she? In another second she remembered falling from her horse, but she was not lying on the ground. There was softness beneath her, and her palm, she now realized, was encountering material—linen, from the feel of it. A bed? Could she be on a bed?

"Are you sure?"

Edith, Pamela identified, and wondered where she was. Opening her eyes, she found herself staring up at a fat pink cupid which in turn was gazing at some manner of goddess, at least she was clad in a chiton, and the cupid was painted on a blue background—a ceiling, of course, but one she had never seen before.

"Ah, she is awake," someone remarked in a voice she had heard before. Her gaze shifted, and instead of the ceiling, she met dark eyes. Unexpectedly, they were not agleam with laughter, but concerned. "Are you in pain?" Mr. . . . the voice . . . *Mr. Questred's* voice demanded.

"I . . . not really, but how . . . ?"

"Pamela, dearest . . ." Edith was bending over her. "Are you much hurt?"

Her feelings were becoming more specific. Her head ached, and so did her shoulders. There was a bar of hurt from one to the other, just below her collarbone. Memory returned, and with it an image of Stargazer rearing. "I fell," she murmured.

"Yes, dear, you did," Edith affirmed. "That low-hanging branch."

"And Stargazer?"

"I expect he must be back in the stables," Edith said.

"I . . ." She hesitated, not knowing quite how she felt and all too aware of the man beside Edith. "How did I get here?"

"Mr. Questred carried you here," Edith explained. "When I could not rouse you, I rode back to the Hall."

"You . . . carried me all this way?" Pamela stared up at him confusedly.

"You were hardly a burden, Miss Cardwell," he assured her. "I only wish my staff had arrived, and my coach. I have only my horse and I did not like to chance taking you back to your home on horseback, being not acquainted with the extent of your injuries. I have sent my man for your father."

"Oh, dear," Pamela said. "He will be annoyed. His calculations—"

"His calculations?" Mr. Questred broke in.

"He is an astronomer, sir—amateur, of course, but dedicated. He will not appreciate the interruption, I fear."

She received a quizzical and slightly disapproving glance. "Seeing to his daughter's well-being is surely of more importance than the . . . er, planetary movements," Mr. Questred observed.

"Of course it is!" Edith exclaimed. "You are being nonsensical, my love." She turned to Mr. Questred. "I expect she is still a bit confused."

"No, I am not," Pamela contradicted. "You know Papa almost as well as I do and . . . Oh, dear."

"Are you in pain?" Mr. Questred demanded quickly.

"No, I do not know what . . ." She broke off, saying reluctantly, "I expect I *am* a bit confused." She had an interior sigh for an admission that was completely untrue. However, she could hardly tell him that she did not know why she had mentioned her father's fixation on the stars. It could be construed as either a criticism or a bid for sympathy, neither of which she had intended. It had been only a statement of fact—but there was no explaining that to a complete stranger. Yet, even as that thought crossed her mind, she found that she was no longer looking on him as a stranger, and furthermore, the antipathy that she had experienced at their initial meeting had vanished. She could only be grateful for the concern he was currently evincing and for the fact that he had carried her quite a distance and had done his best to make her comfortable. She said diffidently, "It was very kind of you to notify my father. I am sure that he must agree."

"I am glad I could be of help," he said. "I think that when you arrive home, you should have a hot bath. It will take out a good deal of the soreness you will necessarily experience.''

''I will do that, of course.'' She nodded.

''Oh, listen,'' Edith said. ''I think I hear a coach.'' She went to the window and was back in a second. ''Yes, he is here. Your father.''

''I will go to meet him,'' Mr. Questred said quickly. ''If you will excuse me ... .'' Without waiting for their answer, he hurriedly left the room.

''Oh, dear.'' Pamela sat up and then groaned as pain shot through her.

''What is the matter?'' Edith hurried to her side.

''I do ache all over,'' Pamela said ruefully. ''But worse than that, Papa will be angry and you may be sure that I will be hearing about the folly of coming here—for the next month!''

''Not if you tell him you had no idea the house was occupied.''

''That will make no difference. He has laid down strict rules that I am not to go beyond our boundaries unless a groom or Tom accompanies me.''

''He has said that?'' Edith looked surprised.

''Yes . . . it's Miss Pringle's notion, I am sure. She insists that since I am betrothed and soon to be wed, I cannot go riding about the countryside as if I were twelve. She says I must remember my position. And Papa has agreed with her. I, of course, have ignored his command—because he is always closeted in his observatory and Miss Pringle spends a good deal of her time in her chamber.''

''Well, you may blame me and say that I led you astray,'' Edith said comfortingly.

''I am sure that will not suffice, though I do thank you.'' Pamela rolled her eyes and braced herself as she heard footsteps coming along the hall. In another moment Sir Robert, with Mr. Questred behind him, had stridden into the room. Coming to the bed, he had an anxious look for Pamela. ''My dear, are you badly hurt, then?''

She had an impulse to hold off the inevitable scolding with a lengthy recital of her various aches and pains, but it would not do for her host to think her craven, as he might were she to make so patent a bid for her father's sympathy. "A few bruises, sir," she said lightly.

"Well, I am glad of that." Sir Robert's gaze hardened. He added, "I must say I was surprised to hear that you were so far from home."

"It was at my suggestion, Sir Robert," Edith assured him quickly. "We had heard that the Hall was to be sold and came to look upon the grounds once more."

"Once more?" Sir Robert echoed. "That would suggest you had visited the Hall before?"

"Only once," Edith said hastily.

"We had heard that the chapel was haunted, Papa," Pamela said, realizing too late that that was just the sort of an excuse to make her father even angrier.

"Had you indeed?" Mr. Questred demanded before Sir Robert could deliver himself to the chill response that was plainly forming upon his lips. "Have I acquired a ghost, then?"

"The late Lady Hermione Hadley," Edith said. "That is . . . she is not precisely 'late'—having been dead at least a hundred years."

"Arrant nonsense!" Sir Robert exclaimed. "Whatever her follies in life, Hermione Hadley is dust and ashes now." He turned to Mr. Questred. "I beg you will not heed this silly female chatter."

"But I find it fascinating, sir," Mr. Questred said. "Understandably, the agents who sold me the property failed to tell me that I might have a phantom tenant . . . or would she consider me her tenant?" He had an interrogative glance for Pamela.

Pamela was grateful to him for what she suspected was a definite intention to smooth her father's ruffled feathers. "She is known to walk only in the chapel, sir."

"Stuff and nonsense!" Sir Robert exclaimed. "It is getting late and we have impinged upon your hospitality far too long, sir. It is time we took my daughter home."

Much to Pamela's surprise, he appeared concerned again as he added, "Are you able to walk, my dear?"

"I have not tried." She sat up hastily and another groan inadvertently escaped her. "My back . . ." she whispered.

"She received a considerable jolt, Sir Robert," Mr. Questred said. "I think it were best if I carried her back to the coach, and then, perhaps, you might have a doctor to examine her."

"Yes, of course. I will send for Mr. MacPherson immediately." Sir Robert nodded.

"A Scottish doctor," Mr. Questred said approvingly. "The very best sort. In my time, I have had cause to be extremely grateful to the breed."

Pamela glanced at him in surprise. There had been a peculiar note in his voice, one that she did not quite understand, and meeting his eyes, she found his glance evasive. "We have always found Mr. MacPherson very capable," she informed him, feeling an odd compulsion to alleviate an embarrassment that she also could not fathom. In the next moment these speculations were in abeyance as, moving to the bed, he said, "Put your arms around my neck, please."

Without really thinking, she obeyed and felt him lift her with an ease she found amazing. She was tall for a woman, and while she was also slender, she was not bone thin, but Mr. Questred held her as easily as if she were the proverbial feather.

As he carried her toward the door, she noticed that save for the large canopied bed, the room was bare of furniture and carpeting. She wondered why he had decided to stay there before the aforementioned staff and his furnishings arrived. It did seem odd, but much about him seemed odd. Oddest of all was her sudden awareness that her earlier anger had completely evaporated. Rather than actively disliking him, she found herself liking him to the point that she was extremely regretful at parting from him and hoped that she would soon see him again—and again and again!

3

Three days after Pamela's accident, Edith came to visit the sickroom. Though Pamela had sustained no broken bones, she had pulled a ligament in her shoulder and bruised her lower back. The resulting soreness had kept her confined to bed with hot bricks close to the injured parts. Much to her relief, however, beyond a few pungent sentences concerning her deliberate flouting of his strictures, her father had said very little about her mishap in the woods or her unsanctioned visit to Hadley Hall. Furthermore, he had praised Mr. Questred's actions—though he had added meaningfully that it was fortunate her rescuer had proved to be a gentleman.

Pamela was rather sure that her father's attitude in regard to the episode was predicated on the fact that an unknown comet streaking through the night sky was absorbing all his attention. Still, his sanction had pleased her, for it opened the way for Mr. Questred to come and inquire after her, as she was sure he must. However, contrary to these hopes, she had perforce to answer Edith's question with a disappointed, "No, he has not come."

"That is odd," Edith commented. "I was sure he would—but possibly he is busy getting his house in order. Sukey tells me that two coaches of servants arrived the day after we were there, and also two drays carrying furniture. There have been two more, and Sukey says the pieces are exceptionally fine, inlaid cabinets, carved chairs and tables, and several oil paintings. He must be extremely wealthy."

"And it sounds as if he has good taste," Pamela approved. "I wonder where he came from. Does Sukey have a notion?"

"She thinks he may be from India—a nabob. That would account for his complexion—the sun is very hot in India."

"Does she know for sure?" Pamela asked.

Edith shook her head. "That's what one of the servants told her, but he was not sure. Perhaps you could ask Mr. Questred when he does come to see you."

"Oh, I could not, and I do not expect he will come to see me. He has not so much as inquired for me." Pamela sighed. "But I told you that."

She received a quizzical glance for Edith. "Perhaps that is just as well. After all, you are betrothed to Tom."

Pamela sat up and shot her friend an indignant look. "What has the one to do with the other?" she demanded in acerbic tones. "Are you suggesting that I have more than a passing interest in him?"

"If the shoe fits . . ." Edith smiled.

"It does not fit!" Pamela exclaimed. "I found him unusual and I . . . I dislike mysteries, that is all."

"But I thought you were passionately fond of mysteries, hence your collection of works by Mrs. Radcliffe. And why do you believe Mr. Questred mysterious?"

"Do not you?" Pamela countered.

"Not really." Edith spoke thoughtfully. "He is only new to the district. I expect that when he has been here longer, everyone will know all there is to know about him—if not through him, through the servants."

"I wonder . . ." Pamela mused. "I have a feeling . . ."

"What manner of feeling?" Edith inquired as Pamela seemed to fall into a brown study.

"It's difficult to be specific . . . No, not entirely. There are his hands, for instance. Did you notice them?"

"His hands?" Edith repeated in some surprise. "No. Should I have? Does he have six fingers, perhaps?"

"No, silly! But they are rough and the palms hard. I noticed that when he carried me to the coach. Our gardener has hands like that . . . laborer's hands. And his nose has been broken. There is also a scar on his cheek. He must have had his share of fights. Yet his manner and his speech are certainly unexceptional. He appears to be a gentleman."

"A designation you were entirely unwilling to accord him at first meeting," Edith reminded her.

"But he is," Pamela said earnestly. "It was just that at first, he did seem bold and . . . and overfamiliar. But afterward, he was uncommonly kind and gentle, too. And . . . " She stared at a tap on the door. "Yes?" she called.

Lucy appeared in the aperture. "If you please, Miss Pamela, there's a gentleman wants to see you."

"A gentleman?" Pamela interrupted quickly, her face brightening. "Who?"

" 'Tis Mr. Bellairs."

"Oh, Tom," Pamela said. "Very well, let him come up."

"Yes, Miss Pamela." Lucy hurried away.

"Tom is back, then!" Edith said excitedly.

"He arrived yesterday evening." Pamela nodded.

"And how is his father?"

"I do not know. You may ask him if he does not tell us, which I am sure he will," Pamela said in tones that were edged with a disappointment she could not quite disguise.

She received a speaking glance from Edith. "Really, I find your attitude incomprehensible and . . ." She paused as Lucy appeared once more.

"Mr. Thomas Bellairs," she announced.

"Come, Lucy," remarked an amused voice. "Must we be so formal? Stand aside, my girl." As Lucy, with a giggle, obeyed, a tall, dark young man entered hastily.

Striding to the bed, he bent to give Pamela a kiss on the cheek. Moving back, he smiled at Edith. "You've come to cheer up the invalid, I see. How are you, my dear?"

"I am getting better," she responded.

He looked down at her quizzically. "And how came you to fall off poor old Stargazer? You cannot have been watching where you were going."

Pamela glared at him. "You speak as if Stargazer were on his last legs! He is still quite a spirited horse. And I rode into a branch."

"Ah, my hypothesis was correct, then. You were not looking where you were going. How many times must I tell you that you must keep your mind—?"

"No more times, please," she interrupted. "It will not happen again."

"A rash and undoubtedly erroneous statement," he commented. "Given your penchant for thinking of three things at once, it will undoubtedly happen again. Still, my dear, I am sorry that you were rendered so uncomfortably by this piece of folly."

Pamela smiled. "I thank you, Tom. And how are you?"

"Never better, now that I am back at Bellairs," he responded with a roll of his dark eyes. "Traveling into foreign parts is not for me."

"Foreign parts?" Pamela scoffed. "Bath? You cannot call that foreign!"

"I can call it a deadly dull city, though," he complained. "And full of desiccated old women and dissipated old men."

Edith looked shocked. "Your father is there."

"I was not including my father, of course, my dear Edith," Tom said blandly.

"Is he any better?" Pamela asked.

Tom shook his head. "Indeed, as I told you he might —he has asked that we postpone the wedding by a fort-night." He looked anxiously at Pamela. "Shall you mind, my dear?"

"Not at all," she said quickly.

He visited a sharper look on her. "I do not know whether or not I am complimented by so hasty an acquiescence."

"Oh, Tom," Pamela said teasingly. "How many references have you made to halters and reins in the last months?"

"But I was funning, as well you know. Still, I expect we will be wed a long time."

Edith looked from one to the other. "I imagine that I have heard less lovelike conversations between a prospective bride and groom—but I cannot remember when!"

Tom grinned at her. "I expect that you, in common with my fair bride-to-be, have been delving into those so-romantic tomes from the circulating library." He suddenly leaned forward and plucked a volume from off the bed. "Ah, here we have *Lord Morton's Secret or: A Bride Revenged!* You know, my angel fair"—he bent a stern look on Pamela—"I shall not allow such trash into my house, once we are wed."

"How do you know it's trash? You've not read it!" she said crossly.

"The title tells it all," he responded. "A murrain on these publishers and their schools of authors. They sow nothing but discord and have been known to reap separations." He tossed the book down.

"I would term that a gross exaggeration," Pamela retorted. "One needs a little gallantry in one's life."

"And a few duels, I expect," he said caustically. "Though why the ladies would imagine it romantic for their husbands or bridegrooms to get punctured for their sake is beyond me."

Edith giggled. "I do not believe we really expect that, Tom."

"Deny it if you can, Edith—that this sort of literature raises your expectations of marriage to ridiculous heights." There was yet a caustic note in his voice.

Turning to Pamela, he continued, "I do hope you are not going to want me falling on my knees and kissing your slipper fifteen times a day!"

"I would never expect such a thing of you," she said sarcastically.

"Good." He smiled at her. "Then you'll not be disappointed."

"And I may read my books in peace?"

"Depending on whether or not I approve the contents."

"You cannot be serious!" Pamela glared at him.

"Of course he's not," Edith said pacifically. "He is only teasing, are you not, Tom?"

"I hope that when we are wed she will dispense with all these frivolities," Tom said doggedly. "Marriage is a serious step."

"Oh, dear, Tom." Edith sighed. "I fear you've sadly missed a mother's leavening influence."

His face changed. He looked unexpectedly sober. "I have missed my mother, true, but what has that to do with anything we are saying?"

"Only that she might have told you that married life does not require an entire change of habit. One might wear a veil briefly but one is not expected to 'take the veil' immediately a ring is pressed upon the third finger, left hand."

"Hear, hear!" Pamela clapped her hands.

Tom's eyes were still on Edith. "I did not suggest that," he said. "But certainly there are more responsibilities to face."

She smiled at him. "You should cross that bridge when you come to it—not anticipate the worst."

"We'll be crossing it very soon," he said, straightening his shoulders—almost as if he were assuming that burden already, Pamela thought with some annoyance. There was a pulse beating at the base of her throat, and as always when she was with Tom, she felt as if she were being enclosed, stone by stone, into a tall tower.

When they were younger, she had enjoyed being with him, but since they had become officially betrothed, he had grown so serious that she scarcely knew him. Furthermore, his mention of censoring her reading matter was not to be taken lightly! She was quite sure that the playmate of her youth could and would be entirely implacable once they were wed. All the indications were present. Also, his passion for Bellair would keep him in the country. He would probably even resent their wedding trip to London and she was positive that nothing would ever convince him to go to Paris. Indeed, her life would not change in any respect save that she would have the responsibilities Tom had mentioned without even the solace of her romances. She was quite sure he meant exactly what he had said about them. She could actually envision him throwing them out the window.

It was a pity he had never read such literature. It would not hurt him to take some instructions from the gentlemen who peopled their pages—or rather from the authors who wrote them and had a very good idea of how a man in love should treat the object of his affections. Tom would be a worse companion than her father, for he would not be spending all his days stargazing, and, she suspected, being ignored was better than being eternally under the supervision of an exacting husband! She stared out of the window and wistfully longed for wings.

"Well, my love"—Tom bent over the bed again to kiss her on the forehead—"I must go." He turned to Edith with a smile. "Good-bye, my dear. You are looking very lovely today—when can we expect to hear of your betrothal?"

Edith looked down. "I will be in London for the Season. I have high hopes of that."

"And so you should," he responded. "Your first Season will undoubtedly be your last."

"I'll bear that in mind and tax you with it later," she returned lightly.

"You'll not need to do that." He bowed over her hand and took his leave.

Once the door had closed on him, Pamela hurled her book against it. "There are times," she said bitterly, "when I actually dislike him!"

"Pamela!" Edith regarded her in consternation. "How can you speak in such a ridiculous manner? Can you not see that Tom is madly in love with you?"

"No, I cannot!" Pamela retorted. "He does not want a wife. He wants a . . . a cow or an ox . . . or some other domestic animal!"

"I cannot believe that I am hearing aright," Edith cried. "You are blind, Pamela. Tom adores you!"

"I do not wish to be adored by a . . . a veritable tyrant, a . . . Napoleon who will dictate what I may read and whom I may see and . . ."

"Oh, my love, he is just talking. Papa has much the same attitude. Mama never heeds him. She does just as she chooses, only she does not let him see her doing it."

"I loathe subterfuge!" Pamela glared at her. "I do not want to resort to tricks and lies. I want . . . I want Tom the way he used to be, charming and full of mischief. I have never seen anyone change so radically!"

"He has only come of age," Edith pointed out. "And, my dear 'tis time you did too. After all, postponements or no postponements, your wedding is not very far off."

"No, it's not very far off," Pamela sighed.

"I wish you knew how very fortunate you are." Edith rose. "I must go," she added.

Pamela, bidding her farewell, was relieved. She had never felt so unhappy or so misunderstood. If Edith had remained, she had no doubt that with her friend taking Tom's part, they would have fallen into a serious argument. It could even have meant an end to their friendship, for, indeed, she had never resented Edith quite so much. And it was not for what she had said, but rather for what she had not said. Elliptically, she had been issuing a warning concerning Mr. Questred. Pamela had no doubt that Edith sensed . . . no, she more than sensed her interest in him. She was actually alarmed by it, which, of course, was ridiculous. She, Pamela Cardwell, would eventually wed Tom. Any other course was unthinkable, and though he annoyed her, she was fond of him. Yet she would like to see Mr. Questred again. And why had he not made an effort to see her? It did not require her continued consideration! She reached for her book and opened at the place where she had stopped reading. The heroine had been in an unfortunate position, immured in a tower and at the mercy of Sir Guy Charteris, a thief whose cliffside castle overlooked a storm-tossed sea.

The hero, unable to approach the guarded road to the stronghold, had been attempting to reach it by that same sea. As described in the book, he was fair with bright yellow hair and deep blue eyes. He was an intrepid sailor and an excellent swimmer and he had just managed to pull himself ashore. However, the image in Pamela's mind was not that of a fair-haired gallant. In his place, she envisioned one who was as dark as Sir Guy but wonderfully handsome and brave. His eyes, needless to say, were almost black, and his skin sun-bronzed. She, watching from her tower prison, saw him overcome all obstacles to reach her. A quavering sigh escaped her. She closed her book and stared out of the window at the tear-blurred distances. Why had he not come to see her? Why, why, why?

It was another two days before Pamela's soreness was gone and she able to ride again. Unfortunately, by that time Miss Pringle, who had been visiting a recently widowed sister, had returned. Hearing of Pamela's mishap, she pronounced herself shocked that the two girls had gone riding without being accompanied by Smith, the groom.

"You are fortunate indeed that you did not meet with

something worse than a mere tumble from your horse,"
her ex-governess and present chaperon had said darkly.
Furthermore, and to Pamela's complete annoyance, she
found she could go nowhere without encountering Miss
Pringle. Even when she walked in the gardens, she
would meet her and be constrained to converse with her
on such boring subjects as the return of the willow-
warbler or how pleasant the spring squill looked in the
adjacent meadows.

Of course, she was allowed to ride with Tom but he
was busy attending to matters concerning Bellair and so
she was neglected while he was away in Bath. Consequently, Pamela's frustration increased, and with it
was an almost passionate longing to see what her
literature-ridden mind had dubbed "the dark stranger"
again. She did hear of him. Everybody, according to
Lucy, was marveling at the improvements he was
making in the house, not excluding the ruined chapel, he
being undisturbed by the possible disapproval of Lady
Hermione.

" 'E seems to be as rich as creases, wotever that
means," Lucy had said, obviously quoting a fellow
servant.

"Croesus was a wealthy king of Greece," Pamela had
explained.

"Oh, but 'e aint' a Greek, at least I don't think so."

Pamela had not elucidated upon the allusion. Instead,
she had asked, "Does anyone happen to know where
he's from?"

"Nobody, an' e' 'asn't much to say for 'isself'n all
the servants is new. 'E 'ired 'em in London'n they don't
know anythin' about 'im either. An' 'e keeps to 'isself a
lot . . . goes off places in the afternoon'n don't return
until late at night or 'oles up in the library. Seems like
'e's bought a great store o' books."

That had surprised Pamela. Mr. Questred did not
have the air of a scholar or student. Indeed, she had the
feeling that he might have served with the armed forces.

Possibly he might even have been a soldier of fortune, the modern equivalent of the knight-errant, off to fight in the cause of justice. She could easily envision him in a brilliant red uniform—the latter-day equivalent, again, of shining armor. And these men, she reminded herself, were often readers or even writers. Had not Cervantes been a soldier, captured by Turks while fighting for king and country? She had reason to regret her original antipathy toward Mr. Questred. Had it not been for that, they might have fallen into a conversation that had not been centered mainly on her aches and pains.

She was thinking about that on the Sunday morning following her recovery. Yesterday she had had a strong desire to go riding in the vicinity of the Hall. Unfortunately, there was no asking Tom to go in that direction and if she managed to elude the vigilance of Miss Pringle, she would have been hard put to explain her presence to Mr. Questred, provided she happened to meet him. Now she was both surprised and annoyed to find herself concentrating once more on one who obviously did not have a reciprocal interest in herself. Nearly a fortnight had passed since her accident and he had not even called to see how she was faring. Yet she could not exorcise him from her mind. He still dominated her dreams and stood in for the hero of every book she read. It would have helped had she been able to discuss the matter with Edith, her one confidante, but not only had Edith not been to see her since her recovery, she was so much in Tom's corner that she would hardly be a receptive listener.

"Pamela, my dear, are you ready?" Sir Robert came into the drawing room.

"Yes, Papa," she responded.

He did not immediately hurry her into the hall. Instead, he regarded her with admiration. "That is a very pretty gown, my dear. One would have imagined the pink must clash with your hair, but it does not. And the bonnet is certainly unexceptional. I have not seen that before, have I?"

It was typical of him to ask such a question, not typical at all to compliment her. She was pleased at that and even more pleased that neither he nor Miss Pringle, who had just joined them, was aware that it had been intended as a trousseau gown but donned in the hopes that Mr. Questred might be present to see it. She was particularly glad that Miss Pringle had been with her sister at the time it was being made. "It was a length of goods I saw in the draper's window and could not resist, the color being one of my favorites, Papa," she explained.

"No one can ever fault your eye for color, Pamela," Miss Pringle said approvingly. "I hope you will include it in your trousseau—the which you will be able to do if you do not wear it after today."

"That is an excellent suggestion. I think I might," Pamela responded blandly. A swift glance in the mirror that hung over the fireplace in the drawing room assured her that her father and chaperon had been quite accurate in their praise. Lucy had taken extra care in combing out her curls and there was a rose sewn beneath the brim of her bonnet. She was sure that Tom would think it very becoming but, regrettably, it was not Tom who was occupying the greater space in her mind. Instead, as she stepped into the post chaise, she was thinking mostly of Mr. Questred.

Miss Pringle, who sat beside her, discerned a beatific expression in Pamela's eyes that quite brought tears to her own faded eyes. Her young charge much resembled an angel, she thought, and one could see, too, that the girl had finally come to realize that she was no longer a child but a maiden, a maiden who was about to become a matron. She hoped that Mr. Thomas Bellairs would prove worthy of so charming and beautiful a bride.

Alighting from the post chaise, Pamela sent a swift look at those members of the congregation who lingered outside enjoying the sunshine on a day that could rightly be termed halcyon. There was a slight dappling of clouds in the cerulean sky, but since they were a week into May, the sun was bright and the breezes gentle. Birds flew back and forth to nests in the eaves of the old church, and green vines softened its stones. In the churchyard, the hawthorn bushes were beginning to bloom.

Pamela did not see Edith immediately, but as she moved toward the church steps, she did sight her talking animatedly to Tom. He was looking very handsome, she had to admit, but in that same moment she forgot him —for there was Mr. Questred, his dark compelling gaze catching and holding her own! She drew in a breath. He was even more handsome than she remembered. Beside him, all other men seemed diminished. None had such height, such broad shoulders, or so slim a waist! He was dressed beautifully in a well-fitting brown coat and beige stockinette trousers strapped under gleaming brown boots. His cravat was well-tied but not intricately and the points of his shirt collar were starched but, again, not exaggeratedly so. She noted with approval that the fobs at his waist were leather rather than gold and his slender fingers were bare of rings. Of course, a ring would have drawn attention to his hands. Fleetingly she recalled their roughness, but forgot it because he was coming in her direction. If only Tom had not seen her and continued speaking with Edith so that she might have an uninterrupted moment with Mr. Questred, her father and Miss Pringle having gone ahead of her into the church. Alas, for that vain hope. Tom had seen her and was coming in her direction with Edith. They must all four meet, and would Edith, the unattached, attract Mrs. Questred? She had not before—but of course she had been at a disadvantage since she, Pamela, had required all of his attention. Edith, was, as usual, looking beautiful. She also appeared more animated than was her wont of late. Her blue eyes were sparkling, and under a becoming bonnet, her golden curls clustered about her pretty face, and never had Pamela wished so strongly that she did not know her!

"My dear . . ." Edith reached her first. "You are looking much more the thing!"

"A picture, indeed." Tom had stepped to her side and now he slipped a proprietary arm around her waist as he fastened questioning eyes upon the approaching Mr. Questred.

Pamela managed a swift greeting for them all and went on to introduce Mr. Questred without mentioning that Tom was her fiancé. However, that fact was brought out almost immediately by one Lady Bicester, who had been a friend of her mother's. As her ladyship continued to visit encomiums upon the engaged couple, saying with a sentimental tear that it was a pity that poor dear Cecily was not present to see her lovely daughter, Pamela could not resist a swift glance at Mr. Questred. She did not meet his eyes. These were fastened on Tom and she noted happily that he was frowning. Did that suggest jealousy? She could only hope so. Yet, what was the use of hoping, when she would soon be wed to Tom? If only Mr. Questred had arrived at the Hall earlier, or—she swallowed a lump in her throat—not at all, so that she might never have known of his existence!

"My dear, where are your wits today?" Tom demanded rudely, availing himself of the license accorded a companion of many years' standing.

"I beg your pardon, Tom. Did you say something?" she questioned.

"I asked if you are still suffering any ill effects from your fall?"

"No, I am completely recovered, thank you." She nodded in Mr. Questred's direction. "This is the gentleman who rescued me, Tom."

"Indeed?" Tom had a pleasant smile for him. "It seems I am in your debt, sir."

"Not at all," Mr. Questred responded politely. "I was glad to have been of service. When, by the way, will this happy event take place?"

"In July," Tom responded.

"If your father does not postpone it again," Pamela said.

"Your father is ill, then?" Mr. Questred asked.

"Yes, he is in Bath availing himself of those ill-tasting waters." Tom grimaced.

"I hope 'tis nothing serious," Mr. Questred said.

"No, a stomach ailment which is yielding to treatment."

"I am glad to hear that." Mr. Questred nodded.

"I thank you, sir." Tom looked toward the church entrance and turned to Pamela. "I expect we'd best go in, my dear."

"Yes," she agreed. As he took her arm, she noticed that Mr. Questred had moved to stand beside Edith. She stifled a sigh and hoped that the vicar would not favor his congregation with one of his longer sermons. She also hoped, for her own peace of mind, that Mr. Questred would not be sitting anyplace where she might see him.

Tom had spoken to her, she realized. "What was that, my dear?" she asked.

"You are certainly abstracted," he complained. "I said that you were looking uncommonly beautiful this morning."

She smiled up at him. "I can return the compliment and say that you are in fine looks yourself, Tom." She was conscious of a certain regret. She had chafed at the thought of her marriage before the arrival of Mr. Questred, but she had been resigned to it, had even expected that she would be tolerably happy with one whom she had known all her life. At this juncture, however, she could only wish that Edmund Bellairs would remain in Bath longer even than that stipulated week. She was not, she assured herself, wishing ill to her future father-in-law, she was only hoping that he would continue to cosset himself as he was undoubtedly doing at present. Having spent a lifetime in the pursuit of self-gratification, he was not likely to change in his old age.

On that pleasant realization, she entered the pew and knelt briefly to pray that Edmund Bellairs remain in Bath indefinitely. She also prayed that she might have the opportunity to exchange a few words with Mr. Questred, even though he would have, she feared, little interest in her, now that he had learned of her betrothal.

Contrary to her expectations, one prayer, at least, was granted. After the services ended, Tom, coming out of the church with Pamela, was accosted by the vicar, who had known him from childhood. Pamela, continuing out of the church in the wake of her father and Miss Pringle, found herself beside Mr. Questred. She smiled up at him and received an appreciative smile in return.

Moving closer to her, he said in a low voice, "I was unable to tell you earlier how very beautiful you are looking this morning, Miss Cardwell."

She was surprised and rather taken aback by a compliment he really ought not to have accorded one who was bespoken. Yet, at the same time, she could not help but be thrilled by his appreciation. She said softly, "I thank you, Mr. Questred."

As they came down the church steps, he further surprised her by adding, "I could wish that we had met before . . ." Without waiting for her response, he continued, "Is your engagement one of long standing?"

She nodded, saying more ruefully than she had intended, "I have known Mr. Bellairs nearly all my life."

"But you cannot have been betrothed so long," he pursued.

"No, that matter was concluded earlier this year— by our fathers." She could not restrain a sigh.

"Ah." He nodded. "A family arrangement."

"Entirely," she dared to add. "I was not consulted. I merely was told of their decision." Meeting his eyes, she found a commiserating look and, at the same time, a regretful look in them. Her heart began to pound and there was a throbbing in her throat.

"Ah, my dear." Tom joined them. "Are you in the mood for a drive?"

She was not, but she did not dare refuse. "That would be lovely," she assented.

"Come, then, my own." Tom turned to Mr. Questred. "We will bid you good afternoon, sir."

"Good afternoon, Mr. Bellairs," Mr. Questred responded. "Miss Cardwell."

"Good afternoon, sir." She gave him a pleasant and, she hoped, properly impersonal smile.

Tom chose to drive his gig down a quiet country road bordered by a stretch of meadow. Giving the horse its head, he broke a brief silence by saying, "Who is this fellow Questred?"

She shrugged. "You know as much as I."

"Not quite. You've had the advantage of another meeting. I've not yet asked you. Why were you so far afield?"

"Did not Edith explain? We went to say . . . farewell to the Hall."

He frowned. "And without escort. Anything might have happened."

"Pray do not read me a lecture. I have had my fill of those already," she said tartly. "Besides, you yourself have been wont to visit the Hall with us from time to time."

"That does not mean that I want my fiancée to—"

"Oh, Tom," Pamela interrupted. "You are being ridiculous. Before I was your fiancée, I was your friend, your comrade, too. And considering the scrapes we've shared, I am not going to have you becoming so top-lofty!"

"I was younger then . . . we were both younger. And what did that fellow have to say to you—after church?"

She was startled by his abrupt change of subject. "He was just passing the time of day."

"I did not like the way he was looking at you."

She gave him a wide-eyed stare. "And how, pray, was he looking at me?"

"I thought him too familiar."

"Surely you must be funning!" she exclaimed, the while she rejoiced at having her own feelings concerning Mr. Questred so quickly corroborated. She added, "I hope you are not going to be jealous of a man I've seen but twice in my life."

"There is something odd about him." Tom frowned.

"Why do you say that?"

"I am not sure . . . it's a feeling I have." He added, "No one here seems to have more than a passing acquaintance with him."

"He has only recently arrived."

"Why did he come here? I have heard that he is a warm man with a lot of the ready. Why, then, did he settle at the Hall? There are many houses in better repair."

"I am not party to his thinking."

"He is very strange-looking."

"In what respect?"

"He is as dark as any Gypsy. His eyes are almost black."

"He is not a Gypsy, however. Obviously he is a gentleman. I am sure that none who have met him would give you an argument as to that." She gazed over Tom's shoulder. "Ah, look at that spread of violets in the field. Did you ever see so many?"

Tom visited a cursory look upon the field in question. "Often," he said impatiently. "Now, as to Questred . . ."

"Why will you continue to discuss this stranger?" she demanded edgily. "Really, Tom, I do not understand you. One would think you were jealous, and surely you have no reason to be—so please, may we not talk of something else?"

"As you wish," he said reluctantly.

By the time they returned from their drive, Pamela's frustration had increased. If Tom did not like Mr. Questred, she would not have the opportunity to converse with him without arousing her fiancé's suspicions. He, in turn, would complain to her father, and since Sir Robert was, she was positive, counting the days until she married Tom and left him in sole possession of the house, he would discourage any attempt Mr. Questred made to see her. However, Tom or no Tom, she wanted to see him again, and judging from the gist of their brief conversation after church, he shared that desire. If they were to meet in secret—what then? Her imagination, fueled by a score of clandestine meetings lovingly described by her favorite authoresses, provided images that brought a blush to her cheek and a sigh to accompany it. She stared out of the window at the passing clouds and wished she might be on one of them—floating she knew not whither. No, that was not true, she did have a destination in mind, and at the thought of it, her cheeks grew even rosier.

4

Pamela stood in the lower hall looking up through the stairwell. She had been there for a quarter of an hour, ever since Lucy had informed her that the master of Hadley Hall had come to see Sir Robert. By dint of listening outside the door of the observatory, Lucy had divined that Mr. Questred was interested in constructing his own observatory in the upper reaches of the Hall. Lucy had further gathered that his interest in heavenly bodies equaled that of Sir Robert!

Was that his only reason for coming?

Pamela, with their brief colloquy outside the church still large in her mind, put her hand to her heart. She was positive that it was beating faster than usual. She could compare her present sensations to those of Geraldine de Gramont in *The Guardsman's Gauntlet or: A Lost Cause*. Every time the heroine of that exciting and ultimately tragic tale saw the young guardsman, she was close to fainting. While she, Pamela Cardwell, was, unfortunately, not subject to swoons, she was fast discovering that palpitations were quite another matter. She did wish that she might also swoon as had the unfortunate Geraldine in the arms of her true but doomed lover. Swooning was something everyone could see, while palpitations were merely uncomfortable and, for the most part, invisible. Of course, she could pretend to faint and he would pick her up and carry her as he had when first they met—such a pity that she had really been unconscious and unable to enjoy that enchanted moment! And . . . Her speculations ceased abruptly as she heard her father's voice.

Of late, Sir Robert had grown slightly hard of hearing
and consequently he spoke more loudly than had been
his wont some years back. She was able to hear him say,
"Very commendable, sir—and I assure you that though
this instrument is old, I cannot believe that any of our
more modern telescopes are any better. The Germans
are masters when it comes to fashioning scientific
instruments. Still, you must judge for yourself when
you visit Mr. Grenville's shop in London."

"I shall do that, sir. I have written down the manu-
facturer's name as well as the address of Mr.
Grenville."

"You will forgive me if I do not see you out, I hope?"
Sir Robert continued.

"I quite understand, sir."

Pamela waited to hear no more. She hurried outside.
After four days of rain, the sun was bright again and she
could have been walking along the carriageway—coming back from a stroll in the woods, perhaps—so that
she might accidentally encounter Mr. Questred as he
came outside. Fortunately, Miss Pringle was in her
room, whence she had retired immediately after the
noonday meal. Her habits never changed, and in conse-
quence, she would not be unexpectedly joining Pamela
outside, and if Mr. Questred wished to speak to her, he
might accomplish his purpose without any undue inter-
ruptions.

Standing near a tree, she saw the front door open and
then *he* appeared. He looked amazingly handsome in a
claret-colored coat and buckskin breeches. As usual, his
linen was spotless and his high leather boots well-
polished. The dark red of his coat was extremely
becoming to his swarthy complexion, Pamela thought.
She wondered if he might not have a dash of Gypsy
blood, like Sebastian, the half-Gypsy hero of *The
Romany Prince,* a novel both she and Edith counted
their favorite. She herself had read it five times. Pamela
quickly dismissed the tale from her mind as Mr.

Questred came down the steps. He appeared thoughtful and she was sure he did not see her. She stepped forward, saying with well-feigned surprise, "Mr. Questred! I did not know you were here!"

His eyes widened and, she thought, brightened. He said, "Miss Cardwell, I hardly dared hope I would have an opportunity to see you today. Your father told me you had gone riding directly after dinner."

It was impossible not to be thrilled at a greeting suggesting disappointment in not seeing her and, at the same time, revealing the fact that he had asked after her. "I have only just returned," she explained, thankful that her father's aerie did not overlook the stableyard, whence she had not been that day, having learned at the last moment that *he* was expected.

"How fortunate for me," he responded. There was a slight frown in his eyes as he continued, "I have been thinking about you. I am told that you are soon to become a bride."

"Yes," she responded, swallowing a sigh. "Mr. Bellairs or, rather, Sir Edmund, as I presume we must call him now, ought to be arriving from Bath at the week's end. He wishes our wedding to take place during the second week in June rather than in mid-July as was originally his intention."

"But that is less than a month away!"

There was chagrin in his tone, and Pamela found her palpitations returning. She also feared that she was suffering a change of color. Keeping her eyes lowered, she said, "Yes, I had not anticipated the change in plan."

"Well, I expect that it is only natural that Mr. Bellairs would want his son to be married soon. He is the sole heir to a great estate, I understand. Bellair, is it not?"

"Yes. It is not far from here . . . just the other side of the woods. Have you seen it?"

"No, but I have heard that the house and grounds are particularly beautiful."

"They are. However, now that Mr. . . . Sir Edmund has finally received the official notification of Arthur Bellairs' death, Tom is thinking of enlarging the lake and planting more trees. He rather fancies a topiary garden, too."

"I see . . . or rather, I do not see, Miss Cardwell. Who is or was this Arthur Bellairs, and what had his death to do with your fiancé's plans for horticultural improvements?"

She was silent a moment, visited by an unexpected pang. "I expect," she said finally, "that I ought not to have mentioned poor Arthur. However, I thought you might have heard about him. It's a subject that seems to arise every time anyone settles in the community."

"I have been rather busy getting my own house in order, Miss Cardwell. Consequently I have not had an opportunity to hear any gossip—or would this come under the heading of 'old wives' tales'?"

"Neither. The subject of Arthur is generally introduced whenever there is a mention of smuggling. Despite our vigilant militia, smugglers still abound in this territory, we being so close to Romney Marsh." She could not restrain a sigh. "It does seem so strange about poor Arthur. I knew him. Of course, I was very little when he . . . when it happened, but even so it was an exceedingly great shock to me. I cried about it for days . . . for weeks."

Mr. Questred was regarding her with some confusion. "I am not sure that I follow you, Miss Cardwell."

She gave him an apologetic smile. "I am sorry. I was not being very illuminating. I probably ought not to have mentioned Arthur. It has been a sore trial to Tom and Sir Edmund . . ." She moved away from the steps and turned toward the garden. "Having introduced the topic, I will tell you about him, but please come with me. I would not like Papa to know that I had been discussing Arthur. He was so surprised and disappointed in him. He does not like to be wrong in his estimate of character, you see."

"I fear I do not see." Mr. Questred's dark eyes lingered on Pamela's face. "But I do understand that whatever happened to the man must have caused you considerable distress."

"Distress?" She raised her eyes to meet his questioning and, she thought, commiserating glance. "Yes, I was distressed," she said slowly, and was visited by a sudden image of the child she had been, weeping into her pillow as she had said over and over again, "I do not . . . I will not believe it." Inadvertently, she repeated, "I did not believe it." Flushing, she added, "I fear I must be confusing you even more!"

"You are certainly raising my curiosity to the . . . er sticking point, Miss Cardwell. But also I am beginning to dislike this Arthur."

"Dislike him, sir? Why?"

"Because I fear he has disturbed you." His eyes roved over her face. "I do not like to see you disturbed."

Their glances locked again. His stare was compelling, almost mesmerizing, Pamela thought confusedly. Various parts of her body had started to throb. She could compare these sensations to nothing she had ever experienced before! She had a sudden impulse to run away from him—but conversely, she had an equally strong desire to remain at his side, and to stave off his possibly imminent departure, she would play Scheherazade and tell him about Arthur, poor Arthur, whose astonishing connection with the smugglers would, at this moment, be a device to keep this fascinating man at her side.

She led him into the garden and thence to the folly, an artful imitation of a Grecian ruin, three pillars and a little marble bench set near a reflecting pool. Indicating the bench, she said shyly, "Will you sit down, sir?"

"If you will." He smiled.

"Of course." She sat on the end of the bench and, as he, too, sat down, a glance into the pool showed her that her cheeks were much pinker than usual. She was blushing! The revelation of that unfortunate condition caused a deeper blush to brighten her cheeks. She looked away and down. Defensively she began, "Arthur was uncommon kind, at least so it appeared to me." As she recounted the never-to-be-forgotten events of that afternoon, Pamela could not vanquish her old indignation. "I cannot believe it," she said on reaching the conclusion of her account. "I still cannot believe it." She looked at him nervously. "But you must not repeat that, nor indeed anything I have told you."

"I promise I shall not." He gave her a searching look. "It appears to distress you that this young man received his . . . er, just deserts."

"It does distress me. It is so hard for me to believe that Arthur acted in so reprehensible a manner."

"You appear to be his sole champion, my dear. Your father knew him, you say. What did he think?"

"Oh, he agreed with the others. There was so much evidence, you see. And yet . . ."

"And yet?" he questioned.

"I do not know. Anyway, he is dead."

"Yes, and that is not surprising, certainly. New South Wales, from all accounts, is no place for the gently nurtured."

"No." She gave him a distressed look. "He must have suffered greatly. He did suffer. We heard that he was . . . flogged."

Mr. Questred nodded. "It's a common punishment for convicts, my dear, for sailors and soldiers, too."

"It's terrible." She shuddered. "And Arthur, who was so gentle and kind . . ."

"Obviously his plight has much affected you, Miss Cardwell."

"He was so good to me," she said defensively.

"And so you will count yourself his champion."

"I do . . . or rather I did."

"You are very sweet, but I fear you are not too knowledgeable in the ways of the world. Was it not

Shakespeare who said, 'One can smile and smile and be a villain'?''

"He was not a villain!" she exclaimed.

"I am sure your fianceé would not thank you for siding so strongly with the late Arthur Bellairs."

"Tom was shocked too. He was very fond of his brother for all there was such a difference in their ages. Oh, I do wish he were not dead!"

"But he must be . . . and I regret we have wasted so much time in discussing him, particularly when there is so much else we might find to speak about in this beautiful garden with its bright spring flowers and . . . its goddess."

"Its goddess, sir?" Pamela repeated confusedly. "I fear we do not have such statuary. There is only a nymph with a water jar on one of our fountains."

"I was not speaking of statuary, Miss Cardwell." His voice deepened. "The goddess is here beside me." He paused, looking into her eyes. "Have you no notion of how very beautiful you are?"

She regarded him incredulously. Feelings of pleasure warred with those of shock, for of course he was far too bold. Yet as she met his dark gaze, she had a strange sensation of being drawn toward him . . . out of herself, compelled by words she realized she had dreamed he might employ. Yet she had never expected that this dream could become a reality.

"Forgive me, Miss Cardwell," he said quickly. "I should not have uttered what was in my heart . . . 'twas most unseemly, particularly to one who is . . . unfortunately betrothed."

Her heart seemed to have shattered into tiny pieces, which, in turn, were speeding through her body and pounding all through it. She also felt very warm, or was she cold? A few shards of common sense, remaining in her heating brain, told her that she ought to dismiss him immediately, but she could not seem to find the words. She said only, "There is . . . nothing to forgive.

I mean, you should not have . . . but . . . Oh, dear.''

He put his arm around her. "Miss Cardwell, I pray you will forgive my impetuous behavior. It is hard, very hard, to remain in your company without wanting . . . much more than you could ever grant me. However, what is the use of talking . . .'' There was a harsh note in his voice as he continued. "You are bespoken, and there's an end to it.'' Releasing her, he rose swiftly. "Would we had met before or not at all.'' Not waiting for her response, he added, "I do not think we had better see each other again. I've not the strength to remain in your company without wanting you.'' Taking her hand, he brought it to his lips, and then, astonishingly, he turned it palm-upward and pressed a long kiss upon it. Releasing it, he turned swiftly and strode from the garden.

For a moment Pamela remained where she was, stunned by the violence of her own feelings. Then she rose and ran toward the carriageway. She was not sure of what she wanted to say to him. She was only sure that she wanted to be near him. Yet, even as she reached that destination, she heard hoofbeats and saw that he was far ahead of her, nearing the gates. In another second he was lost around a bend in the road. Pamela remained where she was, staring into the tear-blurred distances, wishing she might be with him, before him upon his horse—his *palfrey.* Once more, she was mentally clothing him in bright armor—but she was being silly and childish, too, in wanting him to stay. She could not fault him for his abrupt departure. Obviously he was too honorable to continue pursuing her when, as he had said, so sadly, so regretfully, she was betrothed to another.

In the week that followed her encounter with Mr. Questred, Pamela was very busy. Not only was there her wedding gown to be fitted, there was the trousseau she would take with her on what was, astonishingly enough, her first visit to London. There had been a time when she had looked forward to seeing the city with Tom, but now her thoughts flew in another direction, and more than once during the endless fittings, Mrs. Nettlebloom, the mantau maker, had grown impatient, saying with the license accorded one who had been making Pamela's garments since she was in short-clothes, "You are not attending, Miss Cardwell. I told you to pivot. Please pivot so that I might adjust this hem!"

Mrs. Nettlebloom was not the only one to observe Pamela's abstraction. On an afternoon some eight days after her encounter with Mr. Questred, Sir Robert waxed acerbic over her vagueness and angrily demanded an explanation. He was even angrier when Miss Pringle attempted one.

"Young girls on the brink, you know . . ."

"And what would be the meaning of that, pray? What brink?"

"Matrimony, Sir Robert," she responded with a sentimental sigh.

"Stuff and nonsense. The chit has known him all her life! Why should her wits be woolgathering now?"

"Marriage, Sir Robert, is always an unknown country."

Sir Robert sent Miss Pringle into tears by saying, "How would you know, who've never been wed? Oh, by God, will you treat me to the vapors now? Confound you, woman, has everyone in this household gone mad?"

A few moments later he apologized to a red-eyed, red-nosed Miss Pringle and took himself off to his observatory while the chaperon retired to her room. Pamela, glad that she had not been required to furnish any explanations, went outside to the stables.

However, beyond looking at her favorite mount, wishing that she might ride toward the Hall, she found that she was not in the mood for riding, since, of all directions, that was the only one in which she did not dare head. Or . . . could she? And accidentally say . . . While she was turning the matter over in her mind, she was surprised to hear hoofbeats on the carriageway. Her heart close to her mouth, she moved out of the stables in time to see Edith riding up the road. She felt so disappointed that she was hard put not to weep, but of course, it would be Edith. She had quite forgotten that she was expected for tea and a cozy conversation.

Edith, she noted after exchanging greetings, was in better spirits than she had been of late. Her eyes were sparkling and a small smile played about her mouth. In fact, knowing her best friend as well as she did, Pamela guessed that she was brimful of news she could scarely wait to confide. This suspicion was confirmed immediately the grooms had taken her horse. As they walked toward the house, Edith said, "My dear, you will never guess what has happened!"

"I know I will not," Pamela returned. "Lucy's been abed with the quinsy and consequently my only source of information has been cut off—save for Mrs. Nettlebloom, of course, but she did not gossip . . . she was too concerned with my fittings."

Edith appeared relieved and, again, Pamela had no difficulty reading her mind. It was always more fun to spread the word to the uninformed. "Tell me," she prompted.

"Mr. Questred discovered a poacher on his grounds and, can you imagine, rather than summoning his keeper, he dealt with the man himself."

Pamela's hands clenched. Endeavoring to keep her expression merely interested and her voice steady, she said, "Was he much hurt?"

"Badly." Edith nodded. "A broken jaw and three ribs, also broken."

"Oh, no!" Pamela clutched Edith's arm. "Why would he do such a thing. Where is he?"

Edith regarded her in some surprise. "Your concern is misplaced, is it not? As to his whereabouts, I imagine he will be in hospital before he is transported to jail.''

"Jail?'' Pamela stared at her confusedly. "They will put Mr. Questred in prison for assaulting a poacher?''

"Assaulting a . . .'' Edith repeated, and broke into astonished laughter. "I fear I did not make myself clear. 'Twas not Mr. Questred who was hurt—but the poacher.''

"Oh.'' Pamela released a long breath. "He must be very strong, and fearless too. Some of those poachers are known to be dangerous.''

"If this man were dangerous, he met his master. They say that the constable actually remonstrated with Mr. Questred, saying it was better to let the law deal with miscreants, and Mr. Questred laughed in his face and said the law might take his leavings! The constable was furious, but of course Mr. Questred was within his rights.'' Edith grimaced. "I do not admire the man.''

"Do you not?'' Pamela glared at her. "Because he was trying to protect his property?''

"He could have summoned the constable or his own keepers. The beating he administered was savage. Also I have heard that he is a hardened gamester with what my brother calls 'the devil's own luck.' He fleeced poor Gervais Gordon last week.''

"I am sure that Sir Gervais would have done the same to him had he not been bested,'' Pamela replied.

Edith regarded her narrowly. "You have appointed yourself his champion, I see.''

"You do surprise me, Edith.'' Pamela stared at her wide-eyed. "You speak as if we were not together on the day my horse ran into the branch. You cannot remember how kind he was then?''

"He could hardly have left you lying on the ground,'' Edith pointed out.

"I seem to remember that you were extremely impressed by him,'' Pamela retorted. "What has happened to make you change your mind?''

"There is something about him . . .'' Edith frowned.

"This area of the world is much frequented by men with ulterior motives, ingratiating strangers, who speak from two sides of their mouths."

"And you have decided that Mr. Questred is of that company?" Pamela glared at her. "On what grounds, pray?"

"Why did he buy the Hall?" Edith countered. Without giving Pamela an opportunity to respond, she continued musingly, "It is old and in bad repair, but it does have one virtue. It stands alone on a large stretch of ground and is visited by few. Furthermore, it is not far from the Marshes. And why did he visit so harsh a punishment upon that hapless poacher? Had the man seen something he should not have seen?"

"I vow, Edith," Pamela said with an angry little titter, "You have often teased me about my reading of romances—"

"About taking them too seriously," Edith interrupted.

"No matter," Pamela continued stubbornly. "It seems to me that you have all the qualifications necessary to write such a work. You could entitle it *The Mysterious Stranger or: The Smuggler's Roost.*" Pamela prided herself upon a convincing laugh.

"I do not say that I believe him to be a smuggler," Edith said thoughtfully, "but I am not sure I trust him."

"You liked him well enough when we first encountered him."

"Yes, but I have had second thoughts. Why, for instance, did he decide to settle here? What does he want?"

"I cannot imagine." Pamela shrugged. "And why are we squandering so much time in discussing him? It seems to me that I've not seen you for an age, and you've not told me what you plan to wear for the Carstairs ball on Wednesday next."

As she had anticipated, this all-important question

signaled the end of Edith's speculations on the subject
of Mr. Questred. From him they progressed to the
gowns they were having made for this important event.
Subsequently there were the ensembles that would
complete Pamela's trousseau and over tea, Edith, whose
superior knowledge of London had always been a thorn
in Pamela's side, gave her the benefit of that same
knowledge with emphasis upon the delights of being
taken through Carlton House Palace and, even more
intriguing, those that would be on view when the
Vauxhall Gardens opened for the Season.

Until what Pamela herself was beginning to call the
"unfortunate arrival of the disturbing Mr. Questred,"
the Carstairs ball had been an event that had cast a
very long shadow before it, one that stretched into all
the great houses in that particular corner of Kent.

The Carstairs family consisted of Sir Matthew, Lady
Alice, their sons James and Anthony, and their
daughters Felicity and Margaret. It was not often that
all of them were in residence at the same time. Indeed,
in the last two years Lady Alice and Sir Matthew had
spent only six months at Carstairs Court. Three of these
had stretched from mid-December to the first week of
March 1814. The other three had been from August to
October 1815, during which time Anthony, who had
had the great good fortune to suffer only a broken
shoulder, received when his horse threw him during a
cavalry charge at the Battle of Waterloo, recuperated
from that injury and from the shock of seeing so many
less fortunate friends die at his side. Subsequently
Anthony and the rest of his family had returned to
London and thence to the Isle of Man to visit his
maternal relations. Consequently, the fact that they
were in residence at the Court and giving a ball was a
subject for rejoicing. No one in the county entertained
more lavishly than Lady Carstairs, and no dwelling
within miles was so beautiful.

The house had been built in the middle of the

eighteenth century by Sir Anthony Carstairs, a gifted
amateur artist who had taken the Grand Tour in 1740
and had fallen in love with that style of interior
decoration called *rococo,* with the result that the
Court's baroque exterior fronted rooms with painted
ceilings and sculptured pillars, the whole rich with
intricate marble and plaster embellishments running to
the requisite shell shapes, ornamental wreaths, and
alabaster heads. Pastel colors predominated and the
ballroom with its pale green walls, fantastically framed
mirrors, and a ceiling painted with plunging seahorses,
tritons, mermaids, Neptune, and centered by a Venetian
glass chandelier hung with blue, lavender, and pink
glass drops and bearing, amid glass leaves and blos-
soms, a thousand candles, was a sight to inspire legends.

Though most of the invited guests had previously
viewed the wonders of the ballroom, it still elicited
murmurs of rapture, and Pamela, who had never been a
guest at the mansion, looked about her in wonder. Tom
was equally awed.

"It will be a sight to remember." He slipped his arm
around her waist, pulling her close against him, as he
continued, "Something to tell our children." He
favored her with a fond smile, his eyes roving over her
gold silk gown, which he had already pronounced
"most becoming." He added, "I will also tell them how
very beautiful you looked."

It was a most unfortunate choice of words, for in
Pamela's ears it sounded like the crack of doom, as if,
indeed, everything in her life were drawing to a close
rather than being on the very edge of beginning! Pamela
had an instant vision of herself, seated at a tambour
frame, despite the fact that she loathed the very idea of
embroidery—but married ladies seemed to take it up as
a matter of course, and there she would be, working on
some floral design, with Tom seated in an easy chair
reading or, perhaps, playing chess with his father. Sir
Edmund would be nodding, waking only when Tom
said "Checkmate."

She would summon the nurse to take the children to their beds and . . . No! Something deep within her protested: "Not so soon, not so soon!" To go from the staid reaches of her father's house to Bellairs and Tom! She directed a frightened glance at her old childhood playmate, wishing that she could discern in his gray eyes some hint of the mischief that had once lurked there. However, he was not looking at her. He had half-turned and was staring at something or someone behind them. He said wonderingly and not entirely approvingly, "How does he happen to be here?"

"Who?" she asked.

"Questred."

The name brought a throb to her throat. She had not meant to turn so swiftly; indeed, it was more than a mere turn, it was a whirl and elicted a surprised exclamation from Tom, which she hardly heeded as she stared at the man in question.

He was garbed in black satin. In common with nearly all the gentlemen present, he wore knee breeches and white silk stockings. Lace edged his cuffs, and in the fall of white lace at his throat she saw the gleam of a diamond. With difficulty she turned her gaze from him and stared up at Tom. "Why should he not be here?" she asked reasonably.

"When did he become acquainted with the Carstairses?" Tom was frowning now.

"He might have had a previous meeting with Sir Matthew . . . in London or even upon the Isle of Man," Pamela said, her eyes straying toward Mr. Questred. She wished that he would look in her direction, but his dark gaze seemed fixed on some object or person across the room.

"Possibly," Tom admitted. "He has the devil's own luck with cards—maybe he won his invitation."

"I doubt that. And are you suggesting that he cheats?"

"No, but I had an opportunity to watch him play piquet with Noel Gifford at Sir Malory Winston's the other night. He won every hand, and Gifford's no mean player himself.''

''Did you play with him?''

''I challenged him to a game.'' Tom shrugged. ''But he refused me. Indeed, he left a few minutes later.''

''Probably because he had another engagement.''

''It was close on midnight and . . .'' Tom broke off. ''Ah, Father, have you freed yourself from the clutches of Sir Matthew?''

Pamela turned swiftly. Sir Edmund Bellairs had been with them in the coach, but immediately upon entering the ballroom, he had been approached by their host, an old friend, and engaged in conversation. He said now, ''Yes, as you see.'' He smiled at Pamela. ''My dear, I thought you exquisite earlier this evening, but now under the glow from that chandelier, you are a goddess! My boy is indeed fortunate.''

''I thank you, sir,'' Pamela murmured, thinking ruefully that the glow from that same chandelier was not nearly so kind to him. He was looking far from well. His face was bloated, and a network of veins on cheeks and nose caused it to appear unnaturally red. There were broad streaks of gray in his thinning black locks, and his step was infirm. She also noticed a slight tremor in the hand he had placed on her arm.

''You must not thank me for nature's bounties, Pamela,'' he responded gently. He continued, ''I am indeed glad that this marriage will be taking place in a fortnight. I wish to see my lad wed, and so creditably, also.''

''You are very kind, sir,'' she responded, immediately aware that she ought to have bestowed some manner of encomium upon her bridegroom-to-be. Yet, it was just as well that she had not, for in her present mood any such effusion must have sounded patently false. She wished, too, that Mr. . . . or Sir Edmund, as she must remember to call him, were not clutching her arm so tightly. It gave her the sensation of having been captured by him—and that was true: by him and by her own father. *They* had ordained that she marry Tom, and she had weakly yielded to their persuasions.

Why?

Because she had always been fond of Tom, because she had not known what it meant to really experience the "palpitations and the fevers" described by the authors of her favorite romances. She had always been comfortable with Tom—but comfortable, she knew now, was not enough! And that knowledge, unfortunately, had come too late. In thirteen short days she would become Mrs. Bellairs!

"Might I displace my son and claim the first dance with you, my dear?"

"Of course," she responded graciously, thinking that "claim" was another apt use of words. She had been claimed and now stood here figuratively swathed in the Bellairs banner! However, others would soon claim her as partner—out of the corner of her eye she could see several young men gazing at her hopefully. Would that Mr. Questred were of their number. She dared not turn her attention from Sir Edmund and actively seek him out. Her prospective father-in-law would wonder at her abstraction.

She remembered an instance on another evening—an assembly in town. It had taken place just after she had become formally affianced to Tom. Her fiancé and her father had accompanied her there and she had danced more than once with Ernest Townsend. Subsequently her father had scolded her, reminding her that she was bespoken and must needs behave with more decorum. Since he had not been present, she knew that Edmund Bellairs had been his informant, Edmund Bellairs, who wanted her person and, above all, her dowry, which would eventually include her father's house and property, for his son.

There were times when the idea of living in the same house with a man for whom she had conceived a dislike,

for which she had no reason but only an odd cold
feeling, seemed like an intolerable burden. Tonight was
one of those times. She wished that he might have
remained in Bath for another week, another month, a
year—ten years. More than that she wished that poor
Arthur Bellairs were still alive and in possession of the
estate, title, and fortune recently claimed by his stepfather—but in thirteen short days she would be Mrs.
Thomas Bellairs and, eventually, Lady Bellairs.

It occurred to her that thirteen was considered an
unlucky number, and though, in common with her
father, she was not superstitious, she wished it might be
true and that something would occur to prevent this
unwanted coupling! A bitter little smile curled her lips.
If the marriage did take place, thirteen could still be
counted a most unlucky number.

As she had anticipated, Pamela was besieged by
young men desiring dances. Tom, naturally, had
already claimed two waltzes, a country dance, and a
cotillion. The first waltz would go to his father, and
Captain Anthony Carstairs, the elder son of the house,
had secured the fourth. Just as she was beginning to give
up hope, Mr. Questred was at her side to receive her sole
remaining waltz. She had also promised two country
dances, a quadrille, and two cotillions to five other
eager young men. She had, however, left herself free for
another country dance and a cotillion, this in defense of
her feet, she told herself. She *did* become weary at the
end of an evening. She refused to allow herself to dwell
on the possibility that if she were not dancing, *he* might
try to approach her. It was unlikely, but similar situations had arisen, not in her own experience but in a
delightful five-volume novel entitled *The Bandit Bridegroom or: A Stolen Love.*

In that book, the bandit, not really a bandit, of
course, but a nobleman in disguise, had approached the
Lady Livia Tremaine as she awaited the next dance and
had drawn her into an alcove, which happened to have a

pair of doors opening onto a small balcony. He had summarily lifted her over the front of the balcony to the ground below and leapt lightly after her. Moments later, he had placed her on the back of his spirited stallion and they had galloped off into the night, not unlike the lost Bride of Netherby and Young Lochinvar, that eloping pair celebrated in verse by Mr. Walter Scott. She sighed and then chuckled. If Edith had been party to her thoughts, she would not have hesitated to dub her a ninny, and she would have been quite right. It was ridiculous to imagine that despite the presence of that most exciting and mysterious of men, Mr. Questred, that this evening would be more eventful than other similar evenings! Actually, that was not quite accurate —it was already more eventful in that she had braved the fastness of Carstairs Court and, furthermore, *he* was present, even though the chances of his behaving like the bandit or Young Lochinvar were distinctly remote.

Several hours later Pamela, standing beside Mr. Questred and waiting for the first notes of that promised waltz to bring them onto the floor, was devoutly wishing that she could have held to her original intention and remained in the chairs provided for wall-flowers for at least two dances. That had been impossible. She had been besieged by not one but several young men each time she had sought that particular sanctuary. Consequently her feet ached and her dress clung damply to her heated form. Rather than the excitement she had expected to experience when dancing with this one partner she preferred above all others, she could only look forward wistfully to the end of the waltz and the moment when, with Tom and Sir Edmund, she could go in to supper!

"I fear you are weary, Miss Cardwell," her companion murmured. "Perhaps you would care to step out onto the balcony for a breath of fresh air?"

Had he read her mind, or did she look as weary as she

felt? she wondered guiltily, and then sent a lightning glance around the room. She did not see Sir Edmund, would not see him because he had retired some time ago —to play piquet in the cardroom. Tom, she knew, was dancing with Edith. Did she choose to avail herself of this most welcome offer, he would not be aware of it. Still, it would not be *de rigueur* for her to accede to that particular request. Tom would have every right to be angry, and embarrassed too. She said, with a hint of reproach in her tones, "I am not in the least weary, sir. I have been looking forward to our waltz." The moment those words left her lips, she was embarrassed. "I mean . . ." she began.

"I hope you mean exactly what you have just told me"—he gave her a rueful look—"but again I fear I overstep the boundaries that must, of necessity, separate us. I, too, have been looking forward to this waltz all the evening and . . . Now come." He offered his arm and led her onto the floor.

He was an excellent dancer. She had already noted that about him, but had not realized how very gracefully he moved. As she whirled about the vast ballroom, her tiredness miraculously vanished. She was actually regretful when the music ended, and it seemed to her that she saw that same regret in his eyes as he bowed. Then, as he took her hand to lead her off the floor, she felt a small object being pressed against her palm. "I beg you will read this," he said *sotto voce*. "It requires an answer."

Her heart was pounding in the vicinity of her throat again. She dared to glance at the object she had inadvertently clutched and discovered it to be a small, tight roll of paper. She looked up, and meeting his inscrutable gaze, dared to nod her head very quickly. He then moved away.

"Come, then, my love." Tom met her at the edge of the floor. "I am famished, are you not?"

"Entirely," Pamela responded. "And I shall be glad

to sit down, too." She had been hungry and weary, she remembered—but now she felt actually on fire with excitement. What had he written? If only she dared scan that message—but of course, she could not. She must needs wait until she was in her own chamber—and that meant two hours at the least, unless, of course, she were to plead a bad headache, but that would be unkind to Tom, who was obviously hungry. She felt a strange need to be kind to Tom because . . . But she did not want to dwell on reasons, not yet, not until she read what she hoped might be contained in that note!

5

It was not until hours later, slow hours that had inched by like so many creeping snails, that Pamela, safe in her own chamber, in her own bed, dared to unroll the note, slipped from fingers to bosom and out again before Lucy came to disrobe her. Fortunately, the abigail, sleepy and cross, did not quiz her about the ball, as was usually her wont. She performed her tasks hastily and went out as quickly as she might.

The note, rescued from the powder jar, was written in a flowing hand. Though obviously inscribed in haste, the letters were beautifully formed, an example of that penmanship Miss Pringle had lauded and which Pamela had never mastered. That occurred to her even before the sense of the message had seeped into her excited consciousness.

She had been waiting anxiously to read it all through that interminable supper. Its presence between her breasts was a constant reminder of those moments when she had waltzed with Mr. Questred, experiencing a heady excitement because of his proximity and wishing that he had not been forced to hold her so far away, so that only their hands touched as they whirled around the immense floor. So conscious had she been of his note that she had had considerable difficulty concentrating on what Tom or Edith, sitting across from them at the lengthy table, was saying. Fortunately, it being late, Tom blamed her inattention upon the fact that she must have danced holes in her slippers, "and the same with you," he had said to Edith.

"But I am not tired," Edith had hurriedly assured

him. She had spoken no more than the truth. Her eyes were bright and she had appeared excited.

In that moment it occurred to Pamela that Edith had a soft spot for Tom. She wished that he entertained similar feelings for her friend. The match would be eminently suitable. Edith, too, had a sizable dowry, and furthermore, they would get along famously. They were basically much more practical than she herself, their moods did not bring them to the heights or to the depths —and why was she letting her wits wander so far when the note was in her hand to be *read* rather than admired for its beautiful penmanship, surprisingly beautiful, she thought, remembering his rough hands. It occurred to her that she was almost afraid to read what he had written, because . . . But she was not quite sure of her reasons. She held it near the flame from the single candle on her bedstand, and as she scanned it, her excitement mounted with each separate word:

My beloved,
   I am in agony knowing that but thirteen days, brutally short days, remain before you are lost to me forever. Can nothing interfere with this horrid progression? Is it inevitable? Must it follow as the night the day? I have an alternative suggestion that I would present to you. Will you meet me tomorrow afternoon at three in the woods adjoining my property? There is a lightning-blasted elm hard by that grove where you fell and I was able to hold you in my arms for the first time. I must see you, my beautiful angel, my beloved girl . . . tomorrow at three. Do not send me an answer, your presence will be my answer. If you are not there, I will understand that answer, too.
                                    Your adoring and despairing
                                            Sidney Questred
P.S. Best destroy this missive.   S.Q.

She started to put the paper to the flame but found she could not bear to see that thrilling message burn, not yet! She slipped it under her pillow.

"Sidney," she whispered. "Tomorrow . . . oh, yes, tomorrow I will . . . oh, I will meet you!"

Blowing out her candle, she slid down beneath the covers. A glance toward the window showed her a streak of red across the horizon. It was nearly morning. She closed her eyes, wishing that she could sleep until the magical hour of three and awaken to find his arms around her. Unfortunately, she would need to rise at noon in time for the midday meal, else her father would think there was something seriously the matter with her. He might even summon the physician, and nothing, nothing in the world, must keep her from that meeting . . . that *assignation*!

"You've scarce touched your dinner." Miss Pringle bent a stern gaze on Pamela. "And," she continued, "you could not have slept very well last night, rising at so early an hour after arriving home past midnight. 'Tis my belief you should rest this afternoon."

"I fully intend to take a nap," Pamela mendaciously assured her chaperon, glad that Miss Pringle would have been in her chamber for thirty minutes by the time she set out for a certain lightning-struck tree. Nor was there any reason to reveal that she had heard her clock chime every hour from four to eight, when she had finally summoned Lucy to help her into her riding habit. Subsequently she had ridden through the grounds, visiting favorite spots as if, indeed, she would not be seeing them soon again. She could compare her feelings to those of Eustacia Egerton, the eloping heroine of *The Lost Heiress or: Tried to the Limit*.

Poor Eustacia had lived to regret her folly, but of course it had turned out all right in the end, with her fiancé, the man who had loved her all of her life, forgiving her for running away with Oliver Harvey, the bold dragoon, who had been foiled by the hero before he had had an opportunity to rob the heroine of her virtue. Rather uncomfortably, Pamela recalled that Eustacia had not really enjoyed the elopement as much as she had anticipated—having had qualms about leaving Lord Ruxton, her betrothed, behind. However, she reminded herself hastily, Mr. Questred (Sidney) had said nothing about eloping—he had only said he wanted to meet her —but what else could that "alternative suggestion" entail?

She was still cudgeling her brain on that point when at last, after several wrong turns, she arrived at the indicated elm. Unlike Eustacia, she had no difficulty in getting away from home. As usual, her father repaired to his observatory and Miss Pringle to her bedchamber after the midday meal, while Pamela, slipping out of her own bedchamber as soon as she heard the chaperon close her door, reached the side entrance of the house with no difficulty, hurried out, and went to the stables, where she told a rather surprised groom that she was going riding again. She was slightly taken aback not to find Mr. Questred waiting for her. However, as she dismounted and led her horse to the tree, she heard the welcome sound of hoofbeats coming in her direction, and a second later Mr. Questred had leapt from the back of his huge black hunter, and tethering him to a tree, hurried to her side.

"My dear Miss Cardwell, I hope I have not kept you waiting," he said breathlessly.

"No, you did not . . . I just arrived."

"Ah." He had wound the reins of his horse around one hand, but with the other he reached for her hand and brought it to his lips. "I have had such fears that you would think me sadly importunate and refuse to meet me."

He was still holding her hand and gently stroking the palm in a manner that sent little shivers through her. She wanted to pull away—or ought to want to pull away

—but could not. For some reason, she felt oddly
breathless and excited. "I . . . I wanted to meet you,"
she blurted, and was immediately chagrined. "I
mean . . ." she added.

"May I hope that you might mean that you share my
feelings or . . . But I would not wish those on you. I
would not have you tormented as I have been tormented," he said huskily.

"T-tormented?" she whispered. "I . . . do not understand."

"I speak of sleepless nights and days of agony . . .
because I cannot see you, cannot have you at my side.
Oh, my beautiful Pamela, I would not have you suffer
thus."

"But I have s-suffered, sir," she whispered. "Oh,
dear, I . . . I feel so . . ." He was still caressing her hand
in that peculiar way. Was it that which was making her
tremble? She wanted him to release her hand but, again,
she did not. Then he did release it, only to clasp her in
his arms and press a long kiss on her mouth, a kiss such
as she had never experienced in her whole life. She had
read about females becoming weak with love, and now
she felt weak, almost faint. In that moment he released
her and knelt at her feet.

"Oh, God, forgive me, my dearest angel," he said
brokenly. "I am not my own man in your presence."
He looked up at her beseechingly. "Say you forgive me,
my angel."

"I . . . of c-course, I do," Pamela stuttered, caught
between shock and desire. Deep in her mind, she knew
full well that she ought not to forgive such liberties, but
she had been unable to find the words to deny him the
forgiveness that brought him to his knees before her.
"Oh, S-Sidney . . ." She could not restrain the cry that
burst from her. "Oh, what can we do?"

He rose immediately and stared down into her eyes.
"Did you really ask me that? Did you?"

She did not quite understand his question or, rather,

questions. She had a strange feeling that he was speaking not only with his lips but also with his whole being,
his whole *passionate* being, for at last she could really
understand what passion meant and, she suddenly
realized, nothing in her copious reading of romances
had ever prepared her for its actual manifestation!

"Ah, Pamela . . ." He pulled her into his embrace
again, staring at her. She had the feeling that his eyes
filled his whole face. They seemed to be drawing all
resistance from her. She actually felt weak. Geraldine
Guilfoyle of *A Woman's Heart* had experienced a
similar emotion, she remembered, and straightaway
forgot Geraldine as he continued, "Pamela, you will
remember that I mentioned an alternative in my note.
My alternative to your present unhappy situation is a
simple one—I want you to marry me."

"But . . ." She could not quell the name that sprang
to her lips: "Tom . . ."

"Will you tell me that you love Tom?" he demanded
harshly.

"I . . . we . . ." She faltered.

He cut off her protest. "Yes, you may tell me that
you love him, but I'll not believe you—because you are
here with me. You have not remained a stone statue
beneath my kisses, you have responded, do not tell me
differently. If you loved him, would you have
responded? If you loved him, would you have come
here in the first place? Would you?"

He was standing so close to her. His hands were hard
on her arms. His fingers were biting into the flesh, but
she could not even protest that hurtful grasp. She did
not mind the hurt. She did not mind the fact that he was
so close to her. She wanted him to be closer yet, wanted
to feel his mouth on her lips. Yet some lingering thread
of caution made her say weakly, "I do not . . . know."

He released her suddenly and stepped back. His eyes
fairly blazed as he said, "I do not believe that you do
not 'know.' You are here because you feel the way I feel

—have felt since first we met. But, Pamela, are you ready to act upon those feelings, or will you scurry back to your safe little mouse hole and forget all that has passed between us—forget, too, all that could happen were we to remain together?" His hands closed on her shoulders once again. He gave her a little shake. "Answer me, Pamela. Do you want to leave the dark forest and return to the safe sunlight? Is that what you want? Then go, go quickly, and let us never see each other again." He let his hands fall to his sides.

Hardly aware of what she was doing, she grasped one of his hands. Her answer seemed wrenched from her very vitals. "No," she cried. "No, I want to be with you anywhere."

"Pamela . . ." He pulled his hand from her clasp, only to draw her into his arms, and then she was close to him, as close as she wanted to be—as she had wanted to be, she realized, since their first meeting.

Lying in her bed, Pamela heard the clock on her mantelshelf chime eleven. Counting the small tings from the delicate porcelain clock, imported from Dresden by her grandfather, she realized she was hearing it for the last time, would never hear it again, never lie in this bed, never tiptoe across the floor to the door, never set foot upon the stairs which would bring her down two landings to the ground floor and thence to a side door which she had left on the latch after Thomas, the butler, had checked all the entrances and gone wearily up to bed in another wing of the house. Would he be blamed for the fact that the door would be found open upon the morrow? No, there would be other matters confronting that shocked household.

She did not like to dwell on that, nor on her father's anger and Tom's chagrin. He—Mr. Questred—had exacted a promise from her. He had said that she must not leave a note, else they would all be on her trail. She had been sorely tempted to disobey him and at least leave some manner of explanation to temper her father's worry if not his fury—but if he were to pursue them, that would be worse. He might challenge Mr. Questred—Sidney, rather (she could not address the man she was about to marry as "Mister"). Her father might challenge Sidney to a duel as the enraged father had done in *Lady Susan's Marriage or: The Midnight Bride.*

Lady Susan had thrown herself between her furious parent and her lover, and subsequently, wounded unto death, she had expired in the wicked Lord Winston's arms and he had shot himself. Pamela had not been too happy with that particular romance, not liking the ending, especially since the other four volumes had presaged nothing of the kind. Edith, who had lent it to her, theorized that the author had run out of ideas.

Pamela shuddered. Supposing her father were to challenge . . . But he would not; he did not really care what happened to her, hence his stubborn insistence that she marry Tom as soon as possible and leave him in possession of the house, free of all parental obligations. She was equally sanguine about Tom. Most of the time, he treated her like a sister. She was reasonably sure that he would recover from the shock of her elopement very quickly. Edith would do her best to comfort him, Edith, who, she was suddenly positive, really loved Tom in a way that she, Pamela, never could have. True, she had been fond of him, was still fond of him—but having experienced Sidney Questred's kisses, she knew that the chasm that lay between loving and liking was deep. She shivered slightly, understanding completely what one author had meant when she had written, "Annabelle thrilled to his every touch." A few hours ago, Mr. Questred had translated that sentence with his own touching—holding her face between his two hands and letting them slide to her neck and thence to her shoulders, his fingers reaching beneath her collar . . . and then he had stopped, saying huskily, "I cannot

. . . we must part now. Later, when we are wed . . .''

He had left that sentence unfinished, but, she had noted, he had been breathing deeply, almost as if he had been running, and she, much to her surprise, had felt similarly breathless.

Pamela started. The clock had struck the quarter-hour and it was *time*. She slid out of bed and took out the bandbox she had packed after Lucy had bade her good night. She lifted it and then impatiently put it down. She had yet to dress! She had chosen to wear her riding habit because on many occasions she had donned that without Lucy's aid. It had no pesky buttons at the back of the bodice or on the sleeves. It would also be comfortable to wear during the journey—the journey during which they would cover some three hundred miles! She swallowed convulsively. Unfortunately, she did not succeed in swallowing the acrid taste of fear. It did have an "acrid taste," just as several authors said it did! She felt slightly ill, another sensation she remembered from her reading, but she could not stand here enumerating her feelings. It was time to dress, time to follow the plan they had evolved together.

She pulled off her nightdress, and in a few moments she had finished buttoning her bodice. She threw her cloak over her shoulders, and with her boots and bandbox in hand, came out of her room. It was dark in the hall, but she knew her way to the stairs blindfolded and reached them in seconds. As she started down to the first landing, she became aware of a creaking beneath her feet, something she had never heard before or, at least, never noticed before. It sounded so very loud! She threw a frightened glance behind her but saw only darkness. Fortunately, neither Miss Pringle nor her father was a light sleeper. Furthermore, her father's chambers were at the far end of the hall. Finally she was downstairs and in the main hall. She moved to the front door, but that was not the door she was to use! She hurried into the drawing room and stumbled over a chair and fell—but fortunately, on the carpet! She rose quickly, casting a terrified glance behind her. It did not seem to her that she had made much noise, but there was a watchman. Scarcely daring to breathe, she stood still, listening. Had she woken him? No. She was positive she had not.

She moved toward the door she had left on the latch. Supposing one of the servants had noticed that it was open? To her delight, it yielded and she was outside. It remained only for her to go through the gardens and down the slope to the trees, which she would follow until she reached the wall that fronted the main road—the wall she had climbed a thousand times as a child, with Tom at her side. *Tom*. She would not think of Tom. Once he had adjusted his mind to the fact that she was gone, he would probably be relieved. No, not relieved, exactly, but she was sure he would not suffer long. He did not love her passionately. Her eyes were suddenly wet. Why were there tears in her eyes because she was thinking of Tom? Because they had been friends for such a very long time—all their lives—and he would be hurt, terribly hurt, and embarrassed too. She had not thought of that—dared not think about it now, not with Mr. Questred, *Sidney*, awaiting her.

He had not wanted her to steal through the park alone. He had told her he was worried. There might be poachers. Not even when she had assured him that she knew a particular way had he been convinced. "There's but a half-moon tonight," he had said worriedly. "Best let me come for you."

"No, you'd not know the way," she had responded. "You would be hopelessly lost and you might blunder into Bellairs, which lies just beyond our property. Sir Edmund keeps several ferocious hounds."

"Suppose you alert them?" he had demanded.

"They are never ferocious to me."

"No one could be . . ." He had kissed her again.

Thinking of that, Pamela went on down the slope. It

was dark but she knew her way and was at the wall almost before she knew it. She threw her bandbox over it, and searching for the old footholds, was atop it in seconds. She clambered down and stared about her at the road stretching before and behind her, empty in the pale moonlight. His coach would be at the copse around the bend. It was not far. Pamela looked about for her bandbox and found it easily enough. She picked it up and stiffened as she heard footsteps coming toward her.

Swallowing convulsively, she moved back against the wall, and in that same moment a tall shadowy form came into view. The imperfect light from the half-moon obliterated features, but still she knew she was not mistaken in believing that it was Mr. Questred. She opened her mouth but no words came as, suddenly, she was seized with fright and a knowledge of her own folly in agreeing to elope with him. She pressed closer against the wall and must have come in contact with a low-growing bush, for the leaves rustled and the man on the road came to a stop and turned in her direction. To her shock and surprise, a scream actually formed in her throat. She swallowed convulsively, not wanting to utter a sound, but despite that, a little bleat escaped her and the man on the road moved forward quickly.

"Pamela?" he questioned in a low voice. Another step brought him to her side.

"S-Sidney," she whispered.

"My dearest." He slid an arm around her waist.

"I . . . I think . . ." she began.

His arms tightened about her. "What do you think? . . . and why are you here? We had agreed . . ."

"I . . . I was not sure I should . . . Oh, dear, what will Tom think?" she said in a rush. "He will be so hurt and I . . ."

"Have you lost your heart, then?" he asked in a low voice. "If you have, then I will not force you . . ." He drew her against him. "Are you afraid, my love?"

As she stood so close to him, feeling the strength of

his embrace, her incipient fears fled and were replaced by excitement. "No, I am not afraid."

"And you will come with me, my own?"

Something, she was not sure what, made her ask, "Do you really love me, Sidney?"

"Need you ask?" he demanded.

He had answered a question with a question not an answer, but his seeking mouth fastening on her lips was enough to quell her fright and still her protests. In another second he had lifted her up, and possessing himself of her bandbox, he carried her down the road to the waiting coach.

The post chaise was well-sprung and as comfortable as soft cushions and bolsters could make it. Given the roads that stretched from Kent to London, Pamela was not badly shaken even though they traveled at a faster pace than she had ever experienced before. Much to her surprise and disappointment, Mr. Questred, as she still called him in her own mind, rode outside. He had tendered her an explanation for that—one which rendered her extremely nervous.

"My dear," he explained, "though I did my best to clothe all my movements in secrecy, there is always the outside chance that some one of my servants may, in the hopes of a reward, reveal my plans."

"I thought you had told no one," she had begun.

"I have learned that eyes and ears sprout in unexpected places, my love." He had emitted a short laugh which, to Pamela's ears, sounded surprisingly unpleasant. "Indeed, my sweetest girl," he had added, "none should know that better than I."

Oddly enough, those words had made an indefinable impression on her. She thought of them off and on as they got under way, and now, waking from the semidoze into which she had unexpectedly fallen, Pamela found them still embedded in her consciousness. Her reason for this she attributed to the bitter tone in which they had been uttered. It seemed to her to hint of a past

experience which had left him with some bad memories.
With a rush of sympathy she wondered what it might
have been and had at least one answer. Someone must
have betrayed him. Who? She would never know. . . .
Never? If they were to be lovers . . . She was not
thinking clearly. They *were* lovers. She had felt his arms
around her, his kisses on her lips, and it remained only
for them to reach Gretna Green and they would be wed.

"I will be wed to . . . to . . ." she whispered, and was
reluctant to add the other words currently forming on
her tongue: " . . . to a stranger."

It was true! They had met . . . how often? She did not
need to enumerate the times. They were few. Furthermore, they had encompassed not days, not even half-
days; an hour here, an hour there, and now . . . all the
hours of her future would be spent with this man whom,
so unaccountably, she had discovered she loved. And he
loved her. She tried to remember everything he had told
her on their few meetings, but she was not successful.
She needed more reassurances, she needed the reas-
surance of his person beside her in the carriage! She
glanced out of the window. The sky was paling and the
moon looked as flat as a sovereign against that gray-
blue expanse. She directed her gaze toward the road and
glimpsed Mr. Questred as he rode swiftly past. He was
staring straight ahead, a frown on his face. Was he
fearful that they were being followed? She doubted that
they were. Those that might have given chase to an
eloping pair lay in their beds, unaware that she, Pamela
Cardwell, was on the road to London, farther than
London—over the border into Scotland and Gretna
Green, that most infamous marriage mart!

A shiver of anticipation ran through her, to be
quickly followed by another shiver as an unwelcome
realization occurred to her. She was on unfamiliar
ground. Miles of roadway separated her from her home,
her father, Miss Pringle, and Tom. What would happen
when her flight was discovered? What would they

think? She had left no notes, told no one, not even Edith, her one confidante. No, Tom, too, had been a confidant until he had, with her father's blessing, claimed the role of suitor!

She groaned. Tom had always been her true and best friend until he became her lover. It occurred to her that in losing him, she would actually be losing her best friend as well, even if in the last months she had been so resentful toward him. He would be sadly grieved, she was sure, for he had also looked upon her as his best friend. Of course, he had many male friends, but the two of them had grown very close in their lonely childhoods, particularly close after Arthur had gone.

Tears squeezed out of her eyes. All that was at an end —but had it not already been at an end since he had offered for her? It had not been a real offer. It had been instigated by Mr. Bellairs—or rather Sir Edmund, whom she had never liked—greedy Sir Edmund, who wanted Tom to annex her property and join it to Bellair, which he now owned. Poor Arthur. Unbidden, an image of his portly figure appeared in her mind's eye. Had he really been so obese? She was sure that memory did not exaggerate. His body had been truly elephantine!

She sighed as she remembered Arthur's horrid fate. Indeed, it was impossible to imagine him surviving a month in New South Wales . . . and at hard labor! She had read some accounts of the territory. It was incredibly rough and the lives of the convicts were generally wretched. They were brutally treated for the smallest infraction, and Arthur, she recalled, had been flogged. She shuddered. He could never have stood it, nor could he have withstood the hard labor of forcing roads through that difficult terrain. He had never done physical labor of any kind. He had been indulged and cosseted by his doting mother.

"He was spoiled, utterly spoiled," Mr. Bellairs had said.

She remembered him also saying on one occasion, "He had but to crook his little finger and his poor mother, ill as she was, would come running." He had gone on to misquote Hamlet. " 'She might not beteem the winds of heaven visit his face too roughly.' " Mr. Bellairs had added bitterly, "This spoiled child came to believe that everything in his universe had been ordained for his pleasure alone. How easily he fell prey to the blandishments of the smuggling fraternity, who offered him expensive countraband in return for various favors. It is a disgrace that the house of Bellairs will not soon live down."

A disgrace!

And would her father not feel the same about her? Had she not, with this rash action, brought disgrace upon her own house? Arthur's name had been blacked from the family Bible, a weeping little Tom had told her all those years ago. Tom had loved his brother and he had felt bitterly betrayed by him. Now, was he not to experience another, even worse betrayal? A sob escaped her. That had not occurred to her before. In the rush of planning her elopment, she had not been visited by any of the second thoughts that came crowding into her brain at this present moment. She had devoted her whole being to carrying out the plans evolved by herself and Mr. Questred.

What would Tom think?

She swallowed convulsively, wishing that his image did not occupy her mind's eye at present. She blinked but his reproachful face could not be dislodged so easily. Pushing herself back against the velvet-covered squabs, she willed herself to sleep. However, when they rolled into London, Pamela was regretfully awake and so distressed that she could not even appreciate the fact that she had finally arrived in a city she had wanted to see all of her life. Yet, on second thought, there was no reason to appreciate it. Her bridegroom had explained that they would not be remaining there. They would drive across the town as fast as the traffic would allow, and before noon they would be on the Great North Road bound for the Scottish border.

"Why?" she whispered. She stared out of the window, and this time she did not see Mr. Questred. She saw only that they were rounding a cluttered street already filled with people. Raucous cries reached her ears. The street vendors were already out hawking their wares. Groups of apprentices in leather aprons trudged along the narrow way, and above, the houses seemed to lean toward each other, as if wanting to engage in conversation. They were old and battered and ugly in the glow of a sun which, unbeknownst to her, had climbed considerably higher than when she had first beheld it. Other sounds reached her: barking dogs, screaming children, waifs, really, poorly clad and with young-old faces. Obviously they were in a poor section of the great metropolis. Her thoughts fled as the coach came to a jarring stop, catapulting her to the floor. More surprised than hurt, she eased herself back onto the seat and heard a knock on the window. She looked up to find Mr. Questred looking at her anxiously. He opened the coach door.

"I hope you were not hurt," he said.

"No," she assured him hastily. "Why are we stopping?"

"We are impeded by sheep." He smiled. "Lean out, my love, and you will see them."

Obeying, Pamela saw a large flock of sheep complete with dog and shepherd crossing the street. "I never expected . . ." she began, turning her gaze back to her companion, and then, meeting his eyes, she quite forgot what she had been about to tell him. He was staring at her almost incredulously.

"Are you really here, my dearest?" he demanded in a tone so soft and caressing that it made her heart turn over. "Or do I dream you?"

The regrets that had been plaguing her suddenly took

wing. She could imagine them turned into birds, a cloud of blackbirds flying swiftly away. She was really here because she wanted to be with him, and at this particular moment she had no fears about a future spent with a stranger. He was not a stranger! "I am," she said in a small voice. "Neither of us is dreaming."

He moved closer to her, but at that moment the coachman called, "Sir, us can go along now."

Mr. Questred stepped back hastily. "Ah, we can be on our way again and soon we'll be reaching a more felicitous part of the city. I wish we had time to visit some of its famous sites and also the theaters, but it is not our last time here, my darling. Once we are wed, I will show you all of London!"

"That will be lovely," she murmured, trying not to regret the coachman's interruption. She had wanted Sidney's arms around her, had actively craved his kisses —shamelessly, Miss Pringle would have said. But she could not think about shame or betrayal, even though she was guilty of the latter—as far as Tom was concerned—but he should not have pressed her to marry him.

"Come, my angel, close your window. Otherwise you will be treated to the dirt and dust of these streets." His eyes lingered on her face for a second and then he slammed the door shut and Pamela raised her window. In another few minutes they were on their way again.

By the time they were nearing the road leading in the direction of Huntingdon, Pamela had glimpsed some part of Westminster and Mayfair. They had rolled past Hyde Park and she had also seen the bustling stage-coach stop called the Swan with Two Necks. Mr. Questred had gone out of his way to show her the Tower of London and he had promised that when they returned he would be sure to escort her through the armory and also to the Royal Menagerie. He had sub-sequently mentioned Vauxhall Gardens, which had given her a bit of a pang, since Tom, too, had promised they would visit them on the honeymoon which would never take place now. For a brief time Tom had been an uncomfortable presence beside her in the carriage. And had he indeed been making this journey with her, he would have been with her in the carriage, not on horseback—she was sure of that—but she had need to remember Mr. Questred's explanation. Were they being followed? She herself doubted that, but he had sent Charles, one of his men, back along the streets they had traveled to see if, indeed, that were possible. He had returned to assure Mr. Questred that he had seen nothing, but still he had remained concerned and seemed to regret even the time spent at their noon repast in an inn outside London, where they had also changed horses.

Huntingdon had been their original destination, the town where they planned to remain for the night. However, they had made surprisingly good time through London and they reached the outskirts of Huntingdon shortly after two in the afternoon. They again changed horses at the George Inn—an ancient hostelry where, Pamela was told by a proud and informative host, some of Shakespeare's works had been performed in its courtyard by his own company! Later, over tea in the common room, she had learned that in the last twelve hours they had covered nearly 134 miles, farther than she had ever been in her entire life! Indeed, it seemed strange to her that she was yet in England, stranger yet to have heard her native land called small by Mr. Questred, who, when she had mentioned the great distance they had covered, had merely laughed.

"You speak as though we'd traversed a trackless waste," he had said. "These distances are as nothing to what you will find, say, in America or . . . Canada."

"Have you been there?" she had asked eagerly.

"There and elsewhere."

"Oh, I should like to hear about America," she had said eagerly.

"And I will be delighted to tell you about it when we have more leisure, but we still have some traveling ahead of us."

"Could we not remain here?" she had asked. "It is a pretty town."

He had shaken his head. "We have made better time than I had anticipated, my love, but we still have the sun in our corner of the world. We'll lie over in Peterborough." He had glanced over his shoulder—almost, Pamela thought, as if he expected to find someone behind him. He was very edgy and impatient. Though she could not quite understand his reason for haste, she was thrilled at the implications. He wanted to marry her as soon as possible, and then . . . and then . . . she would be Mrs. Questred and . . . then what would happen? She did not know. All the books she had read ended either directly after the ceremony joining the hero and heroine, or just before it. What followed was merely conjecture, though occasionally there were epilogues showing the heroine a year hence with a bonny infant in her arms, generally a boy. Pamela felt her cheeks grow warm. A year hence, would she be cradling Mr. Questred's son in her arms?

"My dear," he had said gently, "a penny for your thoughts."

She had been embarrassed. "I was thinking of . . . nothing."

"I hope you are not afraid."

"How could I be afraid with you?" she had asked.

For some reason, he had flushed. "I am glad of that, and hope to prove worthy of your trust, my love. You are my love, you know. You believe that, do you not?" His dark eyes had been fixed on her face.

For some reason she could not quite fathom, his question had disturbed her. Why did he require those reassurances? Was not her presence in his post chaise proof of her trust in him? Was he suggesting that he feared she might not trust him? It was difficult to fathom the workings of his mind. If only she knew him better. With a little twinge of fright, Pamela had realized that actually she did not know him at all, nor he her, and she had actually anticipated the birth of his child? Panic had surged through her. She had had a sense of time passing far too swiftly—without allowing for proper thought.

He had risen. "Come, my love, let us be on our way."

They were on the road again and Pamela suddenly wished that she was far, far from Sidney Questred, far from the George Inn, now a tiny blot on the lengthening road behind her. She wanted to be home, but home was also behind her, a hundred miles behind her, and by now her frantic father was conferring with an equally frantic Tom and his father, while she had no choice but to go on—go forward with one who was, to all intents and purposes, a veritable stranger! Then she remembered the warm clasp of his hand as he had assisted her into the coach, and the strangeness vanished. She shifted her gaze to the side window and found that rather than being ahead or behind it, Mr. Questred was riding beside the post chaise. Their eyes met momentarily—but long enough to remind her that she was with the man she had loved enough to embark upon this perilous journey which would and must change her entire life.

6

The inn known as the Pilgrim's Staff was located outside Peterborough. It was old, and looked, Pamela thought, as if it had wearied of standing tall against the buffeting of some four centuries' worth of winds and rain. It had huddled in on itself with its timbers all a little bent and awry. Inside, its walls proved to be blackened by the smoke from thousands and thousands of fires. She could well imagine that weary pilgrims must have rested from their journeys under its roof, and had they been as weary as herself? They would have walked the long pitted roads, but they would not have been jounced in a coach for so many hours that she had lost count! She had been so stiff that she could barely negotiate the steps that the postboy placed against the coach door, and Mr. Questred had carried her inside, depositing her in a chair while he conversed with the landlord, a heavyset genial man who seemed impressed by his manner.

Mr. Questred *was* well-spoken, Pamela thought, and from the few observations he had made during their infrequent stops, he was well-educated—but where? She had hoped to know much more about him by now, but to a very great extent, he still remained an enigma. Despite their passionate encounters, she was marrying one whose origins were a mystery. Where had he been born? Where was his family? Was he alone in the world? Her father would want to know that. With a pang, she realized that he would not. Sir Robert had always resented the encumbrance of a daughter—the daughter whose birth had resulted in the death of his beloved young wife. Now he would finally and irrevocably turn his face against her.

Would he? Truly?

There *had* been times when he had been kind to her and concerned, these being mostly during her few illnesses. She could remember a quinsy suffered two years back when he had spent a great deal of each night at her bedside, an indistinct figure in the darkness but withal a most comforting presence. She wished she had not thought of that, nor of Miss Pringle, who would undoubtedly be blamed for her disappearance. She ran her hands through her tumbled locks. She must not allow herself to become plagued by this belated remorse! None of the girls in the novels she had read had been other than dying of love for the men with whom they had chosen to cast their lots. Generally, of course, they had been fleeing from cruel guardians, stern fathers, or wicked uncles, and given these circumstances, it had not seemed to matter that they knew no more about their prospective bridegrooms than she knew about Mr. Sidney Questred. They had blindly trusted, and their instincts had invariably proved to be right—but they were in books, and this was real life!

"My love"—Mr. Questred bent over her—"I have bespoken a private parlor. Let me take you to it now." Before she could respond, he had lifted her from the chair, and though he must have been as weary as herself, not to mention saddle-sore, he carried her effortlessly across the room and up the stairs in the wake of a candle-bearing abigail.

Their chambers, which numbered three, were located on the third floor. Though the ceiling was so low that the beams seemed but a half-inch from Mr. Questred's head, the sitting room, furnished with a table, two padded chairs, and a third straight chair, was surprisingly commodious and already bright with the fire that leapt and crackled on a wide hearth—it having turned surprisingly cold for a late-spring night. There was a door on either side of the sitting room, and still following the abigail, Mr. Questred brought Pamela into a small bedchamber furnished with a four-poster, an armoire, and a dressing table. He deposited her on the bed, which proved to be surprisingly soft. "You will sleep in here, my dear," he said. "And I will take the other chamber."

A breath she had not known she was holding escaped Pamela. "That will be fine," she responded.

His arrangements were similar to those described in novels, but again, this was not a novel, and until this moment, she had not been sure what he would do, given the passionate embraces she had received from him. At this point in time, she was not in the mood for passionate demonstrations of affection; she wanted only to sleep, having already been warned that they would need to rise at dawn. If the truth were to be told, she was too weary even to partake of the repast she had heard him order. All she wanted was for Lucy to come and undress her, but of course she would not. Lucy was part of the life she had left behind forever. Questions arose in her head, and looking up at him, she received a shock. He was not there. While she had been pondering, he had quietly left the room. She found that quick departure unsettling—everything was unsettling—and something which had been lurking in the back of her mind moved forward so that she had perforce to confront it.

"I wish . . ." she whispered. "I wish I had not agreed to come. I wish he would take me home." Tears forced themselves out of her eyes and trickled down her cheeks. It was too late, too late, too late to entertain such wishes. She had made her bed and, at present, she was lying in it! She stiffened at a soft tap on her door and hastily brushed a hand across her wet cheek.

"Yes," she called.

The door was opened by the abigail who had brought them to their accommodations. She was cheerful of demeanor and not much older than Lucy. She gave Pamela a pleasant smile as she said, "Should ye like me to 'elp you prepare for the night, miss?"

A refusal formed on Pamela's tongue and was resolutely swallowed. "I would like that very much, thank you," she said.

The girl worked deftly and quickly. In a matter of moments Pamela was in the nightdress and peignoir she had brought with her. She had also performed her ablutions in the ewer and basin the abigail had provided. She felt much better after the girl—May, her name proved to be—had gone. She also felt unexpectedly hungry, even famished. Undoubtedly Mr. Questred would order a meal, for he, too, must be intensely hungry. Still, she tensed at a tap on the door.

"Yes," she called in a small voice.

The door was pushed open a crack. "We have ham and greens, as well as a pudding and wine, my dear. You must eat, you know. Will you join me or would you prefer to sup in your chamber?" Mr. Questred did not come into the room but spoke from behind the door.

Pamela glanced nervously down at her peignoir. It was a heavy silk, and concealing enough, but still she did feel shy about appearing before a veritable stranger in dishabille. He was not a stranger, she corrected mentally. He was the man to whom she was now affianced, the man whom she would marry in two short days' time, and why should she be shocked by this recollection? She said, "I will be there directly, sir."

"Good," he responded heartily. "I should not have enjoyed my repast half so much, were I required to consume it alone." He left the door slightly ajar and she heard him walk across the room, ostensibly to the table —of course to the table. She had heard a chair being drawn out. She stared at the door, fighting an increasing reluctance to open it any further. Still, she must conquer this ridiculous shyness. The hero of *A Wild Heart or: Lord Tiverton's Fancy* had seen Drusilla, the heroine, in her *shift*! He had yet conducted himself like a perfect gentleman. She had no reason to imagine that Mr. Questred would be other than as respectful as he had been heretofore—but heretofore they had not shared such close quarters, she reminded herself nervously, and she must stop thinking in terms of works of fiction, which had no bearing on real life. She swallowed a lump in her throat, and then, pulling open the door, stepped out, coming to a startled stop just beyond the threshold. Mr. Questred was wearing a brocaded dressing robe!

He rose immediately. "I pray you will forgive my informality, my dear Pamela, but my garments were sadly saddle-worn and I consigned them to the porter's care."

Pamela's cheeks burned. She had never seen a man in such informal attire. Her father, who was always astir at dawn, appeared only in the garments he wore during the day. However, she managed to say shyly, "I quite understand. It must have been a relief to doff them—I know that I feel much more comfortable myself."

"You look charming," he said appreciatively. Moving to her side, he indicated the place opposite his own at the table. "Will you not sit down, my dear?" He pulled out her chair.

"I thank you, sir." She quickly obeyed and was relieved that he did not linger behind her but moved back to his own place immediately. She released a long breath and drew in another, which proved to be scented with the combined odors from the table.

"Oh," she could not help remarking, "I am hungry." Immediately that statement left her lips, she flushed. He would think her greedy.

"Good." He smiled. "You ought to be hungry. You only picked at your noonday meal. Will you have some wine?" Before she could respond, he picked up the bottle and filled her glass. "This," he continued, "will prove relaxing. It has been a tiresome ride. I am myself a trifle saddle-sore. It has been years since I have ridden so far, but we have been fortunate in our route, do you not agree?"

Having nothing with which to compare so lengthy a journey, Pamela contented herself with saying, "I think we must be." It occurred to her that if he found the ride so tiresome, he could have remained inside with her—such a suggestion sprang to her tongue, but out of an encroaching shyness, she swallowed it, wishing devoutly that this feeling of strangeness would pass. Perhaps it would when she knew him better. She tensed, struck once more by the fact that actually she knew very little about him, very little indeed, especially when compared to the knowledge she possessed concerning Tom.

"May I offer you a slice of roast?" Mr. Questred asked politely.

"Yes, thank you," she said shyly.

"And, of course, you will have greens and boiled potatoes."

"Yes, thank you," she said, and then protested as he piled the food on her plate. "You must not give me so much!"

"Come," he said. "You need to keep up your strength, my dear. We have another long day of traveling ahead of us on the morrow."

"Shall we travel as far tomorrow?"

He shook his head. "I cannot think we will. I'll not have you up at midnight, my dear. You may enjoy your beauty sleep until five in the morning." He grinned. "Am I not munificent?"

She made an effort to approximate his teasing tone. "Entirely, sir." She dared to meet his eyes and found his gaze peculiarly intense. It made her feel oddly intimidated. She looked down, her eyes inadvertently straying to the hues of his dressing gown—red, gold, and black with gold threads in what appeared to be an Oriental design. The colors became his darkly handsome contenance, she thought. His coloring was, in fact, much like that of Tom—but how different they were. Tom was handsome, but he did not have the almost flamboyant attraction of Mr. Questred, and of course his eyes were gray and one did not have the sensation of being drawn into them, almost of being drowned in twin pools of blackness.

"Might I offer you some wine?"

Pamela started and flushed. "I have not yet drunk what you have poured for me." She indicated her glass and colored even more deeply, seeing that it was empty. "Oh, I did not realize . . ." she began.

"No, because you are weary and hardly aware of what you are doing," he said sympathetically. "You must have more . . . it will make you sleep."

"Very well." She nodded, staring at the glass as the dark red liquid flowed into it again. Mr. Questred set down the bottle and said softly as he held up his glass, "I propose a toast."

"A toast?" She lifted her own glass.

"To us." He clicked glasses with her. "And to happiness, my love."

"To us and . . . and to happiness," she repeated shyly. She sipped the wine, finding it much to her liking. Yet, as she set down her glass, she felt dizzy. "Oh, dear . . ." she murmured.

"What's amiss?" he inquired.

"I feel . . . dizzy. I think perhaps I . . . I ought to go to bed." The moment those words left her lips, she flushed. It did seem odd to be talking to him in such a familiar manner.

"A lady does not discuss her health or her intentions."

Miss Pringle had told her that years ago. She never should have mentioned that she wanted to go to bed. She was not sure why she should not have vouchsafed this information but, basically, she knew it was wrong— but why? Her mind was going around in circles, she thought crossly.

"I agree that you must go to bed." Mr. Questred rose

quickly, and Pamela, too, got to her feet and felt her cheeks grow warmer yet, as the room seemed to whirl around her. She clutched the back of her chair. "Gracious, I fear . . ."

"I fear that you must retire immediately," he said, and scooped her up in his arms, holding her as easily as if, indeed, she were a rag doll.

"P-please . . ." she giggled, and paused mid-giggle, not knowing why she should feel so merry. In that same second, she saw the door to her bedchamber open mysteriously, but of course it wasn't mysterious. He must have kicked it open, she decided. "I can stand," she told him concernedly. "You do not need to carry me."

"I want to carry you," he said, and brought her toward her bed. Setting her down, he began to unbutton her peignoir.

"I can . . ." she began, and stopped, for he was slipping the peignoir from her shoulders and pulling her covers up about her. She looked up in surprise, and meeting his eyes, was vaguely alarmed. They seemed to bore right through her. "You . . ." she began, and paused, not remembering what she had wanted to tell him.

"You?" he questioned. Then, after a pause, he added, "You are very lovely, little Pamela." Bending down, he kissed her lightly on the lips, and then suddenly he sat on the edge of the bed, and gathering her in his arms, kissed her again, lingeringly, the while his hold tightened almost crushingly.

An excitement such as she had never experienced in her whole life coursed through her, bringing with it a need she barely understood.

In that same moment he released her, saying shakily, "I . . . I did not expect . . . I think I must leave you, my dear." He rose.

"No," she protested. "Do not go."

He dropped a light kiss on her forehead. "I must."

He whirled and went from the room, closing the door softly behind him.

She still felt dizzy, but at the same time, wildly excited. She longed to call him back, but could not, and knew instinctively that he would not obey the summons. She did not know why she was so sure of that. There was so much she did not understand, too much. She slid down in the bed, finding its softness beguiling. The wild pulsing in her throat and the pounding of her heart were subsiding. Her eyelids were growing heavy. She could no longer keep them open. She was really very weary. She needed to sleep, and in another moment that need had been fulfilled.

Another day, and the landscape was changing, growing greener, and the air was crisper—this despite the fact that it was almost summer. Pamela, sitting in the post chaise, barely noticed the passing scenery. She was still thinking about the previous evening, with its revelations and its confusions. The first concerned herself, and the second, the mystifying man whom, in another day, she must needs call "husband." Confounded and yet excited by the memory of his kisses, she alternated between being pleased and angry at his decision to ride outside, sometimes far ahead of the carriage. There were periods when she actively craved his nearness, but there were other times when fear took the place of desire, when she was uncomfortably reminded that she knew nothing about this man, when she pondered the advisability of asking him point-blank to tell her about himself—from whence he had come and why he had decided to dwell in the half-ruined Hall, he, a man of obvious means, at least so it appeared. His equipage, his garments, his generosity to landlords and servants at the inns where they stopped, all suggested that he had no need to watch his expenditures. Consequently he could not be marrying her for her dowry. Yet, was it love alone that motivated him, or did he have some ulterior motive for marrying her? It was a demeaning thought and, unfortunately, it was one which persisted. Despite his words, despite the excitement she experienced at his every touch, she remained uncertain. If only they were not traveling at so swift a pace, if only they had some time in which to be quiet and together—but this day was proving no different from the previous one, save that she actively tried not to think of her father and Tom, their anxiety and pain. They were a part of her past—she was with her future.

Their goal was Kendal, and they reached it at four in the afternoon, a gray town, she thought, and larger than most of those through which they had passed. Yet, though she would have liked to stop there, he insisted on pushing through to a town called Shap, renowned for its abbey, ruined, as were most of them, and barely distinguishable in the gathering dusk. They stopped at an inn, smaller than the one where they had stayed the previous night, but still he was able to hire a private parlor.

She had been both looking forward to and fearing this time spent together. As before, she came to supper in her peignoir and found him in his brocade dressing gown. As before, her warring feelings resulted in a nervousness she could not conceal. He, however, appeared more preoccupied. He spoke little during supper other than to see that she had the choice cuts of meat and large helpings of vegetables. He was, she noted thankfully, more sparing of the wine.

When they finished eating, he rose, saying almost curtly, "We must retire now. We will be reaching our destination sometime in the afternoon, and then . . ." He moved to her side and stood staring down at her. "We will be wed, and I warn you, it will not be a beautiful ceremony such as young girls envision . . . or do they? I know precious little about a woman's mind."

She found his comment—or was it a question?—strangely unsettling. "We dream, or at least I have, of happiness."

"Happiness?" he echoed. He stared down at her. "God knows you deserve it, my child, shut away by yourself, with your father eternally ensconced in his tower. I hope you will be happy. I want you to be happy."

Again, Pamela was confused and disturbed. He had said nothing about trying to make her happy or about his own happiness in being with her. Indeed, she had a sense of withdrawal, as if the man who had embraced her so passionately last night had completely forgotten those moments. He had spoken almost impersonally. "I . . . hope we will be happy," she said shyly.

"We shall . . . we *will.*" He drew her against him, adding in a low voice, "You cannot know what you are doing for me, little Pamela. 'Twill take a lifetime to repay you, and when all is said and done, I do want to see you content."

Again she felt a strangeness in him. "And you also, sir."

He regarded her silently for a moment. "I will be . . . again, when all is said and done." He took a turn around the room and came back to her. "But I fear I am confusing you. I do not want that . . . and now, since we have had a tiring day, I think we had best retire. We will want to be up with the birds again." He moved closer to her and suddenly caught her in his arms, straining her against him until she felt as if the breath must be squeezed out of her. His long kiss stifled the little cry that had escaped her. Then, releasing her, he said in a low voice, "I must not . . . but it is damned hard to be with you and not want you."

Again, her excitement was tempered by shyness, a shyness that precluded any mention of the feelings he had brought to the surface. Indeed, how could she tell him that she wished he would not pull back, that she wished he would continue to hold her so close against him—that she felt as if they were no longer two separate entities, but one. Yet, that bold admission trembled on her tongue and he said, "I did not expect this, believe me."

"You . . . did not expect . . . what, S-Sidney?" She faltered, feeling a pounding in her throat.

"Nothing," he returned gratingly. "You must go to bed, my dear. Again, we will have to rise early if we are to cross the border in good time."

"The border . . ." she repeated, seized by a feeling of unreality. "We will . . . cross the border tomorrow?"

"Yes, tomorrow, my precious." He visited a long look upon her. "Tomorrow," he repeated in peculiarly ominous tones.

Looking into his eyes, Pamela had a strange feeling that he was not really seeing her—that his look was inward rather than outward. She shivered, feeling oddly lonely, as if, indeed, she were here and he on a distant shore. She had an impulse to grasp his hand so that she could feel his reality, but then he smiled at her, a wordless acknowledgment of her presence and of his love for her. He reached out to her and then shook his head.

"I did not expect this," he said wonderingly. "It is becoming harder and harder for me to let you go." A long sigh shook him. Then he brought her hand to his lips. "I will bid you good night, my dearest." Having kissed her hand, he held it a second longer. "You are my dearest, you know. I have never . . ." He broke off, and releasing her hand, added, "But again, my sweetest, good night."

"Good night, Sidney," she breathed, disappointed yet relieved as he moved to the table to extinguish the candles. She went to her room, and as she settled down in bed, she realized that it would be the last time in her life she would be alone if . . . But she did not want to consider that stray "if" that had inserted itself into her consciousness. He would marry her on the morrow. They could not have traversed all of England for any other purpose.

"It would not make sense," she whispered, wishing

that she had not been seized by doubts for which she had no name—but they were there and would not be dispatched until she and Mr. Questred had exchanged their vows—if that were truly his intention. Sleep was not as accommodating as it had been on the previous evening. Pamela lay awake for some little time, and when it did come, sleep brought a host of disturbing dreams in which Tom's face predominated. Expressions of hurt and anger flew across his mobile countenance—but he would not be hurt in the long run, she assured herself upon waking. It would be only his pride that would be wounded, and those wounds would eventually be healed with the help of Edith. She had no doubt that Edith must have been his confidante and comforter. He would have turned to her with questions, and if she had not been able to provide answers, her concern and sympathy might well bind her to him. Pamela did not know what made her so sure about Edith's feelings for Tom—no, that was not true, there had always been an unspoken rivalry between them. It was even possible that Edith had visited her so often in the hopes of meeting Tom. And Edith *was* beautiful. Her fairness contrasted against his darkness . . .

"Oh, I do hope I am right," she whispered. "Furthermore, he will inherit Bellair once Sir Edmund dies."

Judging from Sir Edmund's pasty countenance and trembling hands, she guessed that Tom would not have long to wait.

Pamela had never seen so many people walking two by two. She thought of Noah's Ark, but forgot it as quickly, holding tightly to Mr. Questred's hand—or rather to *Sidney's* hand—Sidney Questred, the man she would be marrying at three this afternoon in the house with the sign that read "Blacksmith" and "Marriages Performed." Mr. Questred's hand was cold—or was it her own that was cold and imparting its chill to his warm flesh? Laughter reached her. A girl, younger than herself, was gazing up at a smiling young man. They were both excited and, she guessed, nervous. Pamela stole a look at Mr. Questred. She failed to catch his eye. He was staring about him or, more specifically, at the crooked dirt road that ran through the village. She had caught him glancing at it more than once. Impossible to understand why, impossible to guess what he was thinking. He did seem abstracted, and that, of course, was only natural. Or was it? There seemed to be a marked difference between his attitude and those of the other men she saw about her. Most of them were devoting their entire attention to their female companions. Mr. Questred, *Sidney,* on the other hand, had not visited many looks on her. He either fixed his attention on the road or stared straight ahead, apparently deep in thought.

What was he thinking about?

Was he entertaining second thoughts?

Did he regret having brought her here?

If he did, it was an odd time to entertain those regrets, for they were here in Gretna Green, a village she found singularly unprepossessing and, aside from the young couples, filled mainly with merchants eager to sell goods which upon close examination proved to resemble those found in stalls at county fairs. There were fans and gloves and stockings. There were bright imitation brooches and piles of brassy-looking "gold" rings. There was one booth hung with nightshifts. Quite a few giggling girls were gathered around it. A cursory glance revealed that the garments were of a most inferior quality and . . . She paused in her thinking as she heard the sound of hooves on the road. Once more her companion looked in that direction, and Pamela winced as his grip on her hand turned viselike. A horseman came into view and she recognized him as Charles, whose duty it was to act as lookout. She tensed. Had they been pursued?

Charles dismounted, and striding toward Mr. Questred, nodded and smiled.

"Very good, Charles," Mr. Questred said on a breath. He pressed a coin into the man's hand. "You've done well."

"Thank you, sir." Charles tethered his horse to a nearby post, and tossing the coin into the air, grinned and ambled into a nearby tavern.

Loosening his grip on Pamela's hand, Mr. Questred smiled down at her. "Well, my love," he said softly, "I think it is time we wended our way toward yonder . . . Dare we address him by the exalted title of 'minister'?"

"Is it . . . time, then?" she asked through stiff lips.

He glanced at the watch that hung on one of the fobs at his waist. "It is close on three. Are you frightened, my own? Do not be. It is a painless . . . operation, the joining of one to another. At least, so I have been told."

She lifted her chin. "I am not frightened," she said.

"Come, then." His arm was around her waist and he moved quickly. As they reached the blacksmith's shed, a giggling young couple emerged from the wide entrance. Pamela heard the girl say hesitantly, "Are we really married, then, Edward?"

"Why would you think we are not?" he questioned.

"I do not feel married, somehow," she complained. "Over that rusty old anvil and the smell of horses so strong . . . and the straw lying about, and all those implements hanging on the walls. Besides, he gabbled the words so fast and chewed tobacco the whole time!"

Her companion laughed. "He's got a passel of folk waiting for him, my love, and as for the tobacco, he's got to pleasure himself a bit—between coupling. But we'll have the real pleasure. Come with me now . . . I've the rooms booked and ready."

"Oh, Edward . . ." She emitted another nervous giggle.

Pamela swallowed a giggle of her own, remembering that Mr. Questred had also booked rooms at the inn.

Would they be heading for them immediately the black-smith pronounced them man and wife? A blacksmith? She could agree with the other bride, especially when she thought of her wedding gown at home, and the church, all those preparations done for naught. She must not think of those, else the pangs of conscience would smite her anew. She eyed the barnlike structure of the smithy dubiously. The vows she was about to exchange with Mr. Questred were sacred and would bind her to his side for life. She wished that thought had not crossed her mind. Was there not something unhal-lowed about a marriage in such a setting?

"Pamela, my love," her bridegroom said softly, "will you not cross this threshold with me?"

She blinked up at him in surprise—realizing that she had been so deep in thought that she must have been standing there for some few minutes. "Yes, of . . . of course," she murmured. As they came in, she stared about her at this old building where so many, many marriages had been performed. And did that not render the dirt floor and the rusty anvil sacred? Surely it must. She tightened her grip on Mr. Questred's arm and moved toward the anvil.

Fresh qualms assailed her as, upon reaching it, they were greeted by a grinning old man in rusty black garments. His linen was dingy, and an odor of sweat and tobacco issued from him. Not far away stood a heavyset woman in a homespun gown. She, too, was grinning and exposing a mouth with a paucity of teeth.

"Well, the two o' ye be a likely-lookin' pair," she commented. She glanced at her companion. "Will you not agree, Jamie?"

"Aye." He nodded and expelled a brown stream of spittle upon the floor. "Your names, please," he demanded.

"Sidney Questred," Mr. Questred said strongly.

"And you, miss?" The smith stared at Pamela, his eyes, small and blue, appraising.

"Pamela Cardwell," she responded in a half-whisper.

She received a knowing look from the smith and a chuckle from the woman as he turned to Mr. Questred. Clearing his throat, he said, "Do you take this woman to be your lawful wedded wife, sir?"

"I do," Mr. Questred said strongly.

"And you, Miss Cardwell, do you take this man to be your lawful wedded husband?"

She hesitated, feeling . . . She was not sure what. Her heart seemed to be pounding in her throat again. She put a hand to her bosom, and then, nodding, said in the merest shred of a voice, "I do."

"Scared, eh? Lots o' 'em is," the smith commented. "But be that as it may, I now pronounce you man and wife. Go in good health."

Mr. Questred drew Pamela into his arms and kissed her lightly upon the lips. Then his arms tightened and he kissed her again, releasing her with obvious reluctance. "Come, my love," he said. "Come and partake of our wedding feast."

She did not move. "But . . . but is that all?" she inquired tremulously.

A cackle of laughter startled her. "That's all, lovey." The woman, who had been standing near the smith, moved forward. "Best take it from Marthy MacNab, 'twill last a lifetime."

Pamela still hesitated. "I thought there would be more . . . words."

"These were enough, my dearest." Mr. Questred put his arm around her shoulders. "We have announced our intentions to wed, and before witnesses. That, my angel, is all that is needed here in Scotland."

"In Scotland . . ." she repeated. "Yes, of course," she said dazedly. Mr. Questred's hand was now on her arm. Her *husband's* hand was on her arm, she amended mentally, but the word still had no reality for her.

"Come," he said gently. "Come, my darling." His arm slipped to her waist and exerted a slight pressure on her so that she had to move, had to turn around and come forth with him into the noisy street. She had a vague memory of that other girl with her young husband—Edward, his name had been. *She* had said she did not feel married, and nor, Pamela realized, did she. She raised questioning eyes to Mr. Questred's face, but he was not looking at her. He was staring at the road that wound through the village, the road they must soon take . . . Where? He had not mentioned any other destination.

"And what is my little bride thinking?" Mr. Questred asked.

She looked up at him. "Am I a bride . . . is it true?" she murmured.

"That we are wed?" He stared at her through narrowed eyes. "We are, my own, and there's none can disprove it. We have announced our intentions before witnesses and . . ." He broke off and then added, "But I have told you that already, my dearest. Come, let us go to our nuptial feast!"

They came into the tavern. He led her to a table, and a short time later he toasted her with a glass of champagne. As she sipped the golden liquid, it occurred to her that in most of the novels she had read, the heroine rarely appeared after the wedding took place. That was usually where the book ended. Yet she was contemplating a beginning, not an ending. She felt a surge of panic. She was contemplating her beginning with a man she barely knew. What had possessed her to consent to this hole-in-the-corner marriage? Then, as she met his dark gaze, her burgeoning doubts were partially assuaged.

"It is good wine," he commented.

"Yes, very." She nodded.

"Pamela"—he leaned across the table—"are you still so frightened?"

She read compassion in his eyes. "I am not frightened, only . . ."

"Only what, child?"

"You must not call me a child," she reproved.

"I am sorry," he said quickly. "But you do seem so very young to me, my darling."

"I am turned twenty. You are hardly old enough to be my father." She spoke lightly, but at the same time, a little thrill of surprise ran through her as she realized that she did not even know his age. "How old are you?" she asked bluntly.

He surprised her by hesitating before answering. "I have recently had my thirty-first birthday."

She laughed. "That is not a great age, sir."

"Possibly not to some," he agreed. "But to others it can seem a lifetime."

"If they have had a hard life," she amplified, wondering if he were referring to himself, and once more she was aware of how very little she knew about him. For some reason, she was reminded of his roughened hands. They suggested that he was no stranger to physical labor. Perhaps he had been in the wars and had been taken prisoner. Were prisoners ever required to do hard labor? She did not believe that officers would be in that position, and he must certainly have been an officer if, indeed, he had ever been in the armed forces.

"What are you thinking, my love?" he asked edgily.

"Th-thinking?" she repeated, and looking at him, found him frowning. "Nothing, only . . ."

"Only what?"

"There is so very much I do not know about you," she explained shyly.

"There is so very much that you have never asked me, my dear little Pamela," he said gravely. "But I can tell you that I do not possess a Bluebeard's closet filled with deceased wives."

"Oh!" she laughed. "I was not thinking about anything like that. But you've not told me where you lived before you came to the Hall or . . . or anything."

"Again, may I remind you that you have never asked, me, my love."

"I know . . ." Pamela was suddenly put in mind of a fairy tale, or rather of a myth, called "Cupid and Psyche"—Psyche, who had asked Cupid, or Love, to reveal his name, and had been punished by his flight. Would Mr. Questred similarly desert her because of her probing questions? She said quickly. "It does not matter."

"But I expect it should." His face changed. "I did not expect this . . ."

"What?" She faltered, wondering if he were hurt or even insulted by her probing.

"I did not expect to love you . . . more each day I've been with you."

"You've not spent much time with me," she dared to say. "You've been on horseback . . ."

He nodded, gazing beyond her into space. "For my own protection," he said strangely. "But I do love you, and I will tell you this. Life has not been easy for me . . ." His eyes were on her face. "I . . . But this is no conversation for a wedding banquet. Just keep in mind that I do love you, my dearest."

She was taken aback by the intensity of his stare—now fastened on her face—and by the tone of his voice. He had sounded almost desperate—but that was ridiculous. She had to be imagining that. "I love you too," she said softly.

He was silent a moment, his eyes roving over her face again. "I hope that you will continue to love me, dearest. Even when you know, as you soon must . . ." He suddenly loosed a long sigh, his eyes narrowing as he stared at something behind her. Then he abruptly pushed his chair back and got to his feet.

Pamela, turning, froze as she saw the tall, grim-faced young man who was making his way through the crowded room. "Tom," she whispered incredulously. "How does he happen to be here? How did he know?"

There were no answers to her questions as Tom, reaching the table, confronted Mr. Questred. "You damned dog," he rasped, striking him across the face.

The voices around them were suddenly stilled as the two men glared at each other.

"Tom!" Pamela also rose. "What . . . what are you doing here?"

He seemed to become aware of her for the first time. "I've come for you, you damned little fool!" he said harshly. He turned back to Mr. Questred. "What will it be, cur? Swords or pistols?"

Mr. Questred had paled. "Where is your father?" he demanded gratingly.

"What does it matter?" Tom asked furiously. "You've not answered me, coward. Will it be swords or pistols?"

"I do not want to fight you, lad," Mr. Questred responded.

"No, Tom, you must not fight!" Pamela clutched his arm.

He wrenched it away from her, his hot eyes on Mr. Questred's face. "I repeat, sir"—he spoke contemptuously now—"Will it be swords or pistols?"

" 'Ave at 'im wi' yer fives, man!" yelled someone at a nearby table. His advice was followed by nervous laughter from others who were interestedly watching the confrontation.

"Where is Edmund Bellairs?" Mr. Questred actually hissed the question. "Where is he? I know he came with you."

"He turned back in Kendal," Tom said in some surprise. Anger coated his tones again as he continued, "Though I cannot guess why my father's whereabouts should concern you, rogue. Will you choose swords or pistols? Or would you prefer my horsewhip across your back?"

"No, Tom, have done!" Pamela cried, moving to Mr. Questred's side. "I love him."

"Be still, you little fool." Tom glared at her. "The less I hear from you, the better it will be. A fine trick you played on me, but no matter. 'Twill do your . . . lover no good to hide behind your skirts."

Mr. Questred stiffened. He said evenly, "I am not afraid to fight you, Mr. Bellairs."

"Prove it, cur!" Tom's fist shot out, to be caught by Mr. Questred, who was breathing deeply.

"Very well, you young firebrand . . . pistols it will be!"

"No!" Pamela shrieked. "No, no, no, please."

"Come, then!" Tom turned toward the door.

"No, you must not . . . please, you must not," she cried again, looking desperately from one man to the other and thinking in that moment that there was a strange resemblance between them. Both were tall, both dark-haired and slim of build. They could have been brothers—but brothers did not kill each other unless they were Cain and Abel. But in what strange channels were her thoughts running? She must not waste time in thinking—she must try to convince them that they must not duel, but inexorably they were striding toward the door. She followed, confronting Tom as they reached the street. "No, Tom, 'twas my fault, you must not."

He thrust her aside. "Go away, Pamela."

An older woman she had never seen before came to her side. "Do not attempt to argue them out of it, my dear," she said in clear, crisp tones. "When men have it in mind to fight, they will fight."

Pamela turned away from her and ran to Mr. Questred. "Mr. . . . S-Sidney, please, I beg you will not fight Tom."

He stared down at her. His expression was regretful. "I did not anticipate . . . Tom," he said strangely.

"I do not understand you!" she cried.

"No matter . . . but you must excuse me now, my dear." He turned away from her and went to talk to a man whom she now recognized as Charles. The latter nodded and moved back into the tavern.

Tom stepped to Pamela's side. "Where is he?"

"There . . ." She pointed and then did not see him.

"Has he bolted, then?"

"He would not!" she flared. "Oh, Tom, I pray you

will not fight. I am not worth you—either of you—
being hurt! Please." She caught his arm.

He pulled away. "No, I begin to think you are not
worth it, Pamela, but you do not deserve to be cozened
by that rascal, whose motives I do not understand.
But . . ." He glared at her. "God, Pamela, have you no
discernment? Never . . . never in my life did I dream you
were so wet behind the ears! It's those damned books
you are forever reading. Edith has told me about
them—"

"I knew you would do well with Edith," she said.
"Go back to her and forget me. Only your pride is hurt,
Tom, nothing more."

He stared down at her, amazement warring with
anger. "Are you saying that I do not . . . did not love
you?"

"Yes, yes, yes, that is what I am saying," she cried.
"I am saying that you agreed to marry me because our
fathers' wanted it."

His eyes widened. "You . . . believed that? You . . .
you did not know that I have loved you all my life?"

"You never said . . ." She faltered, her heart
beginning to pound heavily in her throat again.

"I did not think I had to say it," he cried. Putting his
hands on her shoulders, he actually shook her. "We
were to . . . to be *married*." His voice broke. "God,
Pamela, you are a worse fool than I ever dreamed."

"Oh, Tom, you never told me." Tears filled her eyes.
"You . . . told me nothing of what you felt for me."

"I thought you knew," he said bitterly. "I'm not one
for fancy speeches like that . . . that knave who stole
you from me."

"He did not . . ." she paused, seeing Charles coming
toward them. He said respectfully, "Beggin' yer
pardon, sir, but do you 'ave a second?"

"My groom will act for me," Tom snapped. "And
are you acting for Questred?"

"I am that," Charles assented.

"Please . . . please, it must not come to this," Pamela begged.

"I will fetch him," Tom said, and strode away.

Pamela whirled on Charles. "Where is your master?" she demanded. Before he could answer, she saw Mr. Questred emerge from the tavern with his coachman. "Sidney . . ." She ran to him. "I beg you, please do not fight Tom."

"My dear"—he had a rueful smile for her—"I give you my word that I will not harm him."

"But he may harm you—he's in a rage. I never saw him like this before!"

"It is only natural, my own," he said gravely. " 'Tis obvious that he loves you." He sighed. "I did not think . . . But no matter, the best-laid plans of mice and men, you know. Be assured that my plans included nothing like this. I had hoped . . . But 'twas not to be."

She had listened in growing confusion. "I do not understand you! What plans?"

He did not look at her. "Why, those attendant upon our elopement, child, what else?"

"Are you telling me the truth?" she demanded. "Or . . ." In that moment Tom returned with Martin, his groom, a rangy copper-headed youth Pamela knew very well, since he had been one of Tom's good friends in childhood. She started to greet him and then flushed as she met his cold, unsmiling gaze. Once more the horror of the situation rushed over her. "Please," she cried. "Both of you, I beg you . . ."

"Please, Mrs. Questred, you are to come with me." The coachman was at her side.

She stared at him blankly. "With you . . ."

"The master 'as said so." He looked at her apologetically.

Tom, Mr. Questred, Martin, and Charles were walking away from her—down the street. Various people were staring at them and exchanging knowing glances. Then another man came out of one of the houses and joined them. He was holding a small leather satchel such as doctors were wont to carry, and, she realized, he must be a doctor. She looked up at the coachman. "I must go with them!" she cried.

His hand clamped down on her arm. "No, Mrs. Questred, the master 'as forbidden it."

She stared at him in anger, and at the same time realized that he was calling her "Mrs. Questred," but she could not think about that, not at this moment, not when Mr. Questred and Tom were to engage in this foolish, foolish duel—in which one of them was bound to be hurt. Mr. Questred had assured her that he would not hurt Tom, but Tom could easily hurt him. Tom was a good shot. She had never seen him so angry, and he had said he loved her, something she still had trouble believing—but knowing him as well as she did, she was sure that he was telling her the truth. If she had been aware, would it have made any difference? She was not sure. No, that was not true, could not be true. The feeling she had for Mr. Questred far surpassed anything she had ever felt for Tom, she was reasonably sure of that. However, she must not let herself be plagued by these thoughts, not when the two men who meant the very most to her were planning to slaughter each other, and all because of her foolishness! She looked up at the coachman.

"Please, I must go, please." Tears started to her eyes. "I must go to them and stop them."

"Ye'll not be able to stop them, Mrs. Questred. The master be bound'n determined, an' 'im also. Ye'll 'ave to wait 'ere wi' me."

She glared at him. "You have no right! Let me go! Let me go, I say!"

She might have been speaking to a stone image, she realized. He retained his grip on her arm. "Would ye like to wait in yon tavern?" he asked.

"No!" She stared about her. "I want to . . . Oh, look —what is that?"

He loosened his grip on her arm. "What . . . where?"

Wrenching her arm away from him, Pamela dashed down the street in the direction she had seen Tom, Mr. Questred, and the others take. Vaguely she heard the coachman's angry yell. She only ran the faster, and in a short time she saw open fields. Then, rounding a bend in the road, she came to a startled stop as she heard two sharp reports. Pistol shots!

With a cry of anguish, Pamela looked about her, but saw nothing. She ran farther and staring across a stretch of ground, glimpsed a small group of men, very small, no more than four or five. Though she was sadly winded, she picked up her skirts and continued to run until she was close to them, close enough to see that they were bending over something . . . someone who lay on the ground. Gasping for breath, she approached the group and met Tom's wide-eyed stare. Tom was standing, Charles and Martin were standing, and the little man with the satchel was kneeling beside whoever lay on the ground—but she knew who lay on the ground and came up to them. They protested. They tried to push her back, tried to stand in front of her, but she thrust them aside and knelt beside the fallen man, beside Mr. Questred, who lay on his back, his face nearly as white as his shirt—but his shirt was not white. There was a great red stain near the shoulder, the left shoulder. "Sidney," she whispered, and then looked up at Tom. "You killed him."

"No, no, he is not dead," said the little man, who had moved away when she came. " 'Twas through the shoulder. He'll have fever from it, no doubt, but he's not dead."

"Oh, God," Tom said. "He didn't shoot at me. He did not even try. The bullet went over my head. Why?"

"There's no explaining that, sir." The little doctor shook his head. "But we've got to get him back to his rooms . . . has he booked rooms?"

"Yes," Pamela said dully. "He has."

"Why did he not shoot?" Tom spoke almost plaintively.

"Yer lucky 'e didn't," Charles said. " 'E's a first-rate shot, 'e is. Could shoot the pip out of a card at twenty paces."

"We must get him back to the inn," Pamela cried. "We must get him back."

"Yes." The doctor spoke briskly now. He looked at Charles. "You go and get a plank and some other stout lads to help you, my man."

"That I will." Charles strode off hastily.

"Why . . ." the man on the ground suddenly said.

"Sidney . . ." Pamela stared into his face. His eyes were open. "Oh, Sidney . . ." She caught at his hand, holding it against her cheek, but he was not looking at her. He was looking beyond her to Tom. "You're not hurt, lad?" he asked.

"No." Tom knelt beside Pamela. "But why did you not. . . ?"

"Not . . . you," the fallen man said incomprehensibly. "Not you, lad, not your quarrel, do you see? I thought . . ." But whatever else he would have said went unspoken, for he had fainted.

7

The plank on which they bore Mr. Questred back to the inn had turned out to be a door. Pamela had a vague memory of old doors being recruited to bear the wounded to hospitals and other destinations. She had read about that in a novel, she guessed. She had also read about duels in novels, wildly exciting affairs in which the villain was slain by the hero and everyone lived happily ever after. She swallowed a sob. She must, must, *must* stop thinking about novels—those novels that had wrought such damage in her life, and in the life of the man who lay in the adjoining chamber, and in Tom's life as well, Tom, who was pacing back and forth like a caged beast in the small sitting room that formed part of the "bridal" suite. Even as that thought crossed her mind, he stopped and glared at her.

"What is taking so long?" he burst out. "The doctor said he did not think the wound was dangerous!"

"He only gave it the most cursory look," she said dully. "If he dies . . ."

"He'll not die!" Tom snapped. "I did not aim for his heart. I aimed for his shoulder."

"His left shoulder?" Pamela demanded accusingly. Still accusingly, she continued, "You meant to kill him. Do not tell me differently."

"Damn you!" Tom's voice rose. "I did not!"

"Why did you press the duel on him, then? He did not want it!"

"I am damned if I know." Tom glared at her. "I could have spilled my claret too, and God knows you're not worth so much as a drop of it."

She flinched, knowing that in Tom's eyes she deserved whatever he chose to tell her, but it was hard hearing it from him. "You do not understand . . ." she could not help saying.

"Be assured that I do not! Our wedding was more than . . . than days away." His voice broke again. "How could you do this to me?"

Pamela ran her hands through her already wildly disheveled locks. "I thought . . . Oh, God, what does it matter now? What does anything matter? Oh, why does not the doctor come and tell me if Mr. Questred will live?"

"I tell you he will!" Tom burst out. "However much he deserves to die!"

"He does not deserve to die," she sobbed. "You . . . you do not know him."

"And you do?" he demanded furiously. "How many times have you seen him in the last month and a half? God, you have no more common sense than the veriest infant. The man is obviously an adventurer, else why would he choose to run away with you in this disgraceful manner?"

"Because I was about to be . . . to be . . ."

"Married to me!" Tom finished. "Good God, Pamela, if you were that unwilling to be my wife, you should have said so. Why did you never give me so much as an inkling of what you thought?" Hurt and anger were reflected in his gaze. "You could have said something to me or . . . or to your father."

"Would you have listened? Would he have listened?" she cried. "My father was determined that I marry you. My father and your father . . . do not tell me that you had any more say in the matter than I?"

"You are mad!" he responded roughly. "Do you suppose that my father could push me into anything I did not want too? And as for Sir Robert, do not tell me that he would have acted the tyrant. He was thinking of your own good—"

"He never gave a thought to me," she flashed. "He wanted to be rid of me. He has never forgiven me for my mother's death!"

"Good God, am I hearing aright?" Tom demanded rhetorically. "Let met tell you, Pamela, that he is beside himself with worry."

"I find that very hard to believe," she retorted.

"Do you?" He came to stand in front of her. "God, you have no more sense than . . . than a cat—even less, to say that about him. He was frantic, and Miss Pringle was bedded with the vapors and no one having a notion where you'd gone . . . You did not even leave a note!"

"How did you find out?" she demanded.

"Easily," he rasped. "Your . . . lover told his valet, who could not keep the news to himself but must needs bruit it to all who'd listen, and so we set out, my father and I . . ." He paused, staring at her. "My father," he repeated. "He asked about him, did he not?"

"Yes." She nodded. She added, "You told him that he'd turned back in Kendal . . . Oh, what can it mean?"

"I'm damned if I know," Tom growled. "And to tell his valet . . . did he not realize that 'twas akin to alerting a town crier?"

"He might be from . . . from foreign parts and not knowledgeable of servants' ways in England."

"All servants are the same anywhere," Tom retorted. He stared at her. "There is something very strange about all of this . . . and what did he want with my father?"

Before she could respond, the physician came out, closing the door softly behind him. All the color drained from Tom's face. Through stiff lips he asked, "Well, how is he?"

"As I have explained, sir, he sustained a wound in the shoulder. It is very deep but fortunately it has not touched any vital area. He will live."

"Oh." Pamela sat down suddenly. "Oh, thank God," she said weakly.

"Yes." Tom nodded. "Thank God, indeed. I did not think I'd give him a mortal wound—but there was so much blood."

"Yes, he has lost some blood," the physician said judiciously. "And no doubt he will be feverish—but he seems to be a strong, healthy young man, even though . . ." He paused and turned to Pamela. "Do you know if he has ever served in the navy, Mrs. Questred?"

"No, I . . . He has never said so. Why?"

"No matter. I wondered. However, be that as it may, he will require nursing. I can arrange for a woman to be sent here. There are many in the village who can serve in that capacity. These . . . er, situations are more common than I could wish, you see."

"I do not understand," Pamela began.

"He means," Tom said, "that duels are not uncommon in Gretna Green, is that not so?"

"Quite right, sir." The physician frowned. "Though I wish it might be otherwise."

"So you have said." Tom flushed. "You'd best send for your nurse. And will you continue to look in on him?"

"Yes. My fee—"

"Never mind your fee, man. Whatever it is, I will pay it. And must I see the constable?"

"No, sir, that will not be necessary, since there was no death. The constable, unfortunately, has been called out on another such affair which did not end so . . . felicitously."

"So . . . felicitiously?" Pamela questioned. "With poor Mr. Questred . . ."

"He is still alive," Tom reminded her.

"And why am I standing here? I must go to him." Pamela moved toward the inner room.

"I would not, Mrs. Questred," the physician protested. "He is sleeping. Best not disturb him."

"I would not disturb him. I would only sit beside him."

"A nurse will take your place," Tom said sharply. "You are coming back with me. We will start at once." He turned to the physician. "How much do I owe you?"

"Two pounds, sir."

"And how much will I owe at the end—I mean while he is recuperating from his wound? Tell me, and tell me what I must pay the nurse. Meanwhile—"

"Hold," Pamela cried. "I am not going with you, Tom."

"What?" Tom stared at her incredulously. "Don't be a little fool. You cannot stay here." He turned to the physician. "Mr. Graves, please wait below. We will be joining you directly."

"Very well, sir," the physician responded. "I will be in the common room." He bowed and left, closing the door softly behind him.

"Tom," Pamela said firmly, "I am staying with my husband."

"Husband in name only," he snapped.

She hesitated, knowing that what she was about to tell him must hurt him grievously—but there was no help for it. She was not going to leave the man she loved to the indifferent care of whatever nurses were to be found in this benighted village. She had an instant vision of the woman in the smithy. She had reeked of spirits and she could imagine that the creatures who hired themselves out to tend the sick were the same. She said evenly, "You have forgotten that we have been on the road for three days, Tom. Even before I repeated my vows, I was his wife in every sense of the term."

He paled. "You are lying. He would not take such advantage of you!"

She flushed. "I wanted it," she said.

"You . . ." he said chokingly. "You are a worse fool than I had ever dreamed. And he . . . I am sorry I did not shoot him in his black heart." Turning on his heel, he strode from the room.

Tears filled Pamela's eyes. She had hated the lie, hated to hurt him—but three days ago she had made her choice. She went into the inner room.

The road stretched ahead of him, and dust was in his nostrils, yellow dust, a yellow road by reason of the terrain, by reason of the hot sun beating down on it. His filthy shirt clung to his sweating back. His feet ached. He could feel the sharp pebbles through the worn soles of his shoes. He shuffled rather than walked. They all shuffled, the lot of them, and in common with himself, they carried pickaxes and shovels—the one to beat down the shrubbery, the other to lift the dirt when they reached the place where the road ended, where they would begin the next section themselves. They were not road-builders, they were thieves, murderers, smugglers, coiners, and once-young innocents traduced and condemned to ten years of such labor as he, in all his twenty-and-a-little-over years, had never done.

He stared down at his feet wonderingly. They did not seem *his* feet, these two appendages thrust into broken shoes from which his toes protruded. Neither did his hands, scratched and bleeding, seem *his* hands. He had always taken such care of his nails, and now they were broken and dirty and one of them was smashed.

Now they were at the end of the dirt road and he was digging into the hard earth, or trying to dig, and his back ached intolerably. The men about him cursed and groaned. Words such as he had never heard before, until recently, were in his ears. He had his own words. He said, "I will live, Edmund Bellairs. I will live." He did not cry, "I am innocent." He had repeated that statement into too many unheeding ears. Bligh, Governor Bligh, small, self-assured, pompous, intolerant, had heard the one man who had befriended and believed in him—the doctor he had aided on shipboard—insist that he had been wrongly convicted. Bligh had made answer, staring at him, seeing his rumpled garments and still plump-body.

"I have read the indictment and see no reason for leniency, sir. The youth stands convicted by a jury of his peers. If 'twere not his first offense, he would be hanging by the neck until dead. I have nothing but contempt for one who has abused his station in life and mingled with criminals. To all intents and purposes, he is a criminal himself and belongs where he is. I warn you, sir, against believing every word that falls from the lying lips of scoundrels such as this one. Look at him. He has lived well on his contraband goods. It is time he received the comeuppance he deserves."

The doctor had procrastinated and he had been himself rebuked for his interference and been warned that if he were to take the part of another criminal, Mr. Bligh, the honorable governor of New South Wales, would not know what to think save that he was unfit for his position.

Thus warned, the doctor with a young family to support had apologetically bowed out of his life. Bligh, the Honorable Governor Bligh, assigned him to a road gang rather than making use of his fine education in a more responsible position. He had stressed the ameliorating effects of such a regime for one who had obviously had it too easy for most of his worthless life. The sun burned into him.

"Water . . ." he mumbled. "Water, for the love of God . . . Water."

Water trickled down his throat.

Soft hands were on his forehead, brushing back his tangled hair. "Mia . . ." he murmured. Was it she, the young aborigine girl, whose real name he could not pronounce? Mia, who had come to him one night . . . Mia of the dark face and dark hair . . . beautiful and kind, teaching him about many things. Or was it Aggie, the street girl from London's stews, or Conchita, the Spanish wench, who had led him such a dance . . . when? When he had begun to know his way around and when his anguish and bitterness were pushed to the back of his seething mind in an effort to survive in this hostile land. It was not easy. Betrayers lurked everywhere. He remembered the man from Hythe, a smuggler, who knew the men who had informed against him, knew the judge who had sentenced him, told him an easy way to escape and had then, inexplicably, betrayed him. The flogging that had followed had left him with a back from which the flesh hung in strips. He had nearly died of it, might have died, possibly, had not Mia nursed him . . . as she was nursing him now, giving him liquor to combat the terrible pain . . . but also soothing ointments of her own devising.

"Mia . . . Mia . . ." he mumbled, feeling the pain not in his bleeding back but in his shoulder. His shoulder throbbed and ached. He did not understand why—for the whip had struck only his back, the whip that had been wielded by Edmund Bellairs . . . for later, encountering the smuggler from Hythe, he, grown strong again, had nearly beaten the life out of his betrayer and had his confession that he was in the pay of Edmund Bellairs . . . Edmund Bellairs, who wanted to make sure that his stepson perished in New South Wales. It had taught him something, that episode. It had taught him never to trust anyone again . . . with the exception of Mia, whose tears fell on his face, whose soft hands were the only touch he could stand on his lacerated back. . . .

"My shoulder, Mia . . ." he muttered.

"Shhh, drink this."

Something slid down his throat, bringing drowsiness, one of Mia's native brews. Through her help, he was going to survive, he knew it. "I will not die, Edmund Bellairs," he whispered defiantly.

"Do not think of dying," she murmured.

It was not Mia's voice. Was he with Conchita or Aggie? No, neither of them. He did not know the voice. There had been other women, too, nameless women who had pursued him on the farm, where he had eventually worked as a horse trainer. These were brief passions, easily forgotten, everything forgotten save the machinations of Edmund Bellairs. His shoulder throbbed. He could bear pain, he had discovered that long ago. He could bear anything when he thought of returning to England—to Kent, to Hythe, to Bellair, to Edmund Bellairs, whom he would wound, not kill, no, not kill, there would be no vengeance there, only prison for himself, and he had had enough of prisons. Let Edmund Bellairs, badly wounded, drag himself through the rest of his evil life knowing that the heir of Bellair had returned to wrest his property from him—in payment for ten stolen years.

"I will not kill him," he said aloud. "But he will wish himself dead."

"Shhhh . . . you must sleep."

"I am innocent, Mia," he told the voice. "I knew nothing of the goods they stored in the stone house."

"I am sure you did not, Arthur."

"It was Bellairs . . . he wanted Bellairs."

The soft hand was on his forehead. "Sleep, Arthur, sleep."

He was hot and cold at the same time. His teeth chattered, and then he flung the covers back from him in an effort to combat the terrible heat, the heat of the outback . . . the heat of the hut, where he lay with others of the road gang, the heat of the house on the farm, the heat of the ship's hold . . .

"Best bleed him," an unknown voice urged.

"Must you, sir?"

" 'Tis best."

He felt so weak, weak as a cat, he wanted . . . he was not sure, but weak as he was, he would live. "I will live, Edmund Bellairs," he told that cold mocking face that dwelt in the back of his mind, the face of the man who had bribed militiamen and judges, smugglers, also, those that informed against him and one who had told him how to escape. . . . Was it the flogging that had rendered him so weak? . . . Darkness was hovering over him, an all-encompassing darkness, blackness . . . death?

"Not die . . . not die," he mumbled. "Mund . . . Bell . . . must live for him . . . must live . . ."

"You will live," agreed the soothing voice of the woman at his bedside—the woman who was Mia, Conchita, Aggie, Gertie . . . or the other nameless wenches who had warmed his bed. He threw their names at her and knew somehow without her whispered denials that she was none of these, that she was someone else, but it was too difficult to guess her identity. No, a name *was* thrust into his mind. Pam . . . Pamela, the child Pamela, of whom he had once been fond. Not a child now . . . not . . . Poor Pamela, beautiful Pamela, must not think of her—must think of Edmund Bellairs . . . his second cousin Edmund . . . his stepfather, Edmund . . . his betrayer, covetous Edmund Bellairs!

"The bleeding was necessary, Mrs. Questred. He might be weakened by it, but the fever's lessening. He'll be on the mend now, I promise you."

The sick man on the bed heard the words and the name Questred. He tried to understand where he was and where he had heard that name Questred before. It had a special significance, he knew, a very special significance. He was not sure what. It was very difficult to get his thoughts together. He could envision them as so many sheep scattered over the hills. There were sheep aplenty in New South Wales. He had tended them, a task he had hated less than the others that had fallen to him in his ten years of backbreaking, soul-diminishing servitude, ten years, and not one day of his sentence reduced.

Years back, he had hoped that by good behavior he might be allowed to meet the new governor—Macquarie, who had replaced Bligh—Bligh, whose name was now connected with two mutinies and who had been summarily shipped back to England. However, he had not been able to get an interview with Macquarie. He had gotten no further than a lowly aide, a supercilious creature who had contemptuously explained to the battered, ragged young man that the new governor had already heard too many hard-luck stories from so-called "fallen gentlemen."

He had gone on to remind Arthur that in his six years as a prisoner he had acquired a malodorous reputation, had been early flogged for trying to escape, was known to cheat at cards and to pilfer as well, and there had been the woman who had complained he had molested her. He had been flogged for that, too, brutally. It would have been useless to explain that she had pursued him and had been rejected by him, she the lady of a so-called manor and he a lowly convict laborer.

As for his cheating at cards, they all cheated at cards. As for his pilfering, everybody pilfered. It was the only way to remain alive. He could have named the names of guards who also pilfered, but he never would have betrayed them or anyone else. His honor was important to him for all there was supposed to be no honor among thieves. In five years he had done his share of stealing, and after being rejected by the governor, he had continued—but cleverly, so that he was never detected. His cheating at cards was also clever, learning from those who, in the beginning, had cozened him. His cheating brought him money enough to buy grub and clothes to cover him. And if he gained the reputation of a sharp'un, what did it matter? Nothing mattered to him save staying alive and in condition.

He was also known as a fine athlete. He, who had scarcely liked to trudge the distance between the stone house and Bellair, could run like the wind, could ride anything with a mane and tail, could sail a boat, and use his fists to beat a man to a pulp. He had also learned to shoot and fence. With Edmund Bellairs in mind, he had become expert with both pistol and sword. There were plenty of fine instructors among his convict comrades and there were other lessons to be learned—such as how to please a woman.

The women loved him, the more so because he loved

none of them, taking his pleasure as he chose and going his way alone. They called him hard and a rascal. He could be both. He was what he had been made by time and circumstance, by cruelty and betrayal, by a corroding bitterness and an obsessive desire, nay more than desire—a passion for revenge!

Who was Questred?

The name tantalized him. He was also tantalized by a long, crooked crack in the ceiling over his head. He could not remember sleeping in a hovel with so high a ceiling or with so wide a window. The air that filled his nostrils was fresh, and though sometimes warm, was never as warm as he had come to know it in a decade of sweltering or freezing. Nor was it replete with strange odors—not strange, though, not after ten mortal years in which a lad of twenty had become a man of thirty— but these years were at an end!

Was he on shipboard, then? No, he could not feel the wet deck heaving beneath him and his bed was not the hammock strung between decks where he lay after his hours working an an able seaman aboard HMS *Seraphim,* a heavenly name for a miserable bark, but a bark that was bearing Arthur Bellairs back to England. No, not Arthur Bellairs . . .

He had decided to call himself by a different name, a caution-induced change in case there were a welcoming committee that knew of his release. Sidney for Sydney, the port where he had disembarked a decade ago, and Questred for Quest, for was he not a man with a quest? Indeed, it could be called a knightly quest—to wrest the "castle" from the enemy.

Sidney Questred, yes! He knew the name now. Sidney Questred was bound for home—but first he must needs tend Roger Smith, his fellow seaman. The doctor was guzzling grog in his cabin and old Roger had fallen from the sheets and lay dying. Fortunately he, Sidney Questred, knew something about tending the sick.

He had learned it from the doctor on board the ship

that had carried him to New South Wales, the doctor who had pulled him from his cage aboard that ship, had cured his fever and given him citrus fruits to forestall the scurvy, the doctor who had once so futilely spoken in his behalf and met the sneers and scorn of Captain Bligh, devil take him—the devil take Captain Blight, as he had privately dubbed him. And so now he could drug and soothe the last hours of Roger Smith, and toward the end, the old man spoke to him.

"Lissen, mate, ye been good to me, better'n any I come acrost in many years, 'n afore they toss me to the fishes, I 'ave somethin' for ye. . . . Lemme gi' ye these, 'n let no one know ye 'ave 'em. 'Twill be yer fortune, mate."

Roger had fumbled in his sea-stained shirt and brought out a small leather bag, pressing it into Sidney Questred's hand. " 'Tis a fortune," the old man had repeated. "A fortune, mate. An' me wi' no kith or kin to gi' it to . . . only you 'oo were good to me. I thought to buy meself an 'ouse'n a coach'n four . . . but may'ap ye'll 'ave better uses for it. Take 'em, mate, an' don't let anyone know ye 'ave 'em . . . else yer life'll not be worth two groats."

"I thank you, Roger," he had said.

"Ye speak good, ye know. Yer a gentleman, no matter wot ye done in yer time. God speed ye, lad." There had been a strange rattling sound in old Roger's throat, strange but not unfamiliar to the man who had tended him. He had heard similar sounds when caged with the other convicts on the way to New South Wales and when he had worked with the doctor.

He had not looked at the "fortune" until old Roger's body had been wrapped in sailcloth and consigned to the deep—with a hasty prayer offered by the captain and a silent one from himself. Then, late that night, lying in his hammock, he had taken out the leather bag and through it felt the hardness of them, the roundness of them, and with the light from a lone candle, he had poured the contents of the bag into his hand and seen the incredible soft sheen of twelve large unbored pearls, twelve perfect pearls, a fortune indeed, a legacy won not at the gaming tables but through sheer chance.

"Edmund Bellairs," he had muttered. "Edmund Bellairs," he had laughed softly. "We two will meet on common ground."

"Common ground, Edmund Bellairs. Common ground, Edmund Bellairs, a sow becomes a silk purse, never say that it cannot be done." Thumb and finger pressed against one of the pearls, he held up his hand.

Thumb and finger crooked, the sick man held up his hand, his eyes wide. "A fortune," he mumbled. "A fortune, Edmund Bellairs." He did not protest when his hand was pushed gently down.

The woman beside the bed lifted her hand from the hand of the man she now knew as Arthur Bellairs. She pushed back her heavy hair. It was weighty on her head tonight—the heat had diminished to a degree, but it was still warm, very warm in the small, close room.

The man on the bed still muttered and tossed. Ten days had passed since Tom's bullet had entered his shoulder, and he had yet to look at her with recognition in his eyes. She was thankful that she had decided to shoulder most of the burden of caring for him. What she had heard was strange and horrible, but it was important for her to have heard it and pieced out a tale of anger, anguish, and betrayal, one that she must needs believe because amazingly, ironically, the man on the bed, the man she had married, was none other than Arthur Bellairs, fat Arthur, who had been so kind to her when she was a child, fat Arthur, for whom she had mourned off and on since his imprisonment—fat Arthur, who, after all, was not dead!

How he had changed!

The transformation had been as complete as if a fairy had waved her wand over him, a scourging wand that had warped and hardened that once pliant nature even as it had pared away the fat, replacing it with hard muscles and sinew. It was difficult, almost impossible to understand how that fat, shy, gentle youth had survived the horrors he must have endured before that change had been implemented—but survive them he had, and in the smelting furnaces of New South Wales, the iron in his nature had turned to steel!

Pamela shuddered as she recalled some of his inadvertent revelations. Yet it was easy enough to understand how the privations, the evil companions, and a ten-year sentence had joined to warp and twist a nature once so kind and gentle.

There was nothing gentle about the man who tossed and turned on the bed. Yet there had been one mark of grace, one reminder of the Arthur who had once existed. If Abel, in a sense, had become Cain, the outcast, he had no fear that the Lord would say to him, "Where is Abel, they brother?" Tom's blood had not soaked into the ground to cry out against a murderer. Arthur had deloped and received his brother's bullet.

What did it all mean, this masquerade and their marriage? In the last ten days Pamela had had plenty of opportunity to dwell on that, and to find answers as well, wounding answers, that involved an elliptical purpose and a trap with human bait—herself. It was a hard truth but one that she must needs accept. He had used her to snare Edmund Bellairs, the name most often upon his lips—but, as he had said one night, "Edmund left at Kendal, why is Tom here alone? I want Edmund Bellairs, Edmund Bellairs, Edmund Bellairs. He followed us, I knew he would. He wants the manor . . . why did he leave, why, why, why . . . I cannot shoot my brother."

And it had all become clear: Charles's forays into the towns they had just left to see if they were being followed, and Arthur, with his false assurances that they were not. Arthur, who had made sure that they would be followed. Arthur, who had pursued her not

because he loved her but because he needed her as bait
for a trap set by one whose desire for vengeance and
vindication must have dominated his every thought for
a decade. It had been a hard truth to assimiliate, but she
knew she was not mistaken.

He had pursued her for one reason only. She was the
key to Edmund Bellairs, ambitious Edmund, who was
anxious to annex her property to Bellair and had therefore arranged that Tom, the so-called heir of Bellair,
marry her. He wanted nothing to stand in the way of
that. But why had Arthur gone through the mockery of
this Gretna Green marriage?

She had an answer for that, too. Arthur had guessed
that greedy Edmund would join in the pursuit of the
fleeing couple. He had said as much in the depths of his
delirium. She could supply the other reason. He had not
wished to meet Edmund Bellairs on home ground and so
he had entrapped a foolish, romantic child, had filled
her full of false protestations of his great love for her,
and so won her acquiescence to their elopement.

"Water . . ." the man on the bed muttered. "Water."

She hurried to put a cup to his lips. He drank thirstily.
"We must be in port," he remarked in surprisingly lucid
tones.

"Yes, the ship has docked," she murmured
soothingly, not knowing if he had heard her but not
wanting to excite him.

"And who are you—sweet Nance, come to meet
me?"

His eyes were still closed. Nance was an image inside
his head—an image affixed to a voice he still did not
recognize.

"I've no time for you, Nance, though you are a cozy
armful, I've no doubt. Am I really in England, at last?"

"You are, sir."

" 'Twas a rough voyage . . . the old man died. I'm
rich, do you see . . . Where is he? Where is Edmund
Bellairs?''

"You must sleep now," she said with a soft urgency.

"Sleep . . . no time for sleep. Macbeth hath murdered sleep . . . the innocent sleep that knits the ravelled sleave of care . . . Edmund hath murdered me . . . but corpses may rise from their graves and feast on the living . . . 'tis foolishness, Mia, my love . . . your spirits. There's naught about us save what we can see and touch . . . Why am I so warm? Hold your whip, overseer . . . I'm digging as fast as I may . . . Look at these hands, they bleed, they bleed . . . Why am I so weak? I must be strong! Infirm of purpose, give me the daggers. . . . Pamela, Pamela . . ."

Hearing her name, she started, and looked down at his moon-illuminated countenance. "I am here," she whispered.

"Pamela . . . Pamela . . . charming child . . . means to an end. Hardly fair . . . all is fair in war . . ."

Once she had wept at that particular revelation, but that had been days ago. The repetition carried with it a corroding bitterness and, at the same time, a realization that she had brought this particular sorrow on herself.

In ten days she, Pamela Cardwell, or rather Pamela Bellairs, had shed all vestiges of what she could only describe as her prolonged childhood. She had been totally foolish, blinded by a false romanticism. She had actually thought of herself as a heroine, the heroine of one of those ridiculous novels she had taken so much to heart. She remembered wondering what had happened after the book ended—well, now she knew!

"A ploy," she mouthed. "That is all that I have ever been to him, who knew from the start that I was attracted to him."

That much she had divined from his ravings, and more, yes, much more! Many women had been similarly attracted to Arthur Bellairs. They had, in fact, lain in wait for him like so many "predatory tigresses," his own mocking description of their transparent maneuvers. They had been intrigued by his handsome

face and strong, well-built body, by his air of distinction
and his surprisingly cultivated voice. They had been
equally intrigued by his indifference. He had not been
indifferent to her. His determined pursuit had made him
all the more fascinating, and out of that fascination he
had woven his snare and trapped her—or had she
trapped herself?

She had been unhappy about Tom's seemingly easy
acquiescence to his father's demands. She had been
positive that he had not loved her. Well, she had found
out differently—but that did not matter, could not
matter now. Yet she wished that she had not sent him
away believing that she needed Mr. Questred's name to
help restore the respectability she had forfeited during
their journey. She sighed and reminded herself that it
was useless to dwell on that when there were so many
more important matters that she must consider.

First among these was the man himself, who still desperately needed her care. She expected that any other
woman having found herself so cruelly betrayed must
have left him to the indifferent ministrations of the gin-
swilling beldames who passed for nurses in this village.
She had met one of these and had dismissed the tipsy,
evil-smelling creature before she had so much as crossed
the threshold. She had assumed the main burden of his
care, remanding some of it to little Meg, the landlord's
fourteen-year-old daughter. She was trustworthy and
glad to earn the shillings Pamela offered. There was also
Rob, her younger brother, who helped bathe her
husband and change his linen, wifely duties which, in
the beginning, had brought a blush to her cheeks, but
such sensations had passed very quickly. It had been
impossible to dwell upon her scruples when he was in
such pain and needed her so dreadfully. There was no
time even for the anger and the resentment that visited
her at odd moments. Yes, she had been his victim, but
had he not been a victim also? And was not Edmund
Bellair's cruel betrayal far worse than that which had
been practiced upon her?

Pamela shuddered. The tale which had emerged from his unfettered, fever-ridden consciousness had filled her with horror. Furthermore, despite her own anger, she could not help but admire this man, who had survived against odds which might easily have felled a much stronger man than he had been at the time he was arrested. Yet what a terrible price he had paid for that same survival!

Though she had been only ten when Arthur was taken away, she still remembered his gentleness, his kindness, and his mildness. She remembered, too, his love for books. He had really wanted nothing more than to be left to himself in the library at Bellair or in the halls of Oxford, where, she recalled, he had insisted on remaining another year. She frowned, remembering now that it had been much against Edmund Bellairs' wishes. He had argued with Sir William, Arthur's aged grandfather, Tom had told her, wanting the old man to forbid Arthur to return to the university. The elderly baronet had admired Arthur's scholarship and refused. She winced. His grandfather's death had been hastened by the shock of Arthur's arrest. And that must have pleased Edmund Bellairs—Edmund Bellairs, who had pretended he wanted Arthur to take over the reins of Bellair. He had wanted no one in that particular saddle save himself. Bellair had always meant far more to the man Arthur called stepfather than even to Tom. How he must have chafed at Arthur's indifference! Yet, to have condemned his own stepson and cousin to so terrible a fate . . . nothing could excuse that. It was the work of an out-and-out villain, a monster of cruelty!

She shuddered to think of Arthur as he had been in those terrible early days of his captivity—when he had been thrust into the company of common criminals, men who would have jeered at his heavy body and weak muscles. He had avoided all sports, she remembered. Who would have believed that he would have become a bruising rider—though he had liked to ride, she remembered, but slowly. He had never urged his steeds into a canter—never seemed to vie with the wind as had the man whom she had seen from the window of the post chaise bearing her to Gretna Green. Who would have believed that he could have developed the strong muscles she had seen on his arms and legs—yet, withal, he was slender, and graceful in his movements. Not even his long imprisonment nor the hard labor he had been forced to do had robbed him of his innate refinement— but, oh, God, how he must have suffered! His body was marked from shoulders to feet with scars—the scars from the terrible floggings that she remembered Tom mentioning and which Arthur, too, had relived in his delirium. There had been other scars as well, mute evidence of what his life had been in the brawling reaches of New South Wales. And no wonder his hands were so rough! They had held shovels and pickaxes and hammers on land. On sea he had worked as a common sailor, hauling sail and the like. God knows what other privations he had suffered. Obviously there had been many more.

It was easy to understand his bitterness, understand, too, that he would use any means to effect a confrontation with Edmund Bellairs—but not on home ground, not where his stepfather might turn the tables on him and possibly even thrust him into prison again!

She herself did not understand how that could happen, but he had muttered something of the sort in his delirium. He had hoped to decoy Edmund Bellairs to another dueling ground—here in Gretna Green. If it had been Edmund Bellairs rather than Tom, Arthur's bullet would not have been directed skyward. There had been grace in that. In that last moment, he had harkened back to the Arthur he had been all those years ago when he had been so fond of his little brother. He had spared him, and in so doing, the vengeance he had sought had been denied him. Would it not have been vengeance enough to return to Bellairs and claim his heritage?

No, her common sense told her. It would not have

been enough. He wanted to kill Edmund Bellairs. Yet, to kill him would solve nothing. He would need to flee to France, and in addition to the charge of smuggling, there would be one of murder as well. He would never be able to return to England. What he needed to do was clear his name, and the only way that could be done was to force Edmund Bellairs to confess the truth. But how? Once poor Arthur was on the mend, she would have to see Tom and tell him all she had heard, and that as soon as possible!

The physician had told her that another week would see Arthur clearer in his mind, and then she would leave, thus ridding him of the encumbrance of an unwanted wife, his ploy, his unsuccessful bid to ensure a confrontation with his stepfather. There was a pain in her heart. She had heard of heartaches but had not realized that they were actually physical pain—but again, she could not dwell on that with poor Arthur still so needful and helpless.

In memory of the kindness a shy young man had once shown a lonely child, she would remain with him. In memory of the cruel deception he had practiced upon a vulnerable young woman—on many vulnerable young women, no doubt—she would leave him whenever he was well enough to depend on Meg and her brother.

8

He was trudging down a long, dusty yellow road. The dust was not limited to the road alone. It coated his skin; when he breathed, he felt it entering his nostrils. He knew the road very well, every bump, every stone. It was one of the many he had helped carve into what had been scrubby bushes, jagged stones, and bent trees. He had dug up the bushes, dug out the stones, felled the trees, working until he thought he must drop with fatigue, working beyond fatigue into a nightmare country, where his movements were mechanical and his mind a blank save for that one name which was ground into it, even as the road had been engraved upon the bushes, stones, and trees. *Edmund Bellairs.*

He blinked. The road had mysteriously vanished and he was on a heaving sea watching them hoist a white shape into the moiling waters.

"Edmund Bellairs," he whispered, and hoped that it was not. "He must not die until we meet again, and let my hand be that which slays him."

"No," came the whisper.

"Who speaks for Edmund Bellairs?" he cried. "I will kill whoever speaks in his defense!"

"None will speak in his defense," promised the whisperer. "Sleep, go to sleep, dear Arthur."

Dear Arthur? His mother had called him "Dear Arthur." She had been wont to visit him in dreams. He had loved her greatly, he remembered, resenting her, though—resenting her wedding Edmund Bellairs.

"Edmund is very fond of you, Arthur, dearest. You

146

must be nice to him—now that we, he and I, are to be wed."

"Please do not marry him, Mama!" he had cried. *"Please,"* he addressed the dim vision in the darkness back of his eyes.

"He will be a father to you, my angel. A boy needs a father."

"He doesn't like me, Mama."

"You only imagine that, my love. He's very fond of you."

He had known otherwise—right from the start, he had known that Edmund Bellairs despised him. He had been eager to get away from him on any and all occasions. That was why the stone house had been such a wonderful discovery—because no one knew about it, not even his stepfather. But he had known, had known, had known.

His mother's face faded from his mind. He was not on shipboard anymore. He was in a small atelier and an old man was gazing at the pearls suspiciously, as if he suspected him of thievery. His temper was perilously close to the boiling point, but he managed to restrain the words that threatened to burst from him. If there was one thing he had learned in his ten years of misery, it was restraint! He bore the scars of anger on his body, scars that dated from the period when he was in prison after he, fat Arthur Bellairs, had learned of the cruel trick played upon him by Edmund Bellairs. Anger had been a growling beast inside himself, bursting its bonds and thrust back by his jailers with hurtful blows and in New South Wales by floggings. They had done their best to break his spirit—but his was a spirit that thrived on adversity. He had learned that about himself. He blinked. He was no longer in the jeweler's atelier. He was at Tattersall's. Why?

He was surveying the horseflesh that his newly acquired wealth, a fortune, as old Roger had predicted, had enabled him to purchase. He smiled bitterly. Those at Tattersall's respected his judgment.

"You know horses, sir?" they had said.

He had learned about horses in New South Wales, learned when he was taken from the roads and assigned to a horse farm. He had ridden in Hythe and on quiet country roads. He had never ridden fast and always he had had the best of saddles. At the horse farm, he had ridden untamed steeds, learning to train them through agonizing falls, through the jeering laughter of his fellow workers and his master, too—as he strove to remain on the back of one or another plunging horse. His master had said, "I thought you was a gentleman. Ain't gentlemen supposed to know 'ow to ride?"

"There are gentlemen who know Euclid, Thucydides, and Virgil, you ignorant clod," he had longed to answer, but had not answered, had suffered the falls, sustained the broken arm and cracked ribs, and put his quiet lodgings at Oxford far, far out of his mind. In the end, he had won his master's grudging admiration for an excellent seat on a horse, a strong hand on the reins, and a way with animals that stood him in far greater stead than the theorems of Euclid, the histories of Thucydides, and the poetry of Virgil.

He was no longer at Tattersall's. He was striding through the city, and behind him crept a cutpurse. The creature had been amazed when he, a fine gentleman, at least by the cut of his new garments, had caught him by the throat and addressed him in the cant terms known to that particular fraternity before giving him a hefty boot in the rear and sending him cursing and sprawling in the filthy street. And why were these images passing so rapidly before his eyes? His eyes, he realized, were closed. He opened them and saw something he remembered: the crack in the ceiling!

What ceiling? The ceiling of the room he had hired, of course, immediately upon arriving this afternoon—but why did he feel so weak? And why was he lying down? He had no memory of having gone to bed. He turned, but the movement was hurtful. It had activated a strange pain in his shoulder. Why? Why did his shoulder ache and why was it bandaged? He could feel the bandage now and had a memory of Tom . . . little Tom—no, not little Tom, but tall Tom, who had turned a furious face upon him, and striking him, had demanded a duel. He had not wanted to fight Tom for all that he was Edmund Bellairs' son, Edmund Bellairs, who had left the coach at Kendal. Why?

He could not fight Tom, could not shoot his brother. That would have made him Cain and so he had shot into the air while Tom assumed the role of Cain. No, that was not true. Would he have acted differently if that knowledge had been his? Perhaps not. After all, Tom was the heir of Bellair, or could be, were he, Arthur, dead and buried. Was Tom a murderer too? He was aware of movement beside his bed. He opened his eyes wider, and turning, saw a woman seated in a chair by his bedside. Pamela, of course! Was she not paler than he remembered—and thinner, too?

"Pamela," he said, and was amazed that his voice emerged only as a mere whisper.

She turned quickly, her eyes wide in her pale face. "Arthur, do you know me, then?"

"*Arthur?*"

The name hung between them and there was a pounding in his throat. "Why . . . why do you call me Arthur?" he asked hoarsely.

"I am sorry," she said hastily. "I did not mean to excite you."

"But . . . you said . . ." He tried to speak louder and found it an effort.

"You must not try to talk now," she said concernedly.

He half-raised himself and winced as pain shot through him. "But . . ."

"Please . . ." She gently pushed him back on his pillows. "You are better. The fever broke last night and you have been sleeping most of the day, but you must still sleep. You have been very ill.''

"The fever . . .'' he repeated confusedly. "From . . . from the wound?''

"Yes, it was not a dangerous wound, but there was fever.'' She spoke soothingly.

"How long . . . have I been here?''

"A little over a week.'' She still spoke soothingly.

"A week?'' he repeated incredulously. "I . . . do not remember.''

"You would not remember. It was the fever, you see.''

"And I . . . was out of my head?''

"A bit. You really must go back to sleep,'' she urged.

"Ye 'ad fever, me lad, an' the things you said. I were fair frightened, I were. My old ma, she told me evil intentions come 'ome to roost an' 'oo be Edmund Bellairs?'' Hearing those words, dropped from the mouth of a whore who had tended him some years ago, Arthur winced and, at the same time, a memory of fractured words and phrases arose in his consciousness. "I . . . I must have spoken of many things . . . ?'' It was half a question, half a statement of fact.

Pamela avoided looking him in the eyes. "Yes,'' she answered diffidently.

"And now . . . I stand revealed?''

"Please,'' she begged. "You must go back to sleep. You need all the rest you can get.''

"But . . .'' he started to protest, but in that moment he became aware of a great weakness washing over him. He found, too, that he could not keep his eyes open any longer, and closing them, he knew no more.

Sunshine issuing from an orb that had made its way into the mid-heavens filled the room when Arthur opened his eyes again. Again he was staring at the cracked ceiling, but with the difference that his mind was clearer and he had a vivid memory of that brief conversation with Pamela on what had been the previous afternoon—late afternoon, he guessed. Turning his head, he saw a young girl seated beside him. A hasty glance around the room revealed that Pamela was absent.

"Who are you?" he asked, finding his voice weak but stronger than it had been yesterday.

The girl, a fair, pretty child, visibly tensed, regarding him with a surprise not unmixed with alarm. "I be Meg, sir," she said shyly.

"Meg?" he repeated. "Who is Meg?"

"I be the daughter o' the landlord, sir." She rose quickly. "I'll fetch yer wife. She told me as I was to let her know when you was awake."

Before he could respond, she had hurried out, leaving him to deal with the term "wife." It had sounded extremely odd in his ears. Yet he was married, was he not, and had been for however long he had lain here. Furthermore, he suddenly realized that it was Pamela who had tended him, poor child. The sound of her soothing voice had been in his ears throughout his illness. He had not wanted that. He had expected that the "marriage" would end on the same day it had commenced. Yet, even as that portion of his plan arose in his memory, there were accompanying regrets. He was no stranger to these. They had been in his mind even before he had commenced his journey.

Pamela had been so pathetically vulnerable to his practiced lovemaking that there had actually been times when he had seriously considered changing his plan. Yet each time, the name Edmund Bellairs had blotted out all other considerations and he had proceeded with his scheme. They had embarked upon their journey, and Charles, his trusted scout, had discovered that they were, indeed, being followed by Edmund Bellairs and his son, Tom. In the hours when he had ridden outside the coach, he had seemed to hear the name Edmund Bellairs loud in his ears. "Edmund Bellairs, Edmund

Bellairs''—that spectral sound had blotted out all else
from his consciousness, all else save the thought that
soon he would be face to face with the man, who had
sought to steal his birthright and condemned him to
what he had imagined to be a slow death, a murder with
his own weakness as weapon.

However, if revenge had been his constant
companion during the day, there had been the nights
when, faced with Pamela Cardwell, he could think only
of her tantalizing beauty. He had needed to keep a tight
rein on his feelings during those dangerously intimate
moments they shared in the chambers of the inns where
they stayed. He had wanted to remain with her, wanted
her in every sense of the word, actually regretting the
burning need for revenge that had originally driven him
to take such unfair advantage of her romantic nature.

At the time he had evolved his plan, he had expected
she would go back to Tom, if, indeed, he had
considered her feelings at all. But being with her in such
close quarters, he had become aware, truly aware, that
there was very little left of the child he had known all
those years ago. In addition to being ravishingly beautiful, she was intensely vulnerable and she had a
passionate nature. At a word from him, she would have
fallen into his arms, and he had been forced to bite his
tongue to keep from uttering that word.

And now she *knew*.

How much did she know?

How loquacious had he been in these last days? Had
the damn burst and all the water rushed out, bearing in
those murky depths all the dark denizens, all the
ugliness he had known and kept hidden behind the
enigmatic smile and the bold gaze of Mr. Sidney
Questred? Mr. Questred, whose existence had ended, at
least for the young girl he now called wife.

No one knew the effort that had gone into maintain-
ing that pseudonym in the company of Edmund
Bellairs! It had been an agony to see him, speak to him,

and at the same time to keep his temper in check and his hands—grown strong and powerful through roadwork, through taming wild horses, through countless tasks performed in the last decade—quiet at his sides rather than reaching out to clutch, to catch, to strangle and slay.

He had managed to restrain himself, had played the gallant. Instead, he had worked his wiles on a confused and resentful young girl who was being pushed into a marriage she was not sure she wanted. That Edmund Bellairs wanted it was impetus enough. He had thought then that anything, everything, was grist for the mill that would eventually grind exceeding small and had been at its task already—for ten years that had passed with tortoise tread. His decision had come because he had thought his plan solid and preferable to killing Edmund Bellairs outright. To kill him outright would mean the gibbet, and he had already suffered enough in the name of his stepfather.

"Edmund Bellairs," he groaned.

The girl who opened the door stood still, arrested by the name that had issued from his lips yet again, the name she had heard so often in the past ten days. Even in her present chaotic state of mind, the pity she could not help but feel for poor Arthur Bellairs rose to the surface—and with it was the fear that he might have suffered a relapse. She hurried to his side.

"Arthur?" she questioned tentatively.

He turned his head toward her. He was very pale, but he had been similarly pale since Tom's bullet pierced his shoulder, and now she saw him flush. "Pamela," he mouthed. "Oh, my poor child, I owe you so much."

Relief filled her. He *was* lucid. "We must not speak about that," she answered, and was pleased that her voice sounded natural. "And," she continued, "you must not excite yourself. The doctor has said—"

"The doctor be damned," he exclaimed. "Sit down, please."

She obeyed immediately, seeing that he was already excited. He must be soothed. Yet, as she prepared to explain his condition, he continued, "You *know*, do you not? Yes, of course you do. How much have I said?"

She read fear in his eyes, and shame too—or did she? Did he feel ashamed of the strategem that had changed her from an exciting, loving young girl to a betrayed and suffering woman? She could not dwell on that now, not when he was still in need of the nursing she must yet provide. Despite her own interior anger and anguish, he had suffered enough at the hands of those he knew, of those closest to him. She said steadily, "I know that you are Arthur Bellairs. I know that you were unjustly accused and imprisoned by Edmund Bellairs. If I had been older, I expect I must have guessed that particular truth."

He stared at her incredulously. "You believe me, then?"

"How could I not?" she asked reasonably. "They say that murder will out, and the same must be said for all villainy. I was just ten when you were taken away, but I remember that last afternoon. I remember all you told me about smuggling. I did not think you would willfully lie to me—there was no need. But why, Arthur, why did you not reveal the truth when you returned to Hythe?"

He emitted a sound that was probably intended as a laugh. "I was afraid," he said frankly. "Edmund Bellairs has proved himself to be a man with powerful friends in high places, and in low as well, an ill-assorted group, indeed, but to a man, eager to assist him. I, on the other hand, am a criminal who has served out his sentence—but a criminal all the same. I must needs walk softly for I . . . or rather Arthur Bellairs, is under surveillance and will be as long as he chooses to dwell in Kent. 'Twas more expedient to be Sidney Questred, whom no one knew. Can you not agree?"

She was sorrier for him than she wanted to be. Still,

from the depths of her own anguish she could not help saying, "You might have trusted me, Arthur."

He nodded. "Of a truth, I might have." In a low, shamed voice he continued, "I could not trust anyone, my dear. The Arthur Bellairs that was, trusted everyone —even those he could not abide. I never liked my step-father and he never liked me. As a child I hid from him. I always had the feeling that if we were alone together, he might do me an injury. As a young man I merely avoided him. The child was wiser than the youth. Eventually the youth learned not to be trustful—but the lessons were long in the learning. Edmund Bellairs wants me dead. He took many more steps to ensure my demise than merely seeing that I was transported. He . . ." His voice was rising and now he coughed, his hand against his shoulder.

"Arthur, shhhh." Pamela bent over him with a glass of water in her hand, holding it to his mouth. "You must not talk of this now. I should not have let you continue as long as you have. You must concentrate on recovering your strength."

He drank thirstily. "Pamela," he said hoarsely, "we . . . must speak about many things. I would not have you believe—"

"Shhhh," she said firmly. "I'll not listen to you now. You must sleep."

He closed his eyes, and though he had not meant to obey her, oblivion descended with the ensuing darkness.

Pamela, coming to her own chamber, found herself shaking with a mixture of anger and anguish. Both were directed toward Edmund Bellairs, who had so cruelly betrayed the young man who was both ward and close relation. Yet, was not Claudius Hamlet's uncle? She grimaced. Hamlet was largely fiction, and this was fact —and she had had enough of fiction, enough of high romance to last her a lifetime. Inadvertently she thought of her own sorrow, which, in a sense, stemmed from the same source: Edmund Bellairs. Truly the man did not deserve to live. He was the real criminal. Through his machinations three lives had been twisted out of shape. Arthur's life, Tom's life, and her own.

A long sigh escaped her. If it had not been for Edmund Bellairs, Arthur would be in residence at Bellair and Tom reconciled to the notion that the estate belonged to his brother. As for herself, she would probably have married Tom. Yet she could not mourn the fact that she had not. She did not love him. She did not love anyone, she thought defiantly. That which she had felt for the man Arthur had become had been false, as false as the love he had pretended to feel for her!

She had been a silly, romantic child, and he had known it—and what would happen now? A separation and . . . Was a divorce necessary for this semblance of a marriage? But it was more than a mere semblance; she could not hide that fact from herself. Even though they had not been lovers, she knew him quite as intimately as if they had been. In the past days, she and she alone had nursed him, performing all that he, in his helpless condition, had required. That knowledge was something she could not shrug aside. It would remain with her, and though she might reject him physically and return to her father's house, he would remain with her—closeted in some corner of her brain, never to be ejected, even though love had died. Had it really? How did she feel? She herself was not sure. No, she was sure of her anger and hurt—but when she was with him, other feelings crowded into her mind and heart, feelings that rendered her weak and that must not be, for he did not love her!

He had cruelly, cruelly used her, used her as he himself had been used. He had learned life's lessons from a cruel master, and in the process, he had emulated his teacher. She was glad and relieved that he was on the mend, because soon she would leave him. She was not sure yet what she would do once she reached home. No, that was not true. She did know what she intended to do—but she could not dwell on that at the moment, not while he still needed her. Tears rolled down her cheeks. She had known that she was weeping and she rubbed them away angrily. She would not weep because her lover had betrayed her. She, too, had been guilty of betrayal, the betrayal of poor Tom, who, after all, had proved that he loved her more than she had ever believed. Tom, alas, was the real victim in this situation—the victim of a victim, for surely Arthur Bellairs had suffered far more than either of them. That, no one could deny!

In two days, Arthur was less dependent upon Pamela's ministrations, firmly protesting a continuation of their enforced intimacy. "You have done enough for me, my poor child," he had said, a dark flush on his stubble-coated cheeks. Indeed, he had fallen into the habit of addressing her as the little girl she had once been, as if, indeed, he would obliterate all that had passed between them in the last months. She could not blame him for failing to shoulder the burden of guilt which, if he were to dwell upon it, must necessarily impede his recovery. At least, that had been her first thought. Her second had, however, been far more realistic. She doubted that he was experiencing any real guilt. His desire, indeed his passion for vindication of his supposed crimes had occupied him for ten years— for ten years it had been a cancer eating into his brain, and any device had been grist for that particular mill!

Consequently, once he was able to sit up and take nourishment, to bathe and shave, Pamela set about finding transportation out of the village. There was, she discovered, a coach to Carlisle, where she could make the connection to London and thence to Hythe. Fortunately, she had brought money with her. She did not know what sense of self-preservation had been at work in that decision, but she was glad of it. Inquiries had proved that she had more than enough to pay her fare back to Kent. Yet, once her preparations were completed and she in an old and creaking conveyance, squeezed between two hefty passengers, the tears which had been in abeyance all that morning threatened to fall. It was very difficult to blink them back, more difficult not to think of Arthur and to deal with her decision never to see him again.

Despite his machinations, Pamela's rebellious heart insisted on informing her that it loved him and that that love, once proffered, could not be called back so easily. It could not, for instance, be done in a matter of days. It might take years, it might take a lifetime, and that, of course, was ridiculous, mad, and above all, demeaning to love someone who did not return that love and had, in fact, vilely betrayed it! Still, if she concentrated, she could in time banish him from her mind. However, before she did that, she would do whatever she might to see that he was exonerated of the "crime" for which he had paid so very dearly.

Ten years!

The thought of all he had endured roused her to fury. Though she could never forgive the cruel deception he had practiced upon her, she could understand his reasoning. He had used the only means at his disposal to revenge himself on the man who, like Joseph's brethren, had sold him into actual slavery—and for the many-colored coat that was Bellair. Egypt, she guessed, was a far more felicitous spot to a man from Israel than New South Wales to a gently nurtured young Englishman—and Joseph had not suffered for ten mortal years!

She fingered the gold ring he had slipped on her finger and which she now wore as protection against the possible advances of her fellow travelers. The marriage could be annulled, but not until her husband was restored to his rightful place in his world. Given her own actions, it might be very difficult to set the wheels of justice in motion—but Tom, angry, hurt Tom, would yet help her. She was reasonably sure of that. Tom, also, had loved Arthur, and she was positive that he would be as shocked as she at the machinations of Edmund Bellairs, father or no father. At least she hoped that that might be the way of it. She would have to be careful in sounding him out, and if he proved to be hand-in-glove with Sir Edmund—or rather Mr. Bellairs, since the heir was living and he had no right to the title —but if Tom stood with his father, she would undertake the task herself, no matter what it cost her.

On that same morning, Arthur Bellairs, lying in bed, looked eagerly at the opening door. Pamela was unusually late and he had been worried—but now she had finally arrived and he was feeling well enough for a serious talk, one he prayed he had not postponed too long. Finally he would tell her what he now knew to be no more than the truth. He loved her and might have loved her for a longer time than he had actually realized. He would tell her that, too. He did not want her to imagine that his love sprang from gratitude alone. However, much to his surprise and disappointment, it was not Pamela who stood framed in the doorway, but little Meg, with an envelope in her hand.

"Where . . . where is Mrs. Questred?" he demanded, and was aware of a strange throbbing in his throat.

"She . . . she asked me to gi' you this, sir," Meg told him. She handed or rather dropped the envelope on the coverlet and hastily withdrew.

These actions added to his fears. With trembling fingers he opened a missive which proved to be short and succinct:

My dear Arthur:
     I want you to know that I fully understand your motive in wedding me, and know, too, that you never meant the connection to last as long as it has. I feel that you had reason for your actions,

however hurtful they were to me. I am indeed sorry that matters did not proceed as you had intended.

However, I cannot see why we should be bound together longer now that the plot has failed and you are finally on the mend. Be assured that I will do whatever I can to aid you. I only wish you had trusted me enough to tell me the truth in the beginning rather than resorting to this elaborate and hurtful scheme. Still, I am sure that trust no longer comes easily to you. I am very sorry for that, too. I find, however, that I can forgive all but this pretense of loving. By the time you receive this note, I shall be on my way home.

Pamela

He looked at the door and seemed to see her standing there, as she had stood so often in the last days, a tentative smile upon her lovely little face. Then the vision flickered and was lost. Clutching the note, he slid down under the covers and buried his face in the pillows as tears he had not been able to shed since he was first transported to New South Wales soaked into the rough cotton.

9

The gates of the manor were behind her. Pamela, bandbox in hand, walked slowly up the carriageway toward the house. She felt intensely weary from the long journey, and strangely light-headed, too. She attributed the latter symptom to the fact that she had subsisted mainly on bread and water during the last five days, it having taken much longer to reach Hythe than it had in a well-sprung conveyance traveling all of the day and on into the early morning. Actually, her appetite had deserted her and so had her ability to sleep. She had been unable to snatch more than two or three hours a night, and these had been filled with disturbing dreams. On one occasion she had actually risen from her bed and had had her hand on the doorknob before realizing that she was not occupying a large suite at the inn, but rather a small single chamber, and that, of course, meant that she had not really heard Arthur cry out in his sleep. It had been only a dream, and he already many leagues behind her in Scotland.

Given her state of mind upon leaving the village, she had not expected to miss him, but much to her surprise, she had, *terribly*. In the fortnight that she had cared for him, she had alternated between pity and resentment—but pity had been uppermost, and it remained in that position. Despite his treatment of her, she could understand his fury, his agony, and his overwhelming desire for vindication. If only he had chosen a less underhanded, less cruel method of exacting that vindication, she would have remained with him. As it was, she must needs accustom herself to a long, lonely life, for some-

161

thing told her that she would never cease to love him.

She was nearing the house now, and in her mind's eye she saw the gatekeeper's amazed stare, a stare in which disapproval and shock had been blended. She was gloomily positive that his expression would be duplicated on the faces of all who had known her and who would make a definite effort not to know her anymore—but that did not matter. Living with a father who was extremely reclusive, she was used to loneliness, and that it was now compounded by pain was something else she must learn to endure.

Still, her homecoming would not be easy, especially since she was not accompanied by her husband. Probably there were those who would not believe that a marriage had taken place. Again, that did not matter. All that mattered was Tom's attitude. She had to see him as soon as possible. Yet that particular hurdle was, she knew, even higher than that which she now faced as she mounted the steps, and crossing to the front door, lifted the knocker and sent it crashing against its plate.

As usual, it took the aged butler a few minutes to reach the door. He had a cross, surprised look on his face as he pulled it open. Pamela doubted that there had been many visitors since her departure, and besides, the gatekeeper's son had not gone ahead to announce her homecoming. Meeting the butler's astounded stare, she said, "Good morning, Parsons. Is my father at home?"

"Miss Pamela!" he exclaimed, and much to her amazement, tears gleamed in his eyes. "You are back, then. Come on, come in." He looked past her. "Are you alone, then, Miss Pamela?"

"Yes, I am alone, Parsons," she said firmly, expecting that he would visit a disappoving look upon her, but he did not. He said merely, "I will tell the master."

"No, Parsons," she said quickly. "I will tell him. Is he in his observatory?"

"Yes, Miss Pamela, but would it not be better if I . . . ?"

"Softened the blow?" she finished. "No, you must leave that to me."

A look of respect mingled with relief shone in his eyes. "As you wish, Miss Pamela," he said, standing back so that she might enter.

The staircase, stretching upward, seemed much steeper and much longer than she remembered. Of course, that was all in her imagination, she knew, knew also that though there seemed to be an unfamiliar look about the house, that, too, was in her imagination. As she reached the first landing, she leaned against the balustrade to catch her breath. She felt very weary, too weary, to mount the two remaining flights leading to her father's aerie. Yet she must, and possibly her weariness would stand her in good stead, for she felt drained of emotion and consequently able to bear anything her father said—unless, of course, he would order her from the house. She had not thought of that. She continued on up the stairs, unconsciously counting them as she had been wont to do as a child. By the time she gained the third landing, she was muttering " . . . thirty-five, thirty-six," and there was the paneled door a foot away, facing her. She moved slowly toward it and tapped tentatively on its polished surface.

"Well?" her father called in his most irascible tone of voice.

She hesitated and then pushed open the door. "Good morning, Father," she said breathlessly.

He had been sitting at his telescope but now he rose swiftly, staring at her in amazement richly larded with anger and something else she could not quite define. "You are back," he said in cold, measured tones. "A fine trick you played upon us. Have you no inkling of what we suffered—and where, pray, is your fine bridegroom?"

She had expected no other greeting from him, but as she opened her mouth to answer him, a wave of dizziness passed over her and for the first time in her life Pamela was able to emulate many of the heroines in her favorite romances—by swooning at her father's feet.

She awakened to the strong scent of a vinaigrette and found both her father and Miss Pringle hovering anxiously over her. She looked at them vaguely, feeling extremely nauseated, something the novelists had failed to mention. They had also pictured their heroines gracefully swooning in the arms of their lovers, not in the vicinity of their fathers and on the hard floors. She was about to mutter an apology when, to her amazement, Sir Robert said shakily, "Thank God, she's awake!"

Pamela was even more amazed when, bending over her, he scooped her up in his arms, and holding her protectively against his chest, added, "My dearest child, let me take you to your room."

A few minutes later he deposited her gently on her bed and said in tones that were not quite steady, "My poor little Pamela, forgive me for shutting myself away from you when you most needed my advice. I have been half out of my mind with worry." Sitting on the edge of the bed, he stroked her tangled hair back from her face. "I have . . . missed you, you know," he added, half-brusquely, as if he were afraid of the emotion which seemed close to engulfing him.

She had steeled herself to weather his anger and his scolding, but she was not proof against his unexpected kindness and his self-blame. "Oh, F-Father," she whispered. "I am so . . . so very sorry for everything."

"It is not your fault," he told her. Taking out his pocket handkerchief, he blew his nose. "If I had not shut myself away from you all these years . . . I think I was afraid to show that I loved you for fear I would lose you, too. I cannot tell you how I felt when we discovered you . . . missing."

"Oh, please," she sobbed. "I am sorry."

"Child, it's not your fault. I was wrong to press you into this marriage with Tom. I knew you were not in love with him, but you see, my dearest, I thought that was better. Love can take a fearful toll of the emotions, and when you lose someone . . . But I was thinking of myself, do you see, and perhaps I thought of you as a part of me—and now that you have been widowed, perhaps you will understand.''

She regarded him amazedly. ''But I am not widowed, Father. He is alive. I have left him.'' She trembled, wondering if all his pity had been for her bereavement and nothing more.

''But you fainted, and I imagined . . .'' he began.

''I fainted because I have eaten very little since I left Gretna Green. He did not die of his wound, Father. He is on the mend, in fact, but I . . . I have learned that I was mistaken about him and . . . and . . .'' Her voice broke.

''My dear, you need tell me no more. I thought I had the measure of the man. I quite liked him, but I see I was wrong. He is an out-and-out scoundrel.''

''No, he is not!'' she cried. ''He has been vilely treated, wantonly traduced by those whom he trusted. He . . .'' She met her father's astonished stare and her words died in her throat. Despite his concern, despite his new kindness to her, she must needs remember his long friendship with Edmund Bellairs, so she was not sure that she could trust him. ''He has suffered much himself,'' she finished lamely.

''And has made you suffer more. I beg you will not defend him. I do not want to hear his name again.'' He had spoken sternly, quite in his old manner, but looking at her, he added in a softer tone, ''My dear, you must rest. I will send Lucy to you.''

Astonishingly, he bent to drop a kiss on her cheek. ''Sleep well, my poor child.'' Turning swiftly, he strode from the room, closing the door softly behind him, Pamela, staring at the door, found tears on her cheeks again. She did not know why she was crying. Was it because of her father's unexpected kindness? Was it because she was bone-tired and still weak from her swoon, or was it for the remembered ordeal of poor Arthur Bellairs—and why had Edmund Bellairs told everyone that he was dead? Had it been wishful thinking on his part, or a false report from New South Wales? She lay back on her soft pillows and stared at the ceiling. She was weary of thinking . . . weary of the heaviness of her heart. She closed her eyes and defensively fell asleep.

Though, undoubtedly, the scandal she had engendered was the talk of the community and she herself the subject of endless speculations, Pamela learned in the six days following her return to Cardwell Manor that she was less buffeted by the winds of blame than she might have been had she and her father been less reclusive over the years.

Certainly she would never be welcome at an assembly again, and nor would she be bidden to such houses as she had visited before her scandalous elopement and its inexplicable aftermath that had brought her home without her groom. However, these were few and she found she could easily suffer the defection of Edith, who had returned her note, requesting a meeting, unopened.

Though she had been hurt, she had later reflected that if they had been on speaking terms, her onetime friend would have insisted on having a detailed description of her "exciting adventure." However, Lucy, always a source of information, had told her that Miss Edith and Mr. Tom had of late become "thick as thieves." She had added that she had a wager with Sukey as to when the engagement would be announced.

That particular bit of gossip was in Pamela's mind as she walked toward Bellairs, taking, as she had usually done in the past, the route through the woods, those same woods where Arthur Bellairs had encountered his fate more than ten years ago. An image of that gentle, heavyset youth trudged beside her, providing her with the courage she needed for her coming confrontation with Tom. According to Jim, the lad she had dispatched to discover his whereabouts on three successive days (this being the last of them), he was supervising the removal of a lightning-struck tree that had fallen near the carriageway. It was the opportunity for which she had hoped and waited—the chance to see him alone. That it had come about so soon was another stroke of fortune, for the sooner she saw Tom and unburdened herself of her strange tale, the better it would be for poor Arthur.

Poor Arthur?

A bitter smile twitched at the corners of her mouth. *Poor* in the sense of helplessness was hardly the way to describe "Mr. Sidney Questred." And given Tom's understandable hatred of him, she would have to choose her words with caution—she would need to be doubly cautious indeed if Lucy were right and he "thick as thieves" with Edith, for undoubtedly her onetime friend would have gleefully recounted their meeting with "Mr. Questred," thus adding fuel to his already brightly burning fires. Yet, despite that, despite the terrible resentment he must feel toward her, he had to know the truth. It was a dangerous truth to confide. He could easily tell his father, and then . . . She shuddered at the possibilities.

On the other hand, Tom had loved and sincerely mourned Arthur, saying over and over again that he could not believe him in league with the smugglers—this in the face of Edmund Bellairs' sworn deposition. Indeed, Tom had been soundly whipped for his stubborn stand. Yet, on the other hand, a great many years had passed since Arthur had been transported, and Tom loved Bellair. Would his love for the property he expected to inherit come between him and any feeling he might have for his brother—particularly in view of that said brother's latter actions? No, she was sure that

Tom, once apprised of the truth, must share her horror at his father's schemes. Tom had loved Arthur, and furthermore, Tom was her only recourse and surely he must appreciate the fact that Arthur had not returned his fire.

Her cogitations had carried her through the woods and now she was filled with another fear. Suppose Tom were not there? Would she need to see him at the house, and would he or his father refuse her admittance?

"Not that way!" came a sharp command.

All thought left her mind. She hurried toward the sound and saw Tom standing only a few feet away from her—where the carriageway ran parallel to the woods. Moving forward impulsively, she came to a sudden dead stop, swallowing air bubbles and remembering all that she had done to him. It was unlikely that he would even speak to her, she realized dolefully, but he must. He must!

"Tom!" she croaked, and impelled by Arthur's need, ran forward again.

He stared at her, the color abruptly draining from his face. "You!" he exclaimed hoarsely.

She did not let herself be put off by his apparent anger. Ignoring his two startled workmen, she came up to him. "I must speak to you."

"There is nothing we have to say—" he began.

"It's not about us . . . it's Arthur," she blurted.

"Arthur!" he repeated incredulously. "Arthur?"

"He could have killed you, but he did not," she cried, and knew that with those words she had not meant to utter, she had captured his attention. She continued, "Tom, we must talk. We must. Now."

His gaze, angry but also puzzled, was fastened on her face. "Very well," he assented. "We will talk."

"Not here . . ." she added, once more aware of his men.

"No, not here, of course, not here." Moving toward her, he seized her arm and pulled her urgently back into the woods.

She knew where he was going—to the bank of the stream where as children they had waded and fished. The banks were high and covered with moss, and though it was too late for pollywogs, she had a memory of Tom catching some in a container and telling her later that they had developed little legs and hands and lost their tails. She did not know why this fugitive memory should return to her now—save that it was characteristic of the companionship they had once enjoyed.

The stream was a secret place, the whereabouts of which they had never divulged to anyone else. Tears suddenly arose in her eyes. There was something particularly reassuring that he should choose this spot. Did it mean that he might eventually forgive her for her cruel deception? She could not dwell on that now, and looking at him, her heart sank. His gaze was impersonal, as if, indeed, they were strangers. Yet, be that as it may, he remained her one hope.

He said coldly, "You mentioned Arthur. Why? And what did you mean when you said that Mr. Questred could have killed me? What has one to do with the other?"

"Mr. Questred *is* Arthur, Tom," she cried.

He stepped backward, staring at her incredulously. "Arthur is dead. You know that for a fact. You know we received final confirmation before . . . You knew that before you . . . left."

"It was a mistake or . . . or a lie!" she exclaimed.

He caught her by the shoulders, his fingers biting into her flesh. "What manner of madness is this?"

"Why . . . why do you imagine that the man you know as Mr. Questred deloped? I will tell you why! He would not shoot his brother!"

"His . . . brother," Tom echoed. "I do not—"

"Listen to me," she interrupted. "He had hoped to slay his stepfather. That was the plot, and I was the ploy —the scapegoat, if you like—so that he might snare the tiger, which is why, I suspect, that he did not possess me."

His hands dropped from her shoulders. "What are you saying?" he demanded, his anger obviously rising again. "Why are you lying to me?"

"I am not lying to you now—I lied to you before. There was nothing between us, ever, save that I felt I could not leave him in the care of the village nurses and so invented a reason. But that is unimportant. If I have hurt you, I pray you will not let it influence you adversely when it comes to him. You were fond of Arthur once. You must not turn your face from him now—whatever he has done. Whatever he did was predicated on what had been done to him. And if you still hate him after all I intend to tell you, may I hope that you will not betray him for the sake of Bellair. He has already suffered enough in the name of Bellair. Oh, God"—she met his confused gaze—"you are the only one I could trust, despite all that has happened . . . and despite that, Tom, we must help him and—"

"Pamela," he interrupted. "You are not making any sense!"

"I am," she returned. "Listen to me—will you listen and promise that you will keep this to yourself?"

"Yes," he said stonily. "You know you can trust me." He added bitterly, "You have hurt me very deeply, Pamela, but yes, tell me everything and be assured that it will remain with me."

In the interests of making herself totally clear, she tried to remain as detached from her narrative as possible, but by the time she had recounted the whole of it to Tom, she could hardly speak for weeping, and then, and only then, did she dare to look at him, hoping against hope that, despite what she could only describe as Arthur's machinations, he would have some pity for his brother's terrible and prolonged ordeal. Meeting his eyes, she felt a pulse begin to pound in her throat. She had hoped for sympathy but had half-anticipated disbelief. She had not expected to find his face, dusty from his recent tussle with the tree, streaked with the tears that still filled his eyes.

"Tom, dear," she whispered. "Then you do still feel something for him?"

He nodded. "I loved Arthur. He was uncommon kind to me when I was little—especially on the day Mama died. But do you think my f-father . . . ?" He swallowed.

She knew he must be in agony, but she could spare him nothing, not now. She said, "I can tell you only what I heard."

"Arthur could have . . . lied."

"He was fever-struck, Tom, out of his head. And if you were to see his body, so marked with scars. It . . . it . . ." Her voice broke and it was a moment before she could continued. "I am angry, you know, angry for the deception he practiced upon me. Yet when I think of all he has suffered for ten years, ten long years, and he has been branded as a common criminal, his reputation blackened, that poor young man who . . . who wanted only another year at Oxford. That's what he told me on that last afternoon. He . . . he wanted to read p-philosophy, and instead . . ." Pamela's tears overflowed. "Oh, T-Tom, we must help him."

He put his arm around her, holding her against him protectively as he said huskily, "Yes, yes, we must. I will go to my father."

"You must tell him nothing!" she cried.

"No." He blinked away more tears, and there was a grimness in his tone as he said, "I will let him tell me about Arthur. And then . . . I will go to Scotland."

"Oh, will you, Tom?" she cried thankfully. "He . . . Arthur does care for you. He would be very happy were you to forgive him for . . . everything."

"I pray you will not speak of my forgiving him," he said chokingly. "I would go down on my knees to him. I . . ." He shook his head and swallowed. "Be assured, my dear, I will do everything that is in my power to help him."

"Oh, dear, dear Tom, I was sure you would not fail

me. And I do hope that in time you will . . . forgive me, as well."

"I have done so already," he said slowly. "It is possible that knowing each other so well, we'd not have suited. But enough! It is Arthur who needs must concern us now—though I do not mind telling you, Pamela, that his actions toward you were shoddy in the extreme and, in a sense, toward me."

"He redeemed himself as far as you were concerned, Tom," she said earnestly. "He held his fire, and as for me, I'd have thought that he might trust me, but I believe him when he says that trusting no longer comes easily to him."

"Nor should it," he said mournfully. "My father . . . my own father . . ." He shuddered.

"He did it for you, too," she reminded him, not because of any feeling she had for Edmund Bellairs but because she knew that even given his far-from-circumspect life-style, Tom had a soft corner for his father and must be deeply shocked at this evidence of his perfidy.

She was sure of that when he burst out, "He did not do it for me—but for himself. He has always resented the fact that he was not born of the elder son. Furthermore, he has lost no opportunity in castigating Arthur and pointing him out as a disgrace to the family! Oh, God"—he turned a tortured face toward Pamela— "and Arthur held his fire!"

There were tears in his eyes again. Pamela moved to him and put her arms around him, holding him against her. "It is not your fault, my dearest," she said softly.

"I am my father's son," he groaned.

"And share a mother with Arthur. Do not forget that, Tom, dear."

"I never have." He moved away from her. "And in her name, I vow that Arthur will be exonerated."

She had never loved him half so much as in that moment, but at the same time, Pamela realized that her love for Tom was sisterly, or even motherly—but nothing more—and meeting his eyes, knew that he must soon agree with her. He said, "I will walk you home, my dear, and then I will speak to Father."

"I should like that, Tom," she said, and was aware that she had been wrong. Tom was already her brother. With a little shock, she realized that he was also her brother-in-law, but that, she reminded herself, was a condition that would not last much longer. In that same instant, she also had another realization. A process had been completed this morning—a most necessary process. She, Pamela Cardwell Bellairs, had finally grown up.

10

Tom, walking slowly, very slowly and reluctantly back to the house, came to a stop a short distance from the huge mansion and stared up at its many-windowed facade. Angrily he blinked wetness from his eyes. He was conscious of a hurt that was almost physical. Indeed, it was physical for his throat was aching. His love for Bellair equaled Edmund's in strength, was, indeed, even stronger, for unlike his father, he had grown up within its walls. Yet, equal to his love for his home was his feeling for the brother he had lost and whom he had believed dead.

Arthur had been a figure of fun to many, but the child Tom had loved him with all his heart. It had been Arthur who had comforted him when he had hurt himself and was unwilling to cry in front of his father. Arthur had also read him wonderful stories and had instilled in him a love of poetry. Tom had missed him a great deal when he had gone off to Oxford, and he had always been delighted when he came home, for Arthur had never been too occupied to spend time with the solitary little boy. And on the death of their mother, he had not given him silly platitudes about her having flown to a better place far, far away from himself.

"It is my belief that she will still be with you, Tom, in spirit. You've not lost her, you know."

At that time, he had actually felt that presence, but it had gone with Arthur's inexplicable arrest. He remembered well his father telling him that Arthur's name was to be blotted out of the family bible and never to be mentioned at Bellairs because with his "vile actions" he had brought disgrace upon his family. He also recalled having fled weeping to his room because Edmund had said, "He ought to be hanged, not transported."

"That would have served you even better," he muttered, and came to a dead stop, realizing that he was giving credence to Pamela's story without even sounding out his father on the subject. At least he ought to give him the benefit of the doubt. Yet his life in the ten years since Arthur had been transported was not what Tom admired. True, he had stopped short of bringing his doxies home to Bellair, but still he could not help feeling that Edmund's every action was an insult to the mother he had loved. Indeed, he had, some time ago, come to the reluctant conclusion that Edmund Bellairs had never loved Jocelyn, his wife. He had married her solely because he coveted the estate.

"Why did I never think of that before?" Tom muttered.

Even without speaking to his father, the actions reported by Pamela seemed entirely and terribly logical. The removal of the real heir of Bellair had made it possible for him to inherit and eventually pass the property on to his son. At last he was where he must have longed to be throughout his whole life, occupying the position of eldest son, the undeserved position gained at a price that made Tom shudder.

Yet, as he walked into the house, he realized that he still cherished the futile hope that Arthur might, after all, be culpable and his father right. To lose Pamela and Bellair in such rapid succession was almost more than he could contemplate.

He had loved Pamela nearly all of his life. He had believed that she knew that—but he could not dwell on that. Pamela was lost to him, and Edith . . . well, it was not the time to think of Edith. However, he had found himself very comfortable with her, and certainly she was much more sensible than Pamela, and beautiful too. Still . . . On seeing a passing footman, he banished all thoughts of Edith from his mind.

"James, would you know where my father is?" he asked.

"He'd be in the library, sir."

As Tom neared the library, he wondered how he might broach the subject of Arthur, and was hit by what he believed was the perfect opening. Coming in, he found Edmund frowning over some papers. However, he looked up quickly with a welcoming smile for his son.

"Well, my lad, how does it go with the tree?"

"The . . . tree?" Tom repeated blankly.

"Were you not having the old elm removed?"

"Oh, yes, it's down and will soon be kindling wood." He moved forward to stand at the desk. "Father, I have been thinking about Arthur."

"Arthur?" Edmund repeated in some surprise. "What brought him into your mind?"

"Since we have been aware for quite some time that he is dead, it seems to me that it would be only proper to put up a stone in the graveyard."

"A . . . stone? To commemorate one who has brought a deep and lasting disgrace to the name of Bellair?" Edmund raised his eyebrows. "Good God, Tom, have you no family pride?"

"Several generations back, Lady Alicia Clitheroe was hanged as a witch. The Clitheroes have erected a monument to her memory. As you know, it occupies a very prominent place in the churchyard."

"That was an entirely different set of circumstances. Lady Alicia was innocent—an innocent victim of Matthew Hopkins and his crew of witch-hunters. Your . . . I hesitate even to call him your brother . . . and he is, or was, only your half-brother . . . It was his own villainy that brought about his downfall. Would you erect a monument to a thief and a smuggler?"

"I never heard that he was a thief!" Tom protested.

"It is one and the same! He, a Bellairs, was tried and found to be a common criminal." Edmund was growing red in the face. "I'm damned if I understand your reasoning!"

"I have been thinking about Arthur of late." Tom frowned. "It seems so odd that he, of all people, should have been involved with smugglers. He was so rarely at home, and—"

"He was in communication with them even before he went to Oxford. You know yourself how often he was absent from the house and no one knew his whereabouts."

"I knew them," Tom said. "He went to the stone house."

"And why?"

"I accompanied him there on several occasions," Tom said slowly. "He kept books there . . . his favorite books. He used to read me stories from them."

"And did he escort you to the cellars?" Edmund demanded edgily.

"I wanted to go, but he'd never let me. The stairs were broken."

" 'The stairs were broken,' " Edmund repeated mockingly. "The excuse of a secret drinker."

"He was never bosky."

"He was too clever, too clever by half. Sir Harry Bowers, who was on the bench at the assizes and who is, as you know, an acquaintance of mine, has told me that many a young so-called sprig of fashion had connections such as those made by Arthur, and being found out, suffered accordingly."

"Sir Harry Bowers," Tom repeated. "He was the judge who tried Arthur?"

"The same." Edmund nodded. "A most worthy and upright man."

Tom, with an image of Sir Harry's bloated, porcine features in his mind, felt himself grow cold. He said, however, "I am sure . . . but no one could ever have called Arthur a 'sprig of fashion.' I take it Sir Harry was referring to those devil-may-care youths who went into smuggling on a dare or because they enjoyed courting danger. Arthur was certainly not of that ilk."

"No, he was not, but he had not yet come into his majority, and undoubtedly he needed money, which he received from the smugglers for providing them with a 'safe house,' as it were. There was one of his fellow prisoners who swore to that. I tell you, Tom, Arthur was the very soul of duplicity."

He was doing it too brown, Tom thought. With a sinking heart he was beginning to believe—or had he ever *not* believed—Pamela's woeful tale. He said mildly, "Well, he would not be the only Bellairs whose escutcheon was . . . er, smudged. It seems to me that Sir Christopher Bellairs, who lived during—"

"Sir Christopher was another matter. He killed a man in a duel and had to leave England. 'Twas an honorable combat, not plain thievery. It was fortunate you did not slay that rascal Questred—else you might have followed in Sir Christopher's wake!"

"And so you will not erect a stone to Arthur's memory?"

"You may do it in your tenure. It will never rise in mine!" Edmund glared at him, and Tom, who had been watching him closely, realized that this was the first time his father had looked him directly in the eyes.

"Very well." He nodded. "It was only a thought."

"One that you would do well to cast from your mind." Edmund was once more looking at his papers.

"I'll bid you good morning, Father."

"Good morning, Tom."

On leaving the library, Tom took the stairs two at a time, and ringing for Jacob, his valet, instructed him to pack a small portmanteau.

"Will I be going with you, sir?" the man asked.

"Yes, you will," Tom said. "Pack enough garments for a fortnight, please."

Some two hours later, Edmund Bellairs, going in the direction of the stables, was surprised to find Jacob supervising the loading of the post chaise. "And what would be the meaning of this?" he demanded.

"Mr. Tom's orders, sir," the valet explained.

"Where would he be going?"

"Fishing, Father." Tom came up behind him. "I looked for you in the library and upstairs. I am glad to find you here. I have had an invitation from Andrew Douglas in Inverness. He says that the trout are crowding the streams and that I must come and apply my rod."

"Why did you say nothing about this before?"

"It came by messenger, just after lunch. You were not about. I looked for you. At any rate, I will not be gone above a fortnight. I . . . should like to be away for a bit. I believe you can understand my reasoning, sir." Tom gave him a long unhappy look.

"Oh, yes, that little wretch Pamela has returned home. She ought to be whipped!"

"I . . . would prefer it if you did not mention her name, Father." Tom sighed. "She came to apologize to me this morning."

"And what did you say to her?"

"I gave her to understand that our friendship was at an end," Tom said.

"Such a contretemps," Sir Edmund sighed. "That Questred is a villain for sure . . . But enough. Enjoy yourself, my lad."

"I shall do my best, sir."

A short time later, Sir Edmund, watching Tom's post chaise rumble out of the stableyard, frowned and walked slowly back to the house. His anger was high against Sidney Questred, who had cheated his son out of a fortune and also the chance to annex Cardwell Manor to Bellairs. It was a pity that the man had not died of the wound Tom had inflicted. However, since he had not, there might be another way to make him pay for the interference that had also broken his son's heart. He would give his attention to the matter at such time as

Questred returned to the Hall. As justice of the peace,
he would see that he repented of his act. Summoning
Matt, one of the stablehands, he instructed the lad to
visit the Hall and ascertain when its owner would be in
residence again.

On a morning two days after Tom's departure for
Scotland, Sir Edmund Bellairs pronounced himself
pleased, even elated, to hear from the attentive Matt
that Mr. Questred was once more in residence at the
Hall. He had returned by coach.

"Ain't up to much, from wot I 'ear," Matt told him.
"Took to 'is bed directly after 'e come 'ome."

Concealing the pleasure that had invaded him at this
information, Sir Edmund thanked his informant and
rewarded him with a shilling. Then, without further
ado, he took the path that led through the woods and
which would eventually bring him to the manor. As he
passed a certain glade, he remembered that beyond it lay
the stone house, now reduced to a single wall and a heap
of rubble in the hole which had been the cellar, the
whole pulled down at his direction. He smiled to himself
at a task which had pleased him. In ordering it
destroyed, he had been, in a sense, destroying Arthur
Bellairs, that fat nonentity who, like his father before
him, had stood in the way of his possessing Bellair, an
inheritance his late stepson had not even appreciated.
Well, he was dead of fever in New South Wales—following his flogging, the man he had sent to find out
what he might, had written. He found himself smiling at
the thought of the deep welts that must have criss-
crossed that fat white back. He had once seen a sailor
flogged at sea. His back had been in ribbons when at
last they had cut him down. It was a miracle the man
had not died—but sailors were used to floggings. Fat
Arthur had never been so much as slapped in his days at
Bellair, and there had been times when he himself had
longed to administer a good beating to the sullen, over-

indulged mother's darling who had, until the birth of Tom, made an unwanted third in the household.

Jocelyn, damn the woman, *had* been a fool about him, a fool about many things. She had truly wearied him, but she had given birth to Tom and, unwittingly, sealed Arthur's fate. Tom was a fine son, a lad after his own heart, and now he would inherit Bellair free and clear.

Sir Edmund had come in sight of the manor. He did not usually arrive unannounced, but this news was too good to keep to himself, and he was sure that he would have Sir Robert's sanction in the matter of Sidney Questred's arrest. Even if he were unable to make the charges stick, he would at least see him in jail. He doubted that the wretch would remain in the vicinity long after that. Indeed, it was a marvel that he had had the audacity to return. Certainly he would, at the very least, be shunned by the rest of the community.

By great good luck, the butler who admitted him informed him that Sir Robert was in the library rather than the observatory. He loathed the three flights of stairs leading to the top of the house. In the last six months he had grown regrettably short of breath and his physician had advised him to cut down on his consumption of food and drink. It was ridiculous advice, of course. His grandfather had been a hearty trencherman and a four-bottle man as well. He had lived to the age of eighty-five. It had been the shock of Arthur's transportation that had killed him, and not a moment too soon!

Sitting in the drawing room as he waited for the butler to announce him, Sir Edmund admired furnishings purchased in France when Sir Robert was on his Grand Tour. In the years before he had married, he collected fine furniture and artifacts from all over Europe. These would have passed to Pamela, and some would have enhanced the drawing room at Bellair. The house itself had much to command it, and it, too, would eventually have been the property of Tom and his heirs. He would have been able to use it as a dower house. There was such a structure at Bellair, but it did not equal the Cardwell mansion either in layout or construction. Questred, damn his black soul to everlasting flames, would pay for his abduction *and* seduction of that wretched little chit Pamela, before he was much older.

Footsteps on the stairs caused him to look toward the portal. Pamela was coming down, and for a moment she stood framed in the aperture. He rose immediately. He had no very kind thoughts for her, but he managed a conciliatory smile. "My dear Pamela," he began, and paused as he saw a look almost of horror pass over her face.

"You!" she breathed, and turning a bright scarlet, she fled up the stairs again.

He stared after her in consternation. It seemed to him that he had read dislike, even revulsion in her candid gaze. Was that possible, or was it merely embarrassment because of her own folly and the havoc it had wrought? That must be the explanation, and she had blushed, had she not? She well might, the stupid little fool! However, he must remember that it was not entirely her fault.

Edith Courtney had told him that Pamela was much addicted to the perusal of romantic novels in which such runaway matches abounded. Given what, he had never doubted, was her imperfect mentality (for what woman possessed anything resembling a mind?) she had naturally fallen prey to an accomplished seducer, an obvious rascal, an adventurer, who had wooed her for her fortune, of course. True, Mr. Questred was supposed to have money—but why had he decided to live in the Hall? His servants had said that many of the rooms were shut off, suggesting that he did not have enough of the ready to make the necessary improvements to them. Yes, he had to be a fortune hunter, and poor Pamela has discovered his perfidy too late. It was indeed a great pity that Tom's bullet had not dispatched the rogue! Again he found himself wondering why Questred had not returned Tom's fire.

Had he suffered a belated attack of remorse?

That appeared highly unlikely. Probably he was unused to handling firearms. Tom had said he was most reluctant to duel with him. Probably his weapon was the knife in the back. . . .

"Sir Edmund." Sir Robert, abruptly terminating Sir Edmund's thoughts, entered the room. He had, his visitor noticed, a quizzical look on his face. "Good afternoon."

"Good afternoon." Sir Edmund got to his feet quickly, extending his hand. As he received his host's warm grasp, he said, "No doubt you wonder why I have come here unannounced. I have news which must interest you. I have learned that our Mr. Questred is back at the Hall."

Sir Robert frowned. "Is he, indeed? I wonder that he dares show his face so soon—after all he has done."

"Obviously there is no end to his effrontery. 'Tis my contention that he should be jailed and held on charges of abduction!"

"Abduction?" Sir Robert reddened. "I wish I might agree that that was the case, but I fear that Pamela went with him willingly enough."

"And returned sadder and wiser, I think."

Sir Robert's glance was evasive. "Yes, that might be the case. I have not pressed her for all the details of this unfortunate matter. I have the feeling that when she is ready, she will give them to me of her own accord."

"That shows considerable forbearance on your part, Sir Robert. I must commend you for it. However, to return to my original point. I do not like the idea of that scoundrel living on at the Hall as if nothing untoward had taken place. The fact that your daughter returned *alone* must certainly have given rise to talk. You know how quickly our loose-tongued servants take the pollen from one flower and spread it among others, with even more alacrity than, say, a hummingbird, an analogy which, you must agree, is singularly apt."

"Quite." Sir Robert nodded, his eyes fixed on Sir Edmund's face.

The latter was highly gratified. As he had hoped, he had captured his fellow sufferer's attention. "A day or even five might discourage our fine Mr. Questred from attempting a similar seduction and, at the same time, could result in his leaving this part of the world."

"It would be no more than he deserved," Sir Robert said slowly. "Pamela is not herself these days."

Sir Edmund spoke his relief. "I am aware of that. I saw her a few minutes ago. She hardly looked at me."

"I imagine she connects you with Tom. We are inclined to avoid those whom we believe we have wronged."

"This Questred rascal has much to answer for . . ."

"I agree," Sir Robert returned heavily.

"Then, you will bear me witness?"

"You have my word on it," Sir Robert said. "When will you have the fellow arrested?"

"I see no reason to postpone the matter. He has lately returned to the Hall. I would say tomorrow morning. I might add that the jail is extremely uncomfortable in this hot weather. I think I will let him remain there for a day or two before I have him brought before me. That should discourage him even more about remaining."

"It is a pity we cannot bring him before the assizes. They'll be meeting in the beginning of September."

Edmund grimaced. "Unfortunately, as justice of the peace, I cannot see that this is a matter for that court—though I truly wish there were more serious charges we could level at him. Unfortunately, there are not."

"To my mind, he's nothing but a damned fortune hunter!" Sir Robert exploded.

"Were we to arrest men for that particular sin, we'd have our jails overflowing." Sir Edmund moved toward the hall. "I will send you word when I require your presence."

"That will be much to my liking." Sir Robert's satisfaction was plain. "I am not exaggerating when I tell you that he has broken my daughter's heart."

"Nor would it be an exaggeration to say that poor Tom is equally cast down. I have never seen him in such low spirits. He has taken himself off to Scotland and I am quite sure it's because he cannot bear to be in the same vicinity with Pamela."

"That is highly understandable. Lord, Lord, that Questred has upset a great many apple carts."

"And will think twice before he upsets any more—at least here in Kent," Sir Edmund said grimly. "I have often found my duties as justice of the peace extremely irksome, but I will welcome this one."

In common with many rural justices of the peace, Sir Edmund did not hold court in the town buildings except during the quarter sessions. He set aside a room in Bellair during the autumn and winter. In late spring and during the summer, he chose to avoid discomfort to himself by interviewing such malefactors as poachers and thieves in an internal courtyard. It was here on a morning two days after his conversation with Sir Robert that he set up a table to serve as desk and three chairs. One of these was for himself, one for the clerk, and the other for Sir Robert. Unfortunately, the worthy had sent word that he was feeling poorly and would be unable to attend.

Sir Edmund had a strong suspicion that Sir Robert was concerned over the legality of holding the man on such flimsy charges. He was sorry his friend entertained such qualms. He was sure he would have enjoyed the spectacle of Mr. Questred being brought before him by the two arresting constables.

He had been taken from the Hall on a particularly muggy day and he had protested strongly. In fact, he had struck one of the constables and had needed to be subdued by the other with a strong blow to the jaw that had rendered him unconscious. Subsequently he had been put in the town lockup, a building resembling a small tower and erected three centuries earlier. It was used only to hold prisoners until they could be transferred to the jail. Sir Edmund had ordered that Mr. Questred be kept there for a day and a half, a decision that even the constables had dared to protest.

" 'Tis not usual, sir, an' 'e be passin' ill," the younger of the pair had said, with his companion nodding in solemn agreement.

"Are you questioning my authority, Mr. Smith? Perhaps you would like to join him there and keep him company?" Sir Edmund had responded sweetly, and had the additional pleasure of seeing young Jim Smith, whom he had known since he was a mere lad, pale and shake his head.

Still young Jim had dared to say, "No, sir, but 'e be a *gentleman.*"

"As to that," Sir Edmund had laughed, "many a gentleman has had his head on a pike over Tower Bridge in ages past and many another has had the gentlemanly pleasure of being hanged at Tyburn. As for Mr. Sidney Questred's 'gentility,' that is highly debatable, given his recent actions. Let him remain where he is. I am sure 'tis not the first time he has graced the confines of a lockup."

According to Sir Edmund's directions, the table had been set in the shade and the prisoner would stand in the sunlight of another very warm day, made the warmer by reason of the courtyard being enclosed. He would truly regret, Sir Edmund thought with no little satisfaction, the day he had ever set foot in his part of the world and laid siege to its daughters! Furthermore, he would set out as one of the conditions of the man's release that the marriage between him and poor little Pamela be annulled forthwith! As he had told Sir Robert, he was extremely glad of that appointment to the position of justice of the peace, one he had sought but, at the same time, disdained.

His self-satisfaction increased when, on taking his chair in the courtyard, he said to the waiting constable, "You may bring in the prisoner." He would have been even more pleased had he been able to see the man in chains.

It was immediately evident that, as he had anticipated, Mr. Questred had not benefited from his incarceration. He was very pale. There was a purple bruise on his chin, the which he must owe to the constable's having struck him. His clothing was much disordered, and with the dark stubble on chin and cheeks, he looked a proper rogue. There were dark circles under eyes that were agleam with fury. He was also much thinner than Sir Edmund remembered. Undoubtedly he had not yet recovered from the effects of his encounter with Tom— and would the lad had slain him. He, Sir Edmund Bellairs, could have dealt with the consequences of such an act—easily.

Mr. Questred took a step toward the table and was immediately restrained by one of the constables. Unmindful of the man's interference, he glared at Sir Edmund. "I would like to know the meaning of this . . . this arrest," he said in a shaking voice, though whether this was the result of anger or weakness, Sir Edmund was not quite sure.

"I will let the clerk read the indictment against you," Sir Edmund returned coldly.

"Damn your clerk," Mr. Questred exploded. "I have been informed of that indictment. The charge, I am told, is abduction. I abducted no one! Produce my wife and ask her whether or not she came with me willingly."

"Willingly, sir?" Edmund inquired. "Her father has given me quite another story. It concerns coercion and is, in my opinion, substantiated by the fact that your 'wife' came home alone by stagecoach, I understand, and in a most unhappy condition. And . . ." He paused, staring at the man before him, struck by something he had never noticed before. Mr. Questred resembled someone he knew or had known.

"You had no right to arrest me, no right to leave me in that vile, airless hole—"

"Will you speak to me of rights?" Sir Edmund interrupted. "I am the justice of the peace—"

"And therefore should be concerned with the administration of justice!" Mr. Questred retorted furiously.

Edmund, staring at his prisoner through narrowed eyes, had traced the resemblance. He looked like Tom, he thought amazedly, and also his cousin William, did he not? Yes, now that he had lost so much weight, he did. An image of William's hated countenance arose in his mind to substantiate his suspicions. Mr. Questred definitely had the Bellairs features and build—but Arthur was dead, he reminded himself, had been dead five years or so, according to the intelligence sent to him by the man he had dispatched to find him. How could that be? He had always heard that the authorities in New South Wales kept close tabs on all prisoners sent out from Britain. Yet mistakes could be made, and perhaps Browne, the man he had sent, had wearied of the search and assumed, or even lied—he must have lied. Undoubtedly the man before him was Jocelyn's son—William's son—grown lean from enforced labor and prison fare. Doubts arose again. Sidney Questred had a strength about him that Arthur had totally lacked. Arthur had been a weak slug of a lad.

"You have no right to hold me!" the prisoner rasped.

Sir Edmund summoned his thoughts with an effort. "I have a right in the name of Sir Robert Cardwell, who has issued a complaint against you."

"Then why is he not present to voice this complaint?"

"That is not necessary." Sir Edmund continued to stare at him, remembering suddenly something that had both amazed him and aroused a host of unanswered questions in his mind. In that recent duel, Questred had not returned Tom's fire. He had *deloped,* and Tom's bullet had found its mark. That was the reason for his present pallor and thinness. Will had been similarly thin. Yes, yes, yes, his resemblance to Will, to all the Bellairs men, with the possible exception of himself, who had favored his mother's side of the family, was damning!

"I find it exceedingly necessary," Mr. Questred was saying indignantly.

He continued with his protests, but Sir Edmund was not listening. Years ago, a decade ago and more, that same indignation had coated the tones of a terrified Arthur as he protested his innocence to the stepfather who had pretended to believe him. And now *Arthur* had risen from the dead, thirsting for vengeance! That was the reason for his masquerade!

He could not quite see the connection, but he had a feeling that it was also the reason for his elopement with Pamela. Possibly he had been retaliating against Tom. He could not dwell on reasons at this time! He had to see that *Arthur* remained in custody until he thought of a way to destroy him. Undoubtedly, he must have been released from prison—the ten years were at an end and his papers stating that fact were probably at the Hall. He must needs procure them. It would be a precarious business but he had the upper hand!

He rose to his feet. "You . . . you are here under false pretenses!" He glared at the prisoner. "You are not 'Sidney Questred,' sir. You are a convicted felon, an escaped prisoner from New South Wales, and much as I hate to recognize the relationship, you are my nephew, Arthur Bellairs!"

"Damn you to hell!" Arthur Bellairs leapt at him, his hands, talonlike, reaching for Sir Edmund's throat.

"Constables!" Sir Edmund cried, unnecessarily, for the two men had already leapt to Arthur's side, forcibly restraining him.

"Damn you, I have been released," Arthur gasped.

"And where are the papers to prove it?" Sir Edmund demanded.

"I do not have them on me, but—"

"I presume they are at the Hall?" Edmund interrupted. "Well, we will send someone to fetch them. Meanwhile, Mr. Sidney Questred, as you call yourself—for what reason I cannot divine, since you say you were 'released'—I think you must remain in custody until they are produced. And even in those circumstances, there remains a question as to why you felt it necessary to assume this elaborate disguise." He turned to the constables. "Take my . . . nephew to the jail."

"Damn and blast you," Arthur rasped. "You . . . you . . ." He made another futile move in Sir Edmund's direction and then sank fainting to the floor.

The constables, exchanging shocked glances with the clerk, who had heretofore said nothing, bent over the fallen man.

"There be blood on 'is shirt," one of them remarked.

"Aye, looks as if 'is wound 'as reopened," young Jim Smith said.

"See that someone attends him," Sir Edmund directed. "And afterward, I want you to see that he is taken to jail and placed in solitary confinement—away from the other prisoners. None but the jailer is to have any communication with him. He is an extremely dangerous individual—in league, I happen to know, with a great many of the smuggling fraternity hereabouts. He must be held for the summer assizes."

"But if he was released, sir—" the clerk began.

"If he were released, Mr. Podmore, we will discover that soon enough. And if he were released, why is he lurking about this district under an assumed name? Disgraceful as his past actions have been, this man is my nephew and the heir to Bellair. What is the reason for this strange disguise? Why did he not come forward and assert his claim? Have the goodness to do as I tell you, immediately."

Two hours later, Sir Edmund, conferring with the small, unprepossessing individual who occupied the position of head keeper on his property, repeated strongly and with narrowed eyes, "Those papers must not be found."

"They won't be," the other asserted. "But if 'e was released, won't they know, them wot's in the government?"

"I doubt if they will be attending our summer assizes," Sir Edmund said softly. "And, as I am sure you know, the presiding judge is a very good friend of mine—an old friend who remembers Arthur well enough. Also, by that time we will have produced witnesses who will swear that my nephew has come here to resume his highly profitable smuggling operations. His ten years in New South Wales will not stand in his favor, I can assure you, especially given the fact that he has managed to worm himself into the favor of the local gentry. I see no reason why he should not be hanged this time."

"I still think it would be easier were 'e to die in prison," muttered the keeper with a sly sidelong look.

Sir Edmund was silent for a moment. "It would be to our advantage, surely," he said wistfully. "But 'tis a very chancy thing to do. I am of the opinion that 'murder will out.' Never fear, my man, we have enough to bury him. We'll use murder only as a last resort. Meanwhile, I will send the constable for those papers on the morrow. See that they are missing."

"Shall I burn them?"

"No, let me have them. I will attend to them. It will give me considerable pleasure."

"I'll sleep easier myself," the keeper said.

After the man had left, Sir Edmund rose. He had it in mind to see Sir Robert and describe the events of the morning. Yet, even as he had his hand on the doorknob, he came to a pause, remembering Pamela's strange actions on the day of his visit to the manor. Did she know that the man she had married was none other than

Arthur Bellairs? And what had he told her? The truth,
obviously. Was that why she had left him? No, her
reception of himself suggested that she might have
believed Arthur's accusations, and would she be a
witness for him? Judging from her attitude, there was
that possibility. However, she was married to him, and
a wife could not testify for or against her husband. Yet,
if her marriage were annulled . . . Still, anything she said
could easily be discredited by a clever clerk. She could
also be accused of duplicity, for all knew she had been
betrothed to Tom.

Tom.

Edmund was suddenly reminded of his son's
questions regarding Arthur's stone. They had sprung up
from nowhere, certainly. Or had he been speaking with
Pamela? She had been to see him, he had said, but he
had turned her away and gone to Scotland.

Scotland?

Gretna Green lay over the Scottish border. Was it
possible that Pamela had put a bee in Tom's bonnet?
Was his sudden decision to visit his old friend in
Inverness predicated on Pamela's confidences? Tom
had loved Arthur very deeply as a lad, much as he, Sir
Edmund, had surreptitiously attempted to discourage
his son's affection. Had Pamela informed him that the
man he had shot was none other than Arthur?

It made sense—or did it? Tom had shot Arthur
because he had stolen Pamela from him. Given his
misery over her defection, he would not rush to aid the
man who had betrayed him, the man who, if not
permanently stopped, could inherit Bellair. Tom loved
Bellair more than Pamela, more than life. Tom would
remain squarely in his corner, and as for Arthur's
stone? It could hardly rise above a body buried in
quicklime within the walls of the prison where he had
been hanged. It was a great pity that the practice of
letting corpses of felons hang in chains on their gibbets
until they rotted had been largely abandoned. He could
think of no better monument to Arthur.

11

Pamela was confused. She had heard her father send Thomas, one of their footmen, with a message to Sir Edmund, explaining that he was not well and must needs take to his bed. Consequently he would not be able to attend the hearing that morning.

To her certain knowledge, Sir Robert had never attended one of Sir Edmund's hearings, and furthermore, he was not ill. Earlier that same morning he had eaten his usual hearty breakfast, and after his conversation with Thomas, he had ascended not to his bed but to the observatory. However, when she, concerned about him, had followed him to inquire about his health, he had spoken vaguely about not feeling his best and had regarded her uncertainly, adding obscurely, "I should not have agreed to it, but never mind, I am not there." He had flushed and added, "My dear, we will talk later. I have just secured a translation of Joseph Fraunhofer's work on spectroscopy." Forthwith, he had turned his attention to a large tome filled with complicated diagrams, the sight of which served as a signal that he would be occupied until noon.

Leaving her father, Pamela found herself filled with an alarm for which she had no other reason than the certain belief that Sir Robert had been lying. And what had Sir Edmund wanted with him? And why had he appeared disturbed, regretful, and even guilt-ridden?

Though she had no basis for it, she could not rid herself of the feeling that the meeting he had not attended had something to do with herself. In a sense, she was pleased that her father had not joined Sir

Edmund. The less he saw of that villain, the better. She longed to tell him the truth about his machinations; it was terrible not to be able to trust your own father— but if he were to reveal the identity of the man who called himself Sidney Questred, Arthur would undoubtedly be in danger.

Angry as she was with his deception of her vulnerable self (a self she could no longer claim as her own), she did not want him to suffer any more than he had already. Indeed, every time she thought about his poor scarred back or contrasted his roughened hands with the white, well-shaped, if plump hands of a younger Arthur Bellairs, she shuddered anew at this mute evidence of his ten years in hell. And he had been innocent—that was the worst of it, an innocent man condemned to virtual slavery! Yet thinking of the strategem he had used to decoy Sir Edmund over the Scottish border, she wondered if that terrible ordeal had not rendered him partially mad. Killing Sir Edmund in a duel would have been madness. Forcing him to confess the truth about Arthur's imprisonment was the one way for him to obtain satisfaction, and also it was the one way to clear his name!

Had Tom reached Scotland yet? Had they arrived at an understanding? Would Tom bring Arthur back with him? She did not think him well enough to travel so far as yet, and at least he was safe in Scotland. Pamela ran her hands through her hair. She longed to have answers to these questions, but since she could not gather them from the air, she would go riding. Riding always soothed her. She went to her room. She had left Lucy sewing on one of her dresses—but the girl was not there now. Impatiently she rang for her. Then she laughed. She had forgotten that when in Scotland, she had dressed herself, and despite a lifetime of depending on servants, she had had no difficulty at all!

It was well she had not waited for Lucy, she decided some ten minutes later as she buttoned up her jacket. The girl, amazingly enough, had not yet answered her ring. Then, just as that thought crossed her mind, Lucy came in. She was breathless and apologetic and, at the same time, wildly excited.

"Oh, Miss Pamela," she cried. "You've gone'n changed yourself. I be that sorry, but . . . Oh, Miss Pamela, 'e's in jail 'n they say 'e aint 'oo 'e says 'e is, but 'im wot were mixed up wi' the smugglers all them years ago'n escaped from New South Wales, the good Lord knows 'ow. My Jim says as 'ow nobody's supposed to escape, only 'e . . . Oh, Miss Pamela, I . . . I'll get the vinaigrette."

"No, Lucy," Pamela protested weakly. "I am not going to swoon. Please . . . calm down and tell me exactly what you heard. Oh, God, is he back? He should not have come back. I am sorry, Lucy . . . Go on!"

The girl still looked at her nervously. "Yer white as a sheet, Miss Pamela. 'Adn't I better—"

"No!" Pamela cried, at the end of her patience. "I do not want anything save to hear about Mr. Questred —I presume that is who you mean."

The girl regarded her with a mixture of shock and surprise. "You knew about 'em?"

"I knew," Pamela responded impatiently. "And he did not escape from New South Wales, he served out his sentence and was released."

"Thass wot 'e says, but Jim says Sir Edmund don't believe 'im. 'E's sent to the 'all for 'is papers."

"Oh, God!" Pamela shrieked. "He mustn't. But how did Jim hear about all this?" As she asked the question, she suddenly recalled her father's mention of the hearing. "He . . . he was up before Sir Edmund? Mr. Questred?" she asked faintly.

"He was that, Miss Pamela. This morning."

"Oh what . . . on what charge?"

"Jim says 'twas abduction o' you, Miss Pamela."

"Abduction?" Pamela echoed. "But that is ridiculous. I went with him because I . . . I wanted to go with him."

"Thass wot Jim says . . . 'e says that all o' a sudden

Sir Edmund up'n tells 'im that 'e were Arthur Bellairs wot got convicted o' smugglin' all them years ago. I weren't more'n this 'igh,''—Lucy held her hand close to the floor—"but I remember wot a stir it caused . . . nobody could talk about nothin' else for days.''

"Oh, God, I have to see him,'' Pamela groaned. Another thought struck her. "Does my father know what happened?''

"Thomas were for tellin' im, but nobody wanted to disturb 'im up there.''

"I will disturb him!'' Pamela cried, and dashed out of the room. She reached the observatory in seconds, flinging back the door and meeting her father's amazed and angry stare with an anger that far exceeded his own. "What do you know about Sir Edmund's hearing this morning?'' she demanded.

He blinked at her in amazement. "Hearing . . . I do not understand you. Nor do I understand this . . . invasion. How—?''

"Yes, you do understand me,'' she cried furiously. "I heard you speaking with Thomas. I heard your lying excuses.''

"My . . . lying excuses?'' Sir Robert rose from his chair, glaring at her. "How dare you speak to me in such a manner? Go to your room immediately.''

"I will do nothing of the kind!'' she retorted. "Had Sir Edmund your sanction to . . . to summon my husband before him and charge him with . . . with abducting me?''

"Your husband. He'll not be your husband—''

"Father, answer my question.'' Pamela stamped her foot.

He said defensively, "I did not attend the hearing. But that does not excuse—''

"Father,'' she interrupted, "Mr. Questred is in jail!''

"Jail?'' he questioned in surprise. "Oh, no, my child, 'twas intended as a warning, only.''

"What was intended as a warning?''

"We . . . er . . . heard he was in residence again and Sir Edmund was of a mind to show him that he was not wanted in this community. He asked if I would be his witness and I . . . consented. However, this morning, I thought better of it—rather, I did not think the charge would hold and—"

Pamela broke into this wandering speech. "Hear me, Father, he is in jail! I have just had it from Lucy, whose follower is one of the constables who arrested him. Sir Edmund has put him in jail and not because of me, but because he is Arthur Bellairs!"

"Arthur Bellairs?" Sir Robert repeated. "Oh, no, my dearest, Arthur is long dead. I have it on very good authority."

"You have it on no authority if your informant is Sir Edmund. Mr. Questred is Arthur Bellairs and he has been imprisoned by his villainous cousin and stepfather, who will destroy him. I know it. And all for the sake of Bellairs." Pamela burst into tears.

Sir Robert stared at her incredulously. "You cannot know what you are saying!"

"I do . . . I tended him when he was shot. And if you could have seen his body, his poor body, so marked by the lash, and his hands . . . and oh, God . . ."

"You knew this all along?" Sir Robert demanded. "And told me nothing?"

"Yes, I knew it and did not tell you because I knew how friendly you are with that monster Edmund Bellairs."

He caught her by the shoulders, glaring down at her. "You do not know what you are saying," he repeated. "If this Questred is Arthur Bellairs, why did you not reveal his identity to me days ago?"

"Because I was afraid you'd tell him—Sir Edmund!" she cried.

"As you should have done yourself. Why did you not? And what is this talk of monsters?"

"Edmund Bellairs accused him wrongfully, sent him

to prison on trumped-up charges. I had the whole of it from Arthur!"

"Lies, nothing but foul lies. If this man is Arthur Bellairs, why did he conceal his identity? Obviously he was here to revenge himself on the man who sent him to prison and . . ." He glared at her. "How long have you known he is Arthur Bellairs?"

"I found out only when he was delirious from the wound."

"And why did he not tell you before? What was his motive? Did he perchance wish to be revenged on Tom too? That seems logical."

"It is not logical, Father. He was betrayed by Edmund Bellairs. He hoped to—wrongfully, perhaps—exact some manner of revenge, but—"

"Enough! I have heard quite enough!"

"You have not heard the half of it, Father. When he lay stricken with fever, I heard how he'd suffered in New South Wales!"

"And why should he not suffer?" Sir Robert demanded. "Sir Edmund caught him dead to rights. I will never forget how shocked I was . . . how shocked we all were. You were too young to remember the whole of it . . . to know the ramifications. He was an out-and-out villain. There were witnesses—"

"False witnesses!" she cried. "Introduced by his stepfather!"

"Who did all in his power to have his sentence commuted, who stood up in court and pleaded for mercy because this was a first offense. I wonder that with your unhappy experience you should still believe these lies he has pumped into you."

"You do not understand," she said insistently. "Please, Father, listen to me."

"No." He glared at her. "I will not listen. I think you must be mad—defending this man who has single-handedly ruined your life and kept you from ever holding up your head in this community again. You are ruined, Pamela—do you not realize that you are ruined? There is no man who will ever offer for you now!"

"Father, I do not care about that. I . . . I love him and he is an honorable man, even if he has not always acted honorably. He was desperate, desperate . . . ten years, Father, ten years in New South Wales!"

"I would it were twenty or forty. I would he were dead!" Sir Robert actually thundered. "Go to your room. I do not want to see or hear from you until you have apologized to me for your impudence, and as for Arthur Bellairs . . . Words fail me." Seizing her by the shoulders, he thrust her from the room, slamming the door behind her and locking it.

"Father . . . Oh, God, hear me, hear me . . ." She pounded futilely upon the door. "You do not understand . . . you do not understand."

"Child . . ." Miss Pringle was panting from having run up the stairs. She caught Pamela's arm, saying gently, "You must come with me, dear. You are not yourself."

Tears were running down Pamela's cheeks. "He does not understand. Oh, God, I knew this would happen. I knew it, knew it. And now he will have his way—Sir Edmund will have his way."

Her companion put an arm around her. "Come down, my dear, and tell me all about it. Tell me everything."

"You'll not believe me either," Pamela sobbed.

Miss Pringle gave her a long look and said in a low voice, "I beg you will try me, my dear. I know what it is not to be believed. I know it from a very . . . sad experience of my own. You may think me a dried-up old crone, but years ago I, too, was young and loved someone as I think you must love Mr. Questred, however undeserving he is of that love. Come with me now and tell me what has happened." She reached out a trembling hand and smoothed Pamela's curls. "I'll not betray you. You may have my promise on that—and

also I remember young Arthur very well. I have long
puzzled over that situation.''

"You . . . have?" Pamela breathed.

Miss Pringle nodded, moving farther away from the
door, toward the head of the stairs. " 'Twas as much as
my position was worth to confess it,'' she said in a low
voice. "But, child, I am extremely fond of you, as is
your father, who perhaps is of an arbitrary disposition
and not as discerning as he might be—and given over
too much to study. Come now, to my chamber. We'd
best talk there.''

Shocked and desperate as she was, Pamela,
obediently following Miss Pringle down the hall and
into her small suite, was surprised not only at that lady's
unexpected kindness but also by her chambers, which,
in all the years of her companion's employment, she had
never visited.

They were furnished well enough, but it was the
pictures on the wall that caught her eye. There were only
three, an oil and two crayon portraits. The oil was a
painting of an old house under a darkening sky. It was
beautifully executed and had evidently been done by a
fine artist. One of the crayon portraits depicted a young
girl, her hair swept up in a style of some thirty-five years
ago. The face was piquant without being beautiful, but
the artist had caught a shy smile in eyes that were a dark
gray—the color of Miss Pringle's eyes, she realized
suddenly. The other portrait was that of a very
handsome young man.

"He came to our house to paint my mother's
portrait,'' Miss Pringle said softly. "He painted our
house also, and, unbidden, produced this crayon sketch
of me. At my urging, he made this self-portrait, but he
was even better-looking." She sighed. "My father
found us in this folly''—she pointed to a small Grecian
temple at the side of the oil painting, something Pamela
had not noticed at first glance.

"We were only talking, but his arm was about me and

my father ordered him from the premises that very day. He shut me up in my room for a fortnight, allowing me only bread and water. He called me 'an abandoned woman.' As for the artist, he received no more commissions in that part of the country, for my father spread the word that he was not to be trusted with women. I never knew what happened to him. I never forgot him. I never loved again.''

"Oh, Miss Pringle," Pamela whispered. "I am sorry."

"I thank you, my dear, but there's enough about me. Sit down, Pamela." Miss Pringle pointed to a small chair. She took another chair, moving it near to Pamela's. "Now, tell me the whole of it, and know that anything you say will not go beyond this door."

At the end of her account, Pamela could not hold back her tears, and looking at Miss Pringle, found that she, too, was weeping. "Do you believe me, then?" she asked hopefully.

"I do . . . and though I cannot help but blame him for his deception of you, I understand the reasons. One could not live in such circumstances without one's nature being warped and one's values distorted. Yet there was good in him and that cannot have been obliterated—was *not* obliterated, because he would not hurt his brother."

"No, and his sufferings were terrible."

"Yes, I agree. Poor, poor young man. I have never liked Edmund Bellairs. I should like nothing better than to see him receive his just desserts, but I very much fear that those in this district will sympathize with him."

"I have but one hope," Pamela whispered. "It lies with Tom."

"Tom . . ." Miss Pringle mused. "He is Edmund Bellairs' son but he *is* Arthur's brother too. I do not know . . ."

Despite her hopes of Tom, Pamela found herself equally dubious. "He went to Scotland," she said. "But

of course he must have missed him. Arthur never, never
should have come back so soon! And for Sir Edmund to
. . . to arrest him on such flimsy charges . . ."

"Judging from what I know of him, I would think he
was angered at the failure of his plans. He is a most
acquisitive man. He has never noticed me, but I have
noticed him when he comes to this house. He has cast a
most covetous eye upon some of your father's furnishings. I am quite sure that he was anticipating a time
when your fortune and your property would be in the
hands of his son."

"Oh, if you could only impart some of your observations to Father," Pamela sighed.

Miss Pringle appeared alarmed. "My dear, I should
never dare. The only help I can give you is a sympathetic
ear and perhaps a suggestion or two, when the time is
right, which I hope will be when Tom returns."

Pamela clasped her hands. "Oh, I hope so too," she
said fervently. "Otherwise"—she shuddered—"Sir
Edmund will destroy him."

Miss Pringle sighed. "I wish I might argue with you,
but I fear I cannot. We can only wait and see what Tom
will say, once he knows that his brother is under lock
and key."

"Meanwhile, I will try to see Arthur," Pamela said
with a touch of defiance.

"My dear, your father . . ."

"I shall not tell him," Pamela said fiercely. "I shall
tell him nothing of what I do from now on."

"I pray you'll not think too harshly of him," Miss
Pringle said. "He was greatly cast down over your
elopement. He thought it a betrayal, but notwithstand-
ing his feelings, he was amazingly understanding when
you returned. You must admit that."

"I do," Pamela agreed, "but . . ." Her indignation
rose again. "He might have listened to me when I told
him about Arthur, rather than insisting that he was
culpable."

"He does not think of Arthur as Arthur," Miss
Pringle reminded her. "He sees him in the person of
Sidney Questred, whose actions *were* underhanded, my
love. Years ago, Arthur's so-called machinations were a
great disappointment to Sir Robert. You might call
them his first betrayal. He has been too reclusive, your
father. He has, if you will pardon me this criticism,
spent too much time studying the stars. Consequently he
is inclined to believe what he hears—especially if it is
imparted to him by someone he trusts. Unfortunately,
he does trust Edmund Bellairs."

"If you could only speak to him . . ." Pamela cried.

"As I have told you, that is out of the question."

"Yes, of course it is, and I do thank you. It . . . it is
enough to know that you are in my corner, Miss
Pringle. I wish I'd tried to know you better a long time
ago."

Miss Pringle's gray gaze was very bright. "I am afraid
that I was not very helpful," she said regretfully. "And
at times, I know I was too strict—but I had lost
positions by being too lenient, and it was very necessary
to keep this one."

"I do understand." Pamela caught Miss Pringle's
hand and held it tightly. "I wish life had been a little
happier for you." She glanced at the portrait.

"It was happier than if I'd never known him at
all," Miss Pringle said softly, her eyes straying to the
picture.

Pamela swallowed a lump in her throat. She felt an
uneasy kinship with her companion. The moments she
had spent with "Sidney Questred" before they reached
Gretna Green must needs suffice for the whole of her
life. She was willing, indeed she was determined, to see
that justice was done—if she could possibly manage it.
However, she was quite sure that even loving him as she
still did, she could never forgive him for his heartless
using of her affection. And he, of course, had no feeling
for her. She said, "I think I must go now."

"Very well, my dear. And be of good cheer. I do have faith in young Tom."

"As do I," Pamela said staunchly. She moved out of the room, and hurrying to her own chamber, she drew on her boots. In a short time she was mounted on her favorite horse and on her way to Hythe.

She shuddered as she tethered her horse to a post outside the jail. It was an old building and she had no doubt that its cells were terribly hot in this humid weather. The idea of Arthur being incarcerated there filled her with horror. He could not have recovered entirely from his wound, but that was not the worst aspect of the matter. She could envision his anger, his anguish and despair at being under restraint again, and for crimes he had never committed, including the one which had brought him before Edmund Bellairs this morning—her abduction!

Pamela's anger rose again. How could her father have countenanced so blatant a travesty of justice? His failure to attend the hearing proved, at least, that he had had second thoughts, but these had come too late.

Once inside, Pamela discovered that, as she had feared, the heat was pervasive, even though there were windows here. Were there windows in the cells? Noting a desk where sat a rough-looking individual who was regarding her curiously and, at the same time, with a smile so insolent that she longed to strike it from his face, she moved forward. "I would like to see the prisoner Sidney Questred. I am his wife."

The jailer looked her up and down. "Mr. Questred—or rather, Arthur Bellairs—is in solitary confinement. He is allowed no visitors, miss."

"But I tell you I am his wife!" she cried.

"So you 'ave said, miss," he responded, his insolent stare starting at her feet and traveling slowly up to her face. "I 'ave orders as 'ow this 'ere felon is to be kept by hisself."

"But he is ill!" she cried.

"Ought to 'ave thought o' that afore 'e showed 'is face 'ere, miss. 'E be an escaped convict'n 'e be dangerous. Would've strangled the justice if 'e'd not been restrained. 'E be in irons now."

"Irons!" she cried. "I tell you . . . " But at his sardonic look, her words died in her throat. There was nothing she could say, nothing she could do until Tom returned. He had been gone three days. It would be, provided he had good weather, another three or even four before he returned. She said, "Is there no way I could get a note to my husband?"

The man shook his head. "I 'as orders that no one is to communicate wi' 'im."

"Damn you," she burst out. "Even in the London prisons, inmates are allowed visits from their close relatives."

"I 'as my orders, miss." The jailer's gaze and his insistent use of the title "miss" patently denied her stated relationship while implying another—because, she guessed, she had come unattended.

Her face burning, Pamela left the jail and rode back to the manor. As she was removing her habit, there was a tap at her door. She opened it to admit Miss Pringle.

"Well, my dear?" she asked, adding as she scanned Pamela's face: "I fear you were unable to see him."

"They . . . they have him in solitary confinement and irons . . . and he is so ill, Miss Pringle. This could bring a resurgence of his fever." Her eyes widened. "It could kill him, and that is what he must want, Edmund Bellairs. Oh, God, Arthur cannot remain there throughout August!"

"No, he cannot." Miss Pringle shuddered. "We must pray that Tom returns soon."

"Yes, Tom. Oh, God, make him ride like the wind!" Yet even as she spoke those words, Pamela experienced a sinking feeling. With Arthur out of the way, Tom would inherit Bellair free and clear. But he *had* gone to Scotland. She must not anticipate the worst. She said in a small, trembling, but withal defiant tone of voice, "I do have faith in Tom."

"And I, too, my dear," Miss Pringle said strongly.

On the fourth day of Arthur's incarceration, the seventh day since Tom had gone to Scotland, a summer storm buffeted the manor and muddied the roads. Pamela had heard it lashing the trees early in the morning, quelling the hopes she had entertained regarding Tom's return. It rained steadily all that day, and all that day she thought of Arthur locked in his cell. The dampness must be entering his bones, and she was able to do nothing. She had never felt so unhappy or so utterly frustrated. She had gone as far as to beg Lucy to speak to Jim and see if he could not in some surreptitious way alleviate Arthur's condition. Lucy had obeyed, but returned with the depressing news that none but the jailer saw Arthur. He was in a cell reserved for murderers—with an iron door and only a slit where food could be pushed in, more proof if any such were needed that Sir Edmund Bellairs was determined on his death.

Tom returned a week and a day after his departure. Pamela had that intellligence from Lucy. She also learned, to her despair, that he had caught a cold riding through the storm, and at the doctor's insistence, had taken to his bed. Despite the sympathetic championship of Miss Pringle, she was close to despair.

Lying awake at night in her chamber, she envisioned Arthur, gyves on hands and feet, sweltering in that small hot cell. Even though she had been well aware of the futility of her effort, she had tried to speak to her father about Arthur, begging him to intercede with Sir Edmund, but as she had anticipated, he had rebuffed her coldly, castigating her for her defense of a known criminal. It was on that occasion that she learned one more fact that had filled her with horror.

"He swore that he had served out his sentence and was released," her father had told her, contempt edging his words. "But he lied. The document he mentioned was not found among his papers. Naturally, he said it had been stolen—a likely story."

"It is the truth!" she had cried. "Edmund Bellairs stole it. Oh, God, I feared that would happen."

Her words had brought on another furious quarrel with Sir Robert. He had actually threatened to lock her in her chamber if she did not apologize for leveling such an accusation at his friend. Since, in his present mood, he was quite capable of carrying out that threat, she had apologized, but the breach between them had widened and showed no signs of closing. Her father's every glance contained a quotient of contempt for what he deemed her "folly." Yet, uncomfortable as his attitude was, it did not matter to her; nothing mattered save her hopes for Tom's swift recovery from his indisposition. She longed to send a note to him, but she did not dare, and any hope that he would try to communicate with her, illness or no illness, was dashed as the days passed without so much as a word from or about him.

One afternoon, a fortnight after Tom's return, Pamela, coming into her room after a noonday meal notable for its silence, was close to despair. She was positive that Tom, faced with the fact of Arthur's incarceration, had changed his mind concerning his brother. He was content to let him rot in jail as long as he remained the heir of Bellair!

"Miss Pamela . . ." Lucy entered swiftly, her eyes wide with excitement. " 'E says you should come'n join 'im by the stone 'ouse."

A pulse began to beat in her throat. "Who would that be, Lucy?"

"Master Tom, Miss Pamela. 'E said as 'e'd be there in ten minutes'n if 'e isn't, you should still wait."

"Oh, Lucy." Pamela's eyes sparkled. She threw her

arms around the girl. "Oh, thank God," she said brokenly. "Where did you see him?"

" 'Twasn't me. 'E met Jim'n 'e told me. The 'ouse-keeper, she were cross as anythin' 'avin' Jim show up, but that don't matter, do it?"

"No, that does not matter, Lucy. If Mrs. Moulson is angry with you, I will speak to her."

"That's not necessary," Lucy assured her. "You go join 'im, Miss Pamela. 'E were that eager to see you, Jim says."

"Oh, I will, I will."

Standing by the shattered wall of the stone house, Pamela wished that Tom had not chosen this particular meeting place, with its terrible memories. There was a certain oak where they had been wont to meet as children, but a second later she was painfully sure that he had not chosen that particular spot because of the memories it held for him. She had been sure that she loved him in those years, she remembered regretfully. But she had been a child . . . She paused in her thinking as she heard the crack of a branch. Had someone stepped on it? She moved closer to the wall, and then Tom strode into view. She swallowed a little exclamation of shock. He had grown much thinner and there were dark circles under his eyes. Obviously he had been very ill, and indeed his skin had a transparent look about it.

"Tom, dear, should you have left your bed?" she asked concernedly. "You do not look completely recovered yet."

"I am much better," he assured her. "God," he burst out. "To think that at such a time I should be prostrate with a damned fever, begging your pardon, Pamela."

"I expect it was riding in the rain. You should not—"

"I beg you'll not prate on about what I should and should not have done," he interrupted testily. "Our main concern must be for Arthur—poor Arthur." Tears stood in his eyes. "I've not been able to get him out of my mind. Why in God's name did he come back?"

"I am sure he did not anticipate being accused of . . . of abducting me," Pamela returned bitterly. "Were you able to see him?"

Tom shook his head. "I was at the jail earlier this morning."

"Oh, yes, where you met Lucy's Jim. And they'd not let you see Arthur despite—"

"My father's orders extend even to me, it seems," Tom said bitterly. "And Jim tells me that he's heard . . . Arthur's not well. The heat and those irons . . ."

"I know, I know," Pamela moaned. "I have tried to speak to Father. I hoped I might convince him to intercede with Sir Edmund, but he'd not heed me."

Tom's expression was grim. "I've not spoken to my father. I have only agreed with all he has told me."

"You've agreed?" she demanded confusedly.

He gave her an exasperated look. "Has your understanding left you completely? Of course I have agreed with him. 'Tis the only way to proceed—if we are to help poor Arthur. I think that he suspects even me of being well-disposed toward Arthur. He quizzed me about my journey to Scotland, asking me if I had caught many fish—I think he did not believe that that was my purpose of going. I hope that I convinced him otherwise. God, the net that is being woven about Arthur . . . He is suggesting that he stole the money that enabled him to set himself up at the Hall."

"I told you about the pearls," Pamela said.

"You do not imagine that I could tell him, do you?"

"No. Tom. His papers stating that he was released from prison in New South Wales are missing! Your father is supposed to have sent for them."

"No doubt he did, and no doubt he received them, and no doubt he destroyed them!" Tom said bitterly. "He will tell you that it is for me, so that I might inherit Bellair. That is a damned lie! Bellair means everything to father. He has coveted it throughout his life. All his actions, good and bad, stem from his feelings for that house, denied him because he was the son of a younger son. It has eaten into his brain like rust upon iron. It is a madness with him, a madness that sickens me. My father!" Tom's voice broke. However, he swallowed and visibly pulled himself together.

"In seeming to agree with his treatment of Arthur, Pamela, I have learned the name of the judge who was responsible for condemning Arthur to ten years in New South Wales. He is Sir Harry Bowers . . ."

"I have heard the name," she added. "In the midst of his ravings, Arthur mentioned it."

"Good! That was what I was getting at. I need other names. I had hoped to speak to Arthur, but since that avenue is not open to me, you tended him during his illness. Did he call on others whose names you also remember?"

"Yes, yes," she said eagerly. "There are some I remember, some he mentioned over and over again, like Jonas Culpepper."

"Good—give them to me," Tom urged. "We will seek them out. It may be that one or another of my father's accomplices can be persuaded to reveal the truth."

"Oh, do you think so?" she cried.

"Criminals are only closemouthed when it serves their purpose. Money is often wonderfully persuasive. But we waste time talking. I have brought pencil and paper—give me the names."

She had thought them engraved upon her mind. However, when she tried to produce them, she found herself uncertain. "Ritchie . . . Bigelow or Biggers . . . no, Bigelow . . ."

"Or Biggers." Tom wrote down both names.

"Simon Grant."

"Simon Grant," Tom repeated. "I've heard that name. He's been a guest at Bellair . . . Sir Simon Grant, I think. And who else?"

"Charlie Dobbs and . . . and Ezra Bevis." She regarded him regretfully. "There were others, but mostly they were from New South Wales, and some of them from here were muttered so quickly, I could not catch them."

"No matter," Tom said soothingly. "These five must help us—or rather six—counting Sir Harry."

"Supposing they will not?" she whispered.

"You misunderstand me, my dear. I do not expect their help, except inadvertently or out of fear or for money. I pray you do not expect that, armed with this information, we will triumph in a night." He showed her a saddened face. "Arthur may need to suffer far longer than we choose. I hope only that he will not need to make another appearance in court."

"I hope not too," she cried. "You will take me with you when you see some of these men?"

He hesitated. "If it is safe, I shall."

"I'd not be afraid to accompany you anywhere," she cried.

"Ah, but I will be afraid," he told her firmly. "You must be patient, Pamela."

"But meanwhile poor Arthur . . ." she cried.

"Can you imagine that I do not want to free him as much as you?" he demanded harshly. "Can you not believe that I would rather pull down Bellairs stone by stone than inherit it over his corpse? While I was ill, I dreamed of him by night and thought of him by day. My agony may not match, but it is near enough to your own. My father has betrayed my brother and I must live with that knowledge!"

"Oh, Tom!" Pamela flung her arms around him. "I am sorry. I am sorry for . . . for everything you have suffered, believe me."

His lips brushed her cheek and then he pushed her gently away. "Do not try me too far, infant. I am well on the way to getting over this . . . infatuation, so pray do not stir up the ashes."

"Are they ashes, Tom?" she asked seriously. "I hope so."

He nodded. "There may be one or two dimming embers . . . but Edith is much to my liking. She visited me often during my illness."

"Oh, I am glad," she cried. "I know it . . . it was cruel not to have told you anything, but . . ." She sighed. "I have said enough, I think."

"Enough, yes," he agreed. "I will send you word, and soon."

"Yes, you must—and no matter what happens. Please."

"No matter what happens," he echoed gravely. He lifted her hand to his lips and kissed it. Then he turned, and striding away, was lost among the trees.

Pamela lingered by the broken wall another moment. "Her heart was full to overflowing." She had read that line in one of what she was now inclined to call her "silly" books. Yet that sentiment was not silly. It was true. Her heart did seem full to overflowing because Tom was well on the way to what he always ought to have been—her true friend. She knew now that she had never loved him save as a brother. In a sense, he was a brother now, her brother-in-law. Her eyes filled with tears and she shook her head. That would never be. Directly Arthur was freed, the marriage must be annulled. And he *would* be freed—she was suddenly sure of that. Tom had infected her with his own confidence even though he had told her not to expect an immediate triumph. He had not, however, ruled out eventual success. It occurred to her suddenly that she was very hungry. She had only picked at her food in the last weeks, and if she were to keep up the strength she would need at this trying time, she must eat. With that in mind, she ran back in the direction of the manor.

Ellen Fitzgerald

He nodded. "They may be one or two dimming, others, but I like it much I my liking. She v

12

Pamela, waiting by the stone house for Tom to come, was reminded of that moment a fortnight ago when she had been filled with exuberance and hope. She glared at the leaves on the trees. Not a breath of a breeze moved them. They might have been painted there and set in a gallery for folk to admire. They were two weeks into August and the day was exceptionally hot outside, hotter indoors, broiling in a certain cell where a man had lain in irons for the better part of a month, a sick man whose condition must be worsening with every passing minute. She shuddered, not wanting to contemplate that appalling situation. Yet it was impossible for her to banish it from her mind. It troubled her sleeping and waking. She found herself unable to eat more than a small portion of the food put before her. She had grown thinner, and much of her bright coloring had deserted her. Tom, too, was not looking himself. The burden he bore was just as heavy as her own, for in addition to his concern over his half-brother, there was his great disappointment and shock over his father's machinations. There was also the necessity of keeping Edmund Bellairs from find out what he was doing. The last time she had seen him, he had told her that his father was beginning to question the time he spent away from Bellair.

"Unlike him, I find that I am not a very good liar," Tom had told her ruefully.

Pamela sighed, wondering how much longer Tom would be able to continue searching for those Arthur had mentioned in his delirium. In the last fortnight she had met with Tom three times, and on each occasion he had told her he had been unable to trace any of those persons, with, of course, the sole exception of Sir Harry Bowers. She had, however, been able to dredge up two more names, and though she had no more reason to be hopeful than before, the fact that Tom had sent a message to her within two days of receiving them had activated a tendril of hope within her mind. She wondered what was taking him so long to join her. She had expected that he would arrive before her, as he had on the last two occasions.

At that moment she heard a step behind her and whirled, paling as she saw, not Tom, but her father! His expression was thunderous and he was breathing hard. "Might I ask what you are . . . are doing here?" he panted.

She regarded him with a mixture of fear and defiance, the latter emotion being uppermost. "I am here to . . ." She paused as she heard a merry whistle, an old folk song called "Barbara Allen," one of Tom's favorites. Despite her current confusion and fear, she thrilled to the sound. Tom was whistling, and that meant he must have good news for her—but not for her father. Sir Robert must not be told what had happened. He was still the good friend of Sir Edmund Bellairs.

"You've not answered my question! Whom have you come here to meet? Is it not bad enough that you have disgraced yourself with a criminal, a . . ."

She barely heard what he was saying. He must not know why she was here to meet Tom. He would go directly to Edmund Bellairs. She wanted to warn Tom, but it was too late, for he had emerged from the sheltering trees and come striding toward them. He had been smiling, but the smile vanished swiftly enough once he saw Sir Robert.

"Good God!" Sir Robert glared at him. "Is there no end to your duplicity?" Catching Pamela by the shoulders, he shook her so roughly that her teeth came together on her tongue. "I am ashamed of you . . . ashamed. What is the meaning of this . . . this assignation?"

"Sir Robert." Tom had reached his side. "It is not what you think. As you are a fair-minded man, you must listen to me."

"No," Pamela shrilled. "He and your father—"

"What about myself and Sir Edmund?" Sir Robert demanded.

Tom stared at him. "I cannot think that he would countenance this heinous crime." He was speaking to Pamela now. "You told me he would not attend the hearing, and his reputation is of the best. Furthermore, time is of the essence—"

"Crime? What crime?" Sir Robert interrupted. "Those of your brother?"

Tom faced him. "Those of my father, Sir Robert," he said heavily.

Sir Robert regarded him as if, Pamela thought, he had gone mad. "Your . . . father?" he repeated in accents of horror and disgust. "You would dare speak of him in such terms, you, his son, for whom—"

Tom broke in, "I had wanted to find a witness. I had thought that Pamela could provide me with one sympathetic to poor Arthur's case. You, sir, however, would carry much more weight. And—"

"I do not understand you," Sir Robert interrupted angrily. "You are asking me, your father's friend and neighbor—"

"I told you," Pamela cried.

"Hear me, sir," Tom said steadily. "Sir Robert, I have found a man who is willing to swear before a reputable witness that he was one of the excisemen hired by my father to fill the stone house with contraband and lie in wait for Arthur. He will name not only my father but also Sir Harry Bowers, and there is another who will corroborate his story and furnish one of his own, a onetime smuggler who is near death and wishes to relieve his soul of guilt before he meets his maker, as it were."

"Oh, thank God, thank God!" Pamela cried.

Tom's gaze was on Sir Robert's lowering countenance. "Will you come with us, sir?"

Sir Robert glared at him. "You . . . you'd bear witness against your own father?"

"Arthur is my brother, sir." Tom's eyes were suddenly wet with tears. "My brother, who played the coward and would have refused to duel with me had I not insisted. Subsequently, as you know, he deloped. My father, Sir Robert, has always coveted Bellair for himself and for me." He slammed his hand against the wall of the stone house. "He was unkind to Arthur when he was a lad. He sneered at him and made fun of him because he was so heavy. He quarreled with my mother and told her that she had turned her son into a good-for-nothing milksop. He made her very unhappy even though he knew she was in bad health. I think he was glad to . . . to see her die, because it gave him the free hand he had always wanted—with Arthur. He knew that Arthur was in the habit of coming here. He came here to read, to study, and also because he wanted to be away from my father, who was forever mocking him behind my mother's back. And when she died, there was nothing to keep him from putting a certain onerous plan into action. I have it from the exciseman that he bribed them, bribed Sir Harry also, to bear false witness against the stepson who stood in his way, the stepson who also happens to be his second cousin. It was for Bellair, Sir Robert, all for Bellair!" Tom's voice broke. "I . . . I say: Damn Bellair. It is not worth one hair of Arthur's head!"

"Are you sure?" Sir Robert had paled. "Are you sure of all this?"

"I am sure, Father," Pamela cried. "You'd not heed me when I tried to tell you the truth about Arthur. I tended him night and day after Tom shot him. He was out of his head a great deal of the time, and I heard what he said in the throes of his fever. That is how Tom got the names of the witnesses, the men hired by Sir Edmund to betray him. He cried them out in his delirium. Over and over again he called on them to speak the truth, the real truth!

"Oh, God," she continued passionately. "Think of Arthur as you used to know him. I . . . I remember him well, even though I was only a child at the time. He was so gentle, so kind . . . his head was filled with poetry and philosophy. He was an Oxford student and known to be brilliant! Then think of this shy, quiet young scholar being thrust onto a prison hulk and then into the cages on the ship bearing convicts to New South Wales! Undoubtedly Edmund Bellairs was sure he would die on the voyage out. Many did, but he was determined not to die. Over and over again in the throes of his fever he cried, 'I shall not die, Edmund Bellairs. I shall not die.' And . . . and, Father, I gathered from something he said that the doctor had taken pity on him and spoken to the governor about him—Governor Bligh."

"Bligh of the *Bounty*," Tom said. "His crew mutinied, and in New South Wales . . ."

"The government mutinied against him," Sir Robert finished. "Yes, I remember the incident well. Good God, this was the martinet to whom the doctor applied?"

"Yes," Pamela said. "And Bligh refused to believe him. He said that if Arthur was there, it proved that he had been condemned by a jury of his peers and deserved his sentence. He put Arthur to work on the roads."

"The roads?" Sir Robert repeated incredulously. "Arthur?"

"Yes, Arthur, Father. He labored on the roads in the company of thieves and murderers, the dregs of London's streets. He suffered beatings, stabbings, fever. He was mercilessly flogged—twice. His body, his poor body, is scarred—terribly scarred. His back . . ."

She shuddered. "It's a wonder he survived. But he did survive, and he served every day, every hour of his sentence. He, an innocent man, lost ten years out of his life! And he was released—he had the papers to prove it. That is what he is known to have told them at the jail, and Sir Edmund swears that they were not in the place where Arthur told them to look."

"My father . . ." Tom paused and looked bleakly at Sir Robert. "My father destroyed them. I am as sure of it as if I had been present to see him thrust them into the fire!"

"And he would destroy Arthur—is destroying him— keeping him in solitary confinement and in irons. No one has seen him, and he's been there for . . . for over three weeks." Pamela burst into tears.

"My dearest . . ." Sir Robert drew her against him. "Oh, my poor child." He stroked her hair gently. "I am sorry that I was not more receptive, weeks ago." Turning to Tom, he said in a low voice and with moisture in his own eyes, "I will come with you, and if these men prove convincing, as I am sure they must, I will see that Arthur Bellairs is released from confinement." He frowned, adding, "No matter what his crime, he should never have been placed in a solitary cell and in irons. Why, that is torture, especially in this weather."

"Yes, torture," Pamela echoed. "Sir Edmund wants to see him dead, and soon."

"When can we visit these men?" Sir Robert asked briskly.

"We can go immediately," Tom said eagerly. "Is that possible, Sir Robert?"

"Yes, we'll take my post chaise."

"I will go with you," Pamela said.

"No," her father protested. "It is hardly fit that you—"

"If you do not mind, Sir Robert," Tom cut in, "I think they might be more willing to speak to Arthur's wife."

Sir Robert hesitated, and then, seeming to come to a decision, said, "Very well, we will all go. Come." He turned and strode off across the clearing. Exchanging relieved looks, Tom and Pamela followed.

Willie Noble, the smuggler Tom had mentioned, lived in a tumbledown hovel on the edge of a copse some miles beyond Hythe. As they entered its one room, Pamela was appalled at the odor that permeated the place. It was redolent of sickness and dirt. Dust lay thick on the few sticks of furniture, and the floor was filthy. Sir Robert turned a shocked face toward his daughter. "You should not be here," he exclaimed, but he did not argue as she responded, "I am already here, Father. I have no intention of leaving."

The man they had come to see lay on a cot covered by grayish sheets and a torn blanket. The slatternly woman who had admitted them returned to her seat at his side. Bending over him, she said, "Willie, lad, wake up, they be 'ere now." In a lower aside, she muttered. " 'E be poorly this day. 'E sent to Edmund Bellairs sometime back, but we ain't ever 'eard nothin' from 'im."

Tom said, "I understand. This is Sir Robert Cardwell and this is his daughter, Mrs. Bellairs. They are present to hear what you told me yesterday." He produced a paper. "I took it down—the whole of it, as you know. I will want his signature on it."

" 'E'll gi' it to you, right enough," the woman said. " 'E wants to get it off 'is conscience so's 'e can go to 'is maker wi' less sin on 'is soul. That's wot 'e keeps sayin'."

"One less . . . one less," groaned the man on the bed. His eyes rolled wildly. "It all comes back'n I c'n see it . . . I c'n see it 'ere." He raised a shaking hand to his head. "Be'ind me eyes . . . I can see that young man, fat 'e were, fat'n scared when I says 'e were wi' us on the boat'n 'elped us bring the stuff to 'is cottage. Said as 'ow 'e come out wi' us every time 'e were 'ome from 'is school . . . said as 'ow we paid 'im in brandy an' gold'n perfume for 'is woman. An' all the time 'e were starin' at me an' shakin' 'is 'ead . . . an' sayin' 'e didn't 'ave no woman . . . could believe it . . . 'im so fat'n all. Wot 'appened to 'im . . . wasn't ever wi' 'im we dealt . . . it were wi' 'is stepfather . . . 'e gi' us the safe 'ouse in 'is own cellars . . . an' me it was 'elped transfer some o' it to the stone 'ouse. Fell down the stairs, they was all broken, 'urt my knee . . . 'asn't been the same since. Edmund Bellairs, 'e said 'e'd see I were fixed up . . . didn't.'' He paused, gasping for breath.

Tom said, "This is what he told me yesterday." He bent over the cot. "I have written everything you told me on this paper. Will you put your signature on it— or your X.''

"I can write my name," Will said. "An' I'll do it." He stared at Tom. "Ye've much the look o' 'im, ye 'ave, but yer different. Ye 'ave 'eart . . . 'e 'asn't. Said if I called for 'im again, 'e'd 'ave me transported, an me wot lied for 'im'n swore a false oath afore the judge wi' me 'an on a Bible. I . . . I'll burn for that, I will . . .'' He groaned and shut his eyes.

"Has he fainted?" Pamela whispered with a frightened glance at Tom. "He must sign."

"I'll sign . . . I'll sign . . .'' The man opened his eyes. "Gimme yer paper.''

Putting an arm behind his back, Tom half raised him from the cot while Sir Robert took the paper from his hand and closed the smuggler's fingers around a pencil. Will made a feeble try and stopped. "My 'and be weak. I be dyin','' he groaned. "But,'' he said in a stronger voice, "I'll sign it'n may Edmund Bellairs join me in 'ell.'' He laboriously produced his signature and then lay back again, saying in exhausted tones, "Maybe the flames won't be so 'ot now.''

Tom bent over him. "Thank you, Will. I'll send a physician to you.''

"Too late . . . too late,'' came the faltering answer. "I only wants to die in peace.''

The slatternly woman accompanied them to the door.

" 'E'll sleep now," she said. " 'Tis well you showed up, young man. Must've been the good Lord sent ye . . . this 'as been tormentin' 'im, it 'as.''

Coming out of the house, Tom stared at Sir Robert. "Well, sir?" he demanded. "Did you believe him?"

Sir Robert sighed. "I had no choice. He's on his deathbed. A man does not lie in his last hour."

"No," Pamela said eagerly. "You could tell he was speaking the truth."

"The truth, yes." Tom loosed a long sigh.

Pamela experienced a surge of pity for him and, at the same time, admiration. Tom had always been very close to his father. The revelations of the last week must have hurt him deeply, and even more hurtful was the certain knowledge that he was helping to discredit his own father.

Sir Robert, who had been scanning the paper, said disgustedly, "He names Sir Harry Bowers, too."

"And that must be brought to Sir Harry's attention!" Pamela exclaimed. "I hardly think he'll be so eager to preside over another trial involving Arthur Bellairs." She shuddered. "Oh, God, it is all so terrible."

"Terrible, yes," Sir Robert agreed. He looked at Tom. "Who is your other witness?"

"Abel Graves. As I told you, he is an exciseman. He was with the militia when they searched the stone cottage, and he poured brandy down Arthur's throat and spilled it on his clothes so that he was tipsy when they brought him in. Mr. Graves is no longer an exciseman. By profession he is a fisherman, and he has also done some smuggling. His son is awaiting trial for the same offense. He has appealed to my father and has been told that he can do nothing at this precise time. Mr. Graves is naturally concerned. He has had considerable dealings with my father, and in common with Willie Noble, he swears that our cellars are still full of contraband . . . just as they were on the day that poor Arthur was remanded into custody. And unless my father gives me a signed confession as to the innocence of my half-brother, I will open them for all to see. Will you come with me to meet Mr. Graves, Sir Robert?"

"I will." Sir Robert shook his head. "I am more shocked than I can say." He gave Tom a long look. "You are uncommon brave, my boy. You have my deepest admiration."

"I doubt that my father will agree with you," Tom said bitterly. "I am not looking forward to the moment when I must present him with these facts."

"Oh, Tom, dearest, I am sorry," Pamela said in a low voice.

"I thank you." He spoke brusquely. "And now, let us be on our way again."

"Yes," Sir Robert agreed. "The sooner we collect our evidence, the sooner poor Arthur can be released."

Pamela felt both warm and cold. In a very short time they had achieved the well-nigh impossible. Sir Robert had become an ally and would speak for Arthur were such speech necessary—for they had seen the exciseman and emerged with another signed statement. Arthur would undoubtedly be freed, but still she could not help but feel very sorry for Tom. That he was in agony was evident. Given his old love for Arthur and his strong sense of justice, she did not doubt that he had been doubly shocked at these revelations of his father's perfidy. Furthermore, he had a terrible ordeal ahead of him. He, and he alone, must needs confront Sir Edmund with the irrefutable evidence of his transgressions. It was a scene she preferred not to envision.

Tom walked slowly into the house and across the marble floors of the main hall with its magnificent tapestry rising over the high stone fireplace. His eyes lingered on the sculptured figures that stood on either side of that fireplace. Their faces were those of gargoyles. They had both frightened and intrigued him as a boy, and Arthur had made up stories about them, stories that had always rendered them less frightening.

Despite his father's angry contention that Arthur did not appreciate Bellair, Tom thought differently. Arthur had loved the great house well enough. It was in his blood just as much as his desire for vengeance. Indeed, Bellair in common with that same desire might have kept him alive throughout his terrible ordeal in New South Wales—and soon he would be here with Pamela as his bride. Tom frowned. He was not sure of that. Despite her undoubted concern for him, there was a chance she would never forgive him for his duplicity.

A flicker of hope arose in his mind and vanished. All was over between himself and Pamela, and he did like Edith well enough. In time . . . But he could not think of that now. He must excise all from his mind but his forthcoming meeting with his father.

The butler had told him that Sir Edmund was in the library, and it was there that he must go—down the paneled passageway to the room where, no doubt, Arthur would soon be spending most of his time—or would he? Did books still mean as much to the man who had been molded in the furnace of New South Wales? He . . . Tom came to a stop. While he had been deep in thought, his feet had inexorably brought him to the library door. It was time to stop thinking and to abandon the regrets that had seized him. It was time to speak to his father.

Edmund Bellairs was seated at the large mahogany desk purchased half a century ago by his grandfather. He had been writing, but looked up as Tom entered. "Well, my lad," he said cordially, "I've seen precious little of you in these last days."

Tom said, "I have been much occupied, Father."

"But not with matters pertaining to the estate." Sir Edmund frowned. "Remember that you will inherit—"

Tom had wanted a proper opening, and inadvertently his father had provided it. "I will not inherit Bellair, Father," he said coolly. "I cannot inherit it while the heir, by whom I mean my brother, Arthur, remains alive."

The expression on Sir Edmund's face was replete with self-satisfaction. "I beg you'll not concern yourself over that. Arthur, I have been given to understand, is not well, but if he were to stand trial, he would either be sent back to New South Wales to serve out the remainder of his sentence or he would face a worse punishment."

Tom stared at him in horror. "Are you implying that Arthur might . . . die in that cell?"

Sir Edmund shrugged. "He might be better off dead, do you not agree?"

"No," Tom said slowly. "I do not agree, Father. Oh, God, how could you . . . how could you send an innocent man to . . . to hell and then compound the injury by this foul act!"

Sir Edmund stiffened. He stared at Tom incredulously. "What are you talking about? What arrant nonsense is this?"

"It is not nonsense," Tom replied. "Arthur, as well you know, is innocent of all for which he stands accused. He was vilely betrayed by you and sent into virtual slavery for ten mortal years. How could you, damn you, how could you?"

There was a crash as Sir Edmund, rising, sent his chair slamming against the wall behind him. "What are you saying?" he demanded furiously. "What bloody nonsense are you spouting? How dare you speak to me, your father, in such a manner?"

Tom regarded him coldly. "Do you recall a certain smuggler by name—William Noble?"

Sir Edmund's eyes narrowed. "How did you happen upon William Noble? He is a lying—"

"It was Pamela who first heard the name, Father, when she tended Arthur after I . . . shot him. It was one of the many names he let fall as he lay stricken with fever from the wound. William Noble, for your further information, is on his deathbed, and wishing to divest himself, or rather his conscience, of an intolerable burden, one that he believes will bar the gates of heaven against him, has made a remarkable confession. He has—"

"I do not want to hear it!" Sir Edmund exclaimed. "What has his damned confession to do with me? I barely know the man—"

"You knew him well enough to enlist his services in helping to send an innocent man to prison and eventually have him transported to New South Wales. In his confession he recounts the entire episode and also mentions the sum of money received—an amazingly paltry sum for such a service, Father."

"I tell you . . ." Edmund's face had grown very red. "I tell you that—"

"Let me tell you or, rather, refresh your memory, Father. Mr. Noble has confessed that he and other accomplices stored the contraband that convicted Arthur in the stone house—and at your request."

"He lies, he lies, he lies, damn him, he lies!" Sir Edmund shook his fists at Tom.

"I have his signed confession before a reputable witness who agreed with me that a man on his deathbed would not wish to confront his maker with so heavy a conscience. The witness I have mentioned is Sir Robert Cardwell."

"Sir Robert Cardwell?" His father glared at him. "You . . . you have dared to involve him in this farrago of lies? They are lies, I tell you, lies!"

"And," Tom continued inexorably, "I have also the confession of Abel Graves, signed and witnessed, again by Sir Robert Cardwell, that he, long ago, supplied some of the evidence that incriminated Arthur—such as the brandy he poured down his throat and on his clothes. He has also said that our cellars were full of contraband goods on that day and that they are still used for that same purpose. Yes, even at this late date, Father, he has continued to employ our cellars as a 'safe house' for which you have exacted a pretty penny. You really should have tried to help Mr. Graves's son, Father."

"It's a lie, I tell you, a lie . . ." Sir Edmund roared.

"We have shown the confessions of Messrs. Noble

and Graves to Sir Harry Bowers. Since he, too, figured in these confessions as well known to those men and others in the smuggling fraternity, whose friend he has always been, he appeared much shocked. He has, in fact, issued orders for Arthur's release. It will be his last official act before retiring from the bench. That retirement will take place within the hour, Father. Sir Robert and his daughter are awaiting Arthur's release at this very moment. And . . . " He paused as Sir Edmund whirled on him, his face purple with rage, his eyes nearly starting from their sockets.

"You . . ." His hands fell on Tom's shoulders, shaking him. "You've ruined me, you . . . you've betrayed your own father. How could you? Great Christ, how could you?"

Tom wrested himself from his father's grasp, and moving back, said, "I had no choice. You betrayed my brother, my poor brother, and in a sense, you betrayed my mother. If I had not seen that Arthur received the justice due him, I would have been counted your accomplice. I have no desire to inherit an estate and a fortune that reeks of my brother's blood!"

"You . . . you . . ." Sir Edmund leapt toward Tom and then seemed to shiver. As a tree must at the final stroke of the woodsman's ax, he fell forward full length upon the floor.

"Father!" Tom knelt at his side, knowing even before he looked into the blood-suffused countenance that Edmund Bellairs was dead. Tears rolled down his cheeks. "Father," he whispered, and leaning over him, he pressed Sir Edmund's eyelids over his staring eyes, and rising, rang for the butler.

Standing beside Sir Robert in the anteroom of the jail awaiting the emergence of Arthur Bellairs, Pamela clutched her father's arm tightly. She had caught the swift look that had been exchanged between the constable and the jailer when, at the orders of a shaken Sir Harry Bowers, he had gone to fetch the prisoner.

Three weeks, three weeks . . . The words beat in her ears and fear was a hard lump at the base of her throat. Arthur had barely recovered when he had been placed in custody, and he had been in solitary confinement for three weeks—over three weeks.

"Three weeks and two days . . ." she whispered.

Her father, his eyes alight with compassion, said, "We will see that he has the best of care, my dearest."

She said, "Why is it taking so long to escort him out? And—" She ceased to speak, for she heard footsteps, several pairs of footsteps, she thought, and then her hand flew to her mouth as she saw two sweating constables bearing a plank. On that plank was a gaunt scarecrow of a man, lying limply, one thin arm trailing over the side of the plank and his dark hair plastered against his forehead. He wore only a shirt and trousers. There were iron fetters on his hands and feet and an iron collar around his neck. To Pamela's horrified gaze, he looked more dead than alive.

"Arthur!" she shrieked, and would have run to him, but her father held her back.

"He'll not be able to hear you, my darling," he said in a low, shocked voice. "We will take him home . . ." His glacial eyes fell on the constables. "Strike off the fetters," he commanded.

"Pamela . . . Pamela . . . Pamela . . ." the sick man muttered.

"Shhh, Arthur." The girl at his bedside put a cool length of linen on his brow. "You must sleep, my dearest," she said to his unheeding ears.

"She will never forgive me," he said quite clearly. "I was primed to tell her I loved her . . . but she'll not come back. Oh, God, I must go after her, must find her . . ." He tried to raise himself.

Pamala gently pushed him back against his pillows. "She will forgive you." She had whispered these futile assurances during part of the day and most of the two nights he had lain in her father's house. "Oh,

please . . ." She stroked his hand. "Oh, please know
that I love you . . ." she stared as the door creaked
open.

"Pamela, here is the doctor," her father said in a low
voice.

She rose obediently and moved back from the bed as
Mr. Grimes entered the room. "He looks much better,"
he remarked.

"Do you think so?" she asked nervously. "He's so
pale, and still he does not know me."

"He's had a terrible ordeal, there's no doubting
that." The doctor frowned. "I know that it's wrong to
speak ill of the dead, but Edmund Bellairs has much to
answer for."

"Edmund Bellairs . . ." Arthur murmured.
"Edmund Bellairs . . ." He half-raised himself again.
"I will not die to please you."

"Ah, a hopeful sign!" the doctor exclaimed.

"Hopeful?" Pamela echoed. "He's out of his head."

"Yet he heard the name Edmund Bellairs."

"He has mentioned it often. It's no indication that
he's on the mend," she said dolefully.

"Come, my dear, there is every reason to believe that
he will soon be himself again," the doctor said.
"Believe me, I have had more experience with these
cases than you, capable nurse that you have proved to
be. You must trust me and you must also leave your
husband to me, please."

"Very well," she agreed reluctantly, and came into
the hall, where her father stood with Miss Pringle. "Oh,
if only the fever would break!" she sighed.

"He seems much better to me." Sir Robert put his
arm around Pamela's shoulders.

"He is so thin and pale, and it's been nearly a week."

"It has been three days only since he was brought
here, and he has taken nourishment, which I am told is
also a good sign . . . and you"—Sir Robert gave her a
stern look—"will make yourself ill if you are not more
sparing of your energies."

"Oh, God," Pamela moaned. "If I had not left him, none of this would have happened. I blame myself."

Sir Robert rolled an eye in Miss Pringle's direction. "Please, dear Clarissa, will you talk some sense into my daughter? Tell her that if she'd not left him, which she had every right to do, because he did not treat her properly in the beginning, much as I am ready to agree with you that there were some mitigating circumstances for that . . . However, tell her that if Arthur had not come after her, he would not now be cleared of all charges against him and would not be known as Sir Arthur Bellairs, with the entire community in sympathy with him and ready to clutch him to its collective bosom."

"I am sure she knows that, Sir R-Robert." There was a delicate flush on Miss Pringle's faded cheeks.

He said in a voice that, until the last few days, Pamela had never heard from him, "We have agreed, my dearest Clarissa, that you must address me as plain Robert—or will you call me Sir Robert even after we are wed?"

Despite her anxiety, Pamela smiled at them. Having been wrested from his stargazing off and on since Pamela's elopement, Sir Robert had fallen into the habit of consulting Miss Pringle in regards to his daughter and also the running of the house. In the last few days he had also depended on her for comfort and advice. And much to her surprise, it seemed that Miss Pringle had long looked upon Sir Robert as someone singularly godlike, even though she had admitted that he had a few less-than-Olympian tendencies. At least something positive had come out of this misery, she thought, and paused in thinking as Mr. Grimes emerged from the sickroom. "Oh, how is he?" she cried. "Will the fever never leave him?"

"The fever has broken." The doctor smiled. "I thought it must. He is sleeping quite peacefully. Here, now . . ." he chided as Pamela began to cry. "You must go to bed. You are looking far from well yourself. I do not want two patients on my hands."

Pamela glanced longingly at the door to Arthur's

room, and it seemed as if she would disobey the doctor and resume her place beside his bed. However, at an admonishing look from her father, she sighed and went down the hall toward her own chamber. She wished she might have been able to assure Arthur that she had forgiven him, but . . . Her eyes brightened. Soon they could really talk!

"I do not understand it," Pamela sighed. She looked up at Tom. For the first time in the three weeks that had passed since Edmund Bellairs had been laid to rest, he seemed more like his old self, but it was difficult to keep her thoughts directed toward Tom, concerned as she was over the news he had just imparted to her.

"Of course, I am pleased for you, and it is as it should be. I doubt if Bellair has ever meant as much to Arthur as it does to you. But"—she looked down quickly—"where does he intend to go?"

Tom's sympathetic gaze was on her face. "He did not say. I am damned if I understand any of this. You tell me that during his fever, he constantly repeated—"

"Constantly," she interrupted gloomily. "But since he has been recuperating, he has had very little to say to me. He appears extremely grateful when I come to sit beside him, but he has never made any reference to . . . to anything he said during his delirium."

"Can you not remind him?" Tom demanded brusquely.

"I could not," she responded in shocked tones. "It must come from him, and that it has not suggests that he has changed his mind."

"If he has, he's a fool," Tom said roughly.

Pamela flushed. "You make me feel most ashamed of myself, Tom, dearest, for treating you the way I did."

"That, my sweet, is quite forgotten. As I have said before, I do not think we would have suited each other very well. Indeed, I have come to the conclusion that we knew each other far too well to be other than good friends. In my estimation, there should always be a realm of mystery for lovers to probe."

She regarded him with some surprise. "That is very wise and, I think, entirely true. And, dear Tom, it is ever so much more comfortable having you as my friend. How is Edith?"

She was pleased to see him flush. "I have told her that, scandal or no scandal, I will cut short my mourning period if she will agree."

"And will she?"

His eyes gleamed. "She did not hesitate so much as a moment," he said proudly. "She did, however, admit that her family would protest her decision—but that she would not heed them."

"I am delighted." She added with a slight sigh, "I wish that Edith would be my friend again."

"She is still your friend, my dear. She asks about you often. She . . ." He paused. "I am sure that you will all be together in the days to come." He bent to kiss her hand. "I am going, and if I were you, I would go and sit with Arthur in the garden."

"I had that in mind," she said evenly.

Pamela stood in the roadway until only dust marked the passage of Tom's horse. Some of what he had said depressed her, namely the suggestion that they would all be together in the days to come. It gave her a sense of passing years and of a future in which she, in common with Miss Pringle, would look backward instead of forward. But, she quickly reminded herself, Miss Pringle no longer needed to look back. Two days ago she and Sir Robert had been wed in a ceremony attended only by herself and Tom, who had officiated as her father's best man. The newly wedded couple would soon be leaving for London and a short honeymoon. They seemed gloriously happy. She was very happy for them, but as for herself, though she could applaud Arthur's decision to let Tom remain at Bellair, despite the entail, the implication of that gift depressed her. Undoubtedly Arthur wanted to shake the dust of Kent from his shoes, for which she could not blame him.

He had not confided his future plans to Tom, but she

did not find it too difficult to believe that he preferred to spend the rest of his life in some part of the country where his tragic story was not known. It was even possible that he feared his ten years as a convict in New South Wales would forever set him apart from his own kind. She sighed, remembering what her father had told her, once Arthur had informed him of his plans in regard to Bellair.

"He could remain here. Cardwell Manor would be his when I die. As you know, my love, I am the last of my line. And Arthur would appreciate my observatory."

Perhaps yes, perhaps no, Pamela thought ruefully. Sir Robert was harking back to the Arthur he had known ten years ago. She had never given her father any inkling of the many women with whom Arthur had . . . associated during his stay in New South Wales. His descriptions of his relations with them had been, on occasion, embarrassingly graphic. It was quite possible that he had grown weary of her during the fortnight of his recovery.

She was nearing the small summerhouse where he was sitting. He was still weakened from his ordeal in the jail, but the doctor had pronounced himself entirely pleased with his progress. In another two weeks or even less, he would be well enough to return to the Hall or . . . to go where he would. As the crow flies, she thought with a touch of melancholy.

He had been staring moodily at the grounds, but he looked up as she came across the grass. His eyes remained somber. She wondered what he was thinking and found herself momentarily regretful that there was no touch of fever to loosen his tongue. Immediately she was as ashamed as though she had actively ill-wished him. It was an ill wish to want . . . She dismissed or tried to dismiss the deviant thoughts that crowded her mind. She was smiling quite naturally when at length she stood in the doorway of the summerhouse. She kept her hands close to her sides because of an absurd desire to touch him as she had sometimes during the nights when he had called out to her, had wanted her, then.

"I was saying farewell to Tom," she told him. "You were uncommon kind to him."

"It was little enough," he said softly. "It was little enough to give him—and you—for what you both have done for me."

"To . . . give me?" she said on a breath.

"I . . . I watched you with him," he said. "I want you to know that I am deeply sorry that I stood between you, but you have settled your differences, have you not —and it only needs for me to return the freedom I took from you."

"The . . . freedom?" she whispered.

"We were married," he said in a low voice. "A few words only, but a binding tie. Yet it should be easy enough for you to procure an annulment. I do not blame you for wanting me gone. But though you might not credit it, I do want you to know that I love you and—"

"Oh, Arthur," Pamela cried. "I beg you will say no more!"

He reddened. "I am sorry. I had not meant to embarrass you. But you have looked so sadly at me of late, and Tom—I owe Tom so much."

She was suddenly angry. "And so you thought you might present me to him as one more parting gift?" she demanded sarcastically. "A house, complete with bride?" As she met his perplexed stare, laughter suddenly replaced her anger, and running to his chair, she knelt beside it. "Oh, Arthur, you fool! Tom is recently betrothed to Edith—and did you not realize that I forgave you long ago?"

He stared at her almost uncomprehendingly. "No," he said slowly. "I did not know that. Is . . . is it true?"

She did not answer him, save with the kiss that she joyfully pressed upon his lips, and in another moment she felt his arms close around her. He held her as tightly as his yet-diminished strength would allow, which was, as it happened, quite enough to demonstrate that whatever their past differences, he agreed that they had finally reached an understanding.

Epilogue

The visitor, having been upstairs and down in the smart red-brick house on Cheyne Walk in Chelsea, was pleased to sit in the well-stocked library with its lovely Chippendale desk, its floor-to-ceiling bookcases, its Aubusson carpet, and its comfortable chairs. From the window, she obtained a view of the Thames, yet despite the spacious library and the other rooms of the house, all of which she had pronounced charming, she still looked at her hostess with wide eyes and said, not altogether approvingly, "You prefer this to the *real* country, Pamela?"

Pamela smiled at her. "It's so convenient for Arthur, as I think I wrote you, Edith. Chelsea is not quite London, though I expect it might be in years to come. Arthur thinks it will eventually be gathered into the London fold. He is very far-seeing."

"I understand that he has that reputation in the House." Edith spoke as wisely as if she were not repeating information fed her by Tom. She added, "He has done well. His speech on prison reform was, I understand, extremely stirring."

"It's a subject he knows," Pamela said dryly. "He does not believe it made much of a dent in current parliamentary thinking, but he will continue to pursue it."

"Well, I expect one can understand that," Edith allowed. She shivered slightly. "Ten years . . . out there, and then to come back to—"

"I beg you'll not dwell on ancient history, dear," Pamela interrupted, a note of protest in her soft voice. "I should not like him to come in and hear you. He and Tom should be back soon."

"Do you never discuss it?" Edith asked curiously.

"There is so much else to discuss," Pamela said. "Time, fortunately, does not stand still."

"But will you tell your children?"

"Yes, when little Arthur is old enough to understand it, I expect we will, before he hears it from others at school. We will tell Jocelyn, too."

"Tom wanted to name our daughter Jocelyn," Edith said with a faint note of complaint in her tone.

"I think Charis is sufficiently pretty," Pamela commented. "And your little girl could easily be one of the Graces for which she is named—if the watercolor you sent me is any criterion."

Edith's face softened. "She is, is she not? Tom adores her. He is a very good father. You should see him with Will and Terence. They are such rambunctious boys. I beg him not to encourage them in all their mischief— but he will."

"I wish we might have had twins. Perhaps this time we will. Oh!" Pamela blushed and put a hand to her mouth. She gazed ruefully at Edith.

"You are breeding again?" Edith asked.

Pamela nodded. "But I beg you'll not tell Arthur until—"

"He does not know?" Edith shot her a disapproving look.

"I was sure of it only this morning," Pamela explained. "And as you know, Arthur met Tom practically at dawn to take him to see some of the new buildings springing up in the city."

"London is certainly expanding. We were here five years ago, and I vow I scarcely recognize some of it. And it is so noisy. Do you never miss the country?"

"We see enough of the country in the summer when we visit Papa and Pringle."

"Papa and Pringle," Edith echoed disapprovingly again. "I heard Will call them that and I gave him a good scolding."

"They do not mind," Pamela assured her.

"I think it is very disrespectful," Edith said in the tones of one determined to find fault.

"Oh, Edith, where has your sense of humor gone?" Pamela cried. "You never used to be such a . . . stick!"

"A stick?" Edith repeated indignantly. "You and Arthur might want your children to behave like . . . like wild abor . . . abor . . . whatever . . ."

"Aborigines?" Pamela supplied coldly.

"The very thing," Edith snapped. "You and Arthur have no sense of position. As a member of Parliament and—"

"His Australian experiences have ruined his character, is that what you mean, Edith?"

"No, of course that is not what I mean." Edith suddenly smiled. "Oh, dear, Pamela, I am sorry. I *was* sounding stickish, do forgive me." With a rare burst of candor she added, "I expect I am only envious. Tom is so wrapped up in Bellair, and so am I, of course. I do love it—but I should like to live in London some part of the Season, and it would be delightful to go to Paris now that it is so pleasant again. You have been there three times and Arthur is speaking about going to Vienna and Venice, too, while all Tom can talk about is the price of fodder and grain. I try to be satisfied. I am satisfied most of the time, for I truly adore him, but . . ."

Pamela arose and dropped a kiss on Edith's cheek. "Oh, my dear, I know. We both read too many romances."

Edith put her arms around her friend and they clung to each other for a moment. Then she moved away, saying self-consciously, "I did not mean to lay my woes upon you. They are such small ones, and truly I am content. I have loved Tom far longer than you imagine . . ."

"I know," Pamela said. "We have discussed that before . . . and I will tell you again that he never would have been happy with me, nor I with him. We'd been friends too long. Surely that makes sense to you."

"Wonderful sense, and I agree. He is happy with me and I expect I am glad that he never wanted a political

career. It must be very hectic for you on occasion—all
those dinners one must give, and being charming to the
right people. Does it not weary you at times?''

"No, nothing against Papa, but growing up so alone,
I have found that I enjoy people. And Arthur is an
excellent host.''

"Tom would be also, I am sure. Oh, dear, I am
growing envious again.'' Edith paused as they heard
voices in the hall beyond the library.

In another moment the door had opened and Tom
entered, followed by Arthur. "Well"—he smiled at the
two women—"did you miss us?"

"Not in the least," Edith sniped back at him. "We
were extremely pleased that you were not here—else
we'd not have had the opportunity to discuss you
behind your back.''

Arthur laughed. "Should our ears have been burning,
then?"

"Like an autumn bonfire," Pamela teased. "Can you
imagine," she added, looking from her handsome,
stylishly dressed husband to his equally handsome, if more
carelessly clad brother, "how we could have failed to note
the resemblance between them all those years ago?"

"They are amazingly like," Edith agreed.

"I am complimented," Arthur said.

"And I." Tom clapped Arthur on the shoulder. "I
have reason to be. From what I am able to divine, you
are a power in the House.''

"I fear I do not deserve that particular encomium,"
his brother protested. "I am regarded as a gnat with a
long sting.''

"Which is as it should be," Tom said heartily. "I
myself would not mind speaking out on the problems
that beset farmers here—much less in the colonies.''

"I wish you would," Edith said wistfully.

Tom shook his head. "I do not possess Arthur's silver
tongue, and furthermore, each time I come to London,
I am the more eager to take the road for home, are you
not, my love?"

"Of course," Edith answered with a valiant smile. "Shall we be leaving soon?"

"Not so soon," Pamela protested. "You have been here but three days."

"Oh, I expect we will go tomorrow." Tom stared down at his wife, a mischievous gleam in his eyes. "I have been to Tattersall's and purchased a pony for Will and a gelding for Terry. And you, my angel, must have had your fill of shopping?"

"I have." Edith bit down a sigh. " Fancy, I have bought a gown *ready-made,* and with the new leg-o'-mutton sleeves. It is becoming. I do like the styles. I hear the skirts will be even fuller next year."

"I imagine," Tom said, "that you would be even more positive of the styles were you to go to Paris."

"I imagine I would," Edith said. "But since such a journey is unlikely—"

"Not as unlikely as you might imagine," Tom interrupted. "I am having the cattle sent home tomorrow. They will compensate the boys for not joining us on our Parisian journey."

She blinked up at him, saying in faltering accents, *"P-Parisian* journey . . . You are funning me, Tom, and I do think it too bad of you."

"No." He put his arm around her waist and smiled down at her. "With matters all right and tight at home, I see no reason why we should not go to Paris. I myself have long had a hankering to visit the city. I thought you must agree, but if you will miss the children . . ."

"No, I shan't ever . . ." Edith shrieked. "I mean, I would, but . . ."

"Enough," Tom laughed. "I take it then that my plan has your approval?"

"Oh, it has, it most definitely has. Oh, Tom . . ." With a most uncharacteristic abandon, Edith flung her arms around her husband's neck and kissed him. Her embrace was returned with fervor, and then they broke apart, both a little red-faced.

"You will f-forgive me?" Edith turned to Pamela.

"There's nothing to forgive, my dear. I am delighted for you." Pamela caught Edith's hand. "And you will enjoy it! When will you leave?" She looked at Tom.

"We will leave tomorrow," he said. "And I think we will be there for a fortnight. Who knows"—he smiled at Edith—"we might even visit Italy."

"Italy," Edith breathed.

"Why not?" her husband demanded. " 'Tis time and past that we had the Grand Tour—but meanwhile, I think we'd best dress for the opera."

"Yes . . . the opera," Edith murmured. "Is this really happening or am I dreaming?"

"Ask me again when we are in sight of Notre Dame or the Tuileries, my love."

"I think I *must* be dreaming," Edith said.

"When you make the channel crossing, you will be sure you are not. Let us hope that the weather will continue fine tomorrow," Tom said.

"If it does not, I shall have no complaints," Edith breathed. "Paris. Oh, Tom! And tonight, *The Marriage of Figaro!* It is heaven." She turned to Pamela. "It was lovely, our visit, my dear, and I shall look forward to this evening."

"I, too, and I am very happy for you," Pamela responded. "You and Tom will have to visit the Opera and the cafés and go dancing . . ." She executed a whirling waltz step.

"Dearest, be careful, your condition . . . " Edith began, and flushed. "Oh, dear, I am sorry, my love, it just slipped out."

"What . . . are you not feeling the thing, Pamela?" Arthur asked anxiously.

"You would never know it if she is not," Tom said warmly. "I cannot remember when I have seen you in such looks, Pamela."

"I thank you." Pamela managed a smile. "I am in very good health, thank you. And now we'd best see you to the door."

After the door had closed upon their departing and,

in Edith's case, apologetic guests, Arthur looked down at Pamela with some concern. "Why was Edith worried about your health? Is there something you've not told me?"

"It's something that I had just learned myself and inadvertently let slip to Edith," Pamela sighed. "I do not think she'd have said anything had she not been so excited and flustered by Tom's surprise. Isn't it lovely? She's been longing to see Paris. I wonder what put it into Tom's mind . . . ?" She looked up at Arthur and knew. "You did."

"A word to the wise . . ." he acknowledged.

"But however did you manage it?" she said wonderingly. "I thought he was as rooted in Kent soil as one of his elms!"

"I told him that travel is broadening. I said that he would profit by the experience and . . . But no matter, we are getting far from the subject of you, my love. What did Edith mean?"

"We are expecting another addition to the family, my love. I hope you do not mind."

"Mind!" he repeated. "Oh, my dearest, but how do you feel? Are you—"

"Arthur!" Pamela stood on tiptoe to slip a hand over his mouth. "How can you be so entirely nonsensical? Do you not recall the ease with which I produced the rest of our family? I am in the very pink of condition and—"

"Oh, my darling." He caught her in a tight embrace and then hastily released her. "I am sorry." He flushed. "I must be careful."

"No, you must not." She pouted. "Not for at least another three and a half months."

Thus encouraged, Arthur pressed a long kiss upon her lips.

"Ahhh"—she smiled—"now that was something like, but please . . ."

"Please what?"

"Please do it again, because—"

But whatever else she might have said was silenced as her husband happily obliged.